LIKE I WISHED

HEATHER BAY BOOK TWO

CHARLIE NOVAK

Copyright © Charlie Novak 2022

Cover by Natasha Snow

Editing by Susie Selva

Formatting by Pumpkin Author Services

All rights reserved. Charlie Novak asserts the moral right to be identified as the author of this work.

This novel is entirely a work of fiction. Names, characters, places, and incidents are the products of the author's imagination or are used fictitiously. Any resemblance to actual events, locales, organizations or persons, living or dead, is entirely coincidental.

For Noah.
May there always be low angst love stories built on horniness and soft vibes.

CHAPTER ONE

Noah

My head was pounding, and there were stars bursting behind my eyes despite the fact I hadn't even opened them. The darkness was spinning, and I felt bile rising in my throat, even though it seemed like my body was refusing to actually throw up. Everything hurt, and I heard the pitiful moan that escaped my lips before I realised I'd made it.

I shifted slightly, realising I was lying down, possibly in bed, judging by the way something heavy and soft shifted across my skin. I'd managed to lose my shirt and jeans at some point, but since I had no memory of even making it to bed, I had no idea when or how that had happened.

The last thing I remembered was being at Lane and Oliver's housewarming party the night before, drinking something Laurie had made. Daquiris maybe. They must have been stronger than I'd thought, although I'd always been a lightweight, so it didn't take much to knock me on my ass. Figuratively and literally.

I'd known Lane and Oliver for years because we'd grown up together, and they'd dated as teens before falling out just before Oliver left for university. Then, four months ago, he'd moved back to Heather Bay, the small Yorkshire town the rest of us called home, to renovate his late grandmother's cottage, and Lane had been the site manager.

They'd ended up reconnecting and realising just how much they'd missed each other, which was incredibly sweet, at least in my eyes. Oliver had originally been planning to sell the cottage, but he and Lane had wound up moving into it instead and had spent the last few months doing it up. Last night was the first time they'd had us all round to show us the result of all their efforts.

What was supposed to have been a chilled night with my friends, celebrating an incredible milestone for two of them, had turned into one big mess. I knew Lane and Oliver would forgive me for ruining their evening, but I didn't know if I'd forgive myself. I'd been such a fool.

I groaned again and rolled onto my back. I'd been curled into a ball, probably in some subconscious hope that it would help, and it must have done because as soon as I stretched out, my body rebelled.

God, I was never drinking again. I was too old for this.

I'd been too old for it at my twenty-first birthday when my best friend, Alex, had insisted we all do a line of tequila shots off the bar. Chucking my guts up in the middle of Newcastle city centre had not been the highlight of my evening, but unfortunately, it was one of the only parts I remembered.

Alex had also been three sheets to the wind and this close to picking a fight with a group of lads over something petty, but he'd been sweet enough to take me back to my uni house and sit with me while I clutched the toilet and muttered nonsensically. He'd always looked out for me ever since we'd first met.

I assumed he'd been the one to bring me home last night.

With a deep breath, I decided it was time to open my eyes. The spinning and dizziness couldn't get any worse, and at least if I opened them, I'd be able to check the time and assess the damage. Although I assumed I'd slept away at least half of Sunday already.

My eyes fluttered open, and I was immediately struck by two thoughts.

The first was that the dim light actually made the spinning slightly better.

And the second was that this wasn't actually my room.

Or my house.

The room I was in had a sloped ceiling that led down to an enormous set of curtains that ran along the entire wall opposite the bed. I assumed there were windows behind them since that was the source of the light. The walls to my left and right were both painted a warm, pale yellow, and as I tilted my head, a move I instantly regretted, I saw the wall behind the bed was made of exposed brick.

The bed I'd found myself in was enormous, but only the

side I was currently occupying was disturbed, which meant I hadn't had company.

That made sense, but I still didn't know where the fuck I was. This definitely wasn't mine or Alex's room. It wasn't either of the spare rooms in Lane and Oliver's cottage either. Theo and Laurie's flat was too small and the wrong shape to have a room like this, so that ruled them out, and it wasn't Will's farmhouse either since there was a notable absence of accompanying farm noises in the background.

That only left Spencer.

Fuck. Was I at Spencer's house? In Spencer's bed?

I groaned and threw my arm over my face. As if my morning couldn't get any worse, there was now a *very* strong chance I was in my best friend's older brother's bed. The older brother who I'd known since I was seven and had had a crush on since I was thirteen.

The older brother who was kind, funny, charming, and Hollywood levels of gorgeous.

And also completely and utterly straight.

"What am I doing?" I muttered to myself or at least tried too. My words came out hoarse and choked like I was missing half my vocal cords. I groaned again, self-pity creeping in around the edges of my immense hangover.

I lifted my arm and glanced at the side of the bed, hoping I'd be able to find my phone. Then I'd be able to message Alex and ask him what the fuck had happened.

My phone wasn't on the neat, wooden bedside table. But there was a large glass of water and an open box of paracetamol.

I smiled because the gesture was so adorably Spencer.

There was a note too, scrawled on a small, green Post-it Note.

Good morning!
Drink the water and take two pills. I put spare clothes on the armchair for you. Come down when you're ready, and we'll have breakfast!
Spencer =D

I chuckled, then groaned as my muscles protested the idea of laughing. Why did everything hurt so much? I couldn't remember falling over, and I wasn't even thirty.

Perhaps this was my body's way of reminding me not to let Laurie make me any more drinks.

Ever so slowly, I slid into a sitting position. My pace would have given a sloth a run for its money, but it worked because I made it into an upright position without feeling the need to throw up. My head was still throbbing, but the dizziness had started to ebb, and I considered that progress.

The water in the glass was still cold, which meant Spencer couldn't have left it out for me that long ago, but the sheer relief the cool liquid brought me dissolved any embarrassment I might have felt at that realisation. Besides, if Spencer was the one who'd brought me back here, he'd probably seen me in a far worse state.

I barely remembered to take the paracetamol before I drained the glass, wishing it would magically refill itself. Now that I'd had one glass, my body was craving more. But the only way to get that was going to be to get up, and that prospect felt like climbing Everest.

It was either that or stay here until Spencer came to check on me again, and I didn't know when that would be.

With another deep breath, I slowly pushed the duvet off me. Spencer must have stripped my clothes off when we came back because I was just in my boxers and socks. I felt my face flame, and I wished I could magically disappear.

I'd dreamt about Spencer undressing me for *years*, but none of those fantasies had involved me being so flat-out wasted that I couldn't remember any of it.

"Shit," I muttered under my breath, scrubbing my face and feeling the brush of weekend stubble under my palms. What the hell had I said to Spencer last night? Had I told him how I felt? Had I gone even further and started waxing lyrical about how fucking beautiful he was or the details of the sordid fantasies my imagination had concocted over the years?

There was no coming back from that if I had.

Spencer might be sweet enough to laugh it off, but I'd never be able to look him in the face again. I might as well just move to the Outer Hebrides and become a hermit.

But the biggest problem was that I couldn't get out of the house without seeing Spencer, and even if I did, I wouldn't be able to escape him for long. He was my best friend's brother and business partner as well as a regular at our Friday nights at the pub. I couldn't just stop going to those because I wanted to avoid Spencer and didn't want to find out the truth about my drunken antics. Alex would be bound to catch on quick, and then he'd get the truth out of me with just a pointed look.

It would be better to rip the plaster off now and spend the rest of my life apologising.

The wooden floor was cool under my feet as I swung my legs out of bed, looking around the room for the armchair Spencer had mentioned in his note. It was hard to miss—a large, squishy-looking yellow armchair sat in the far corner with a neat pile of clothes folded on it.

Nausea and dizziness threatened to overwhelm me as I stood, and I had to put my hand on the bedside table to steady myself. I squeezed my eyes shut and took a deep breath, letting it out slowly while silently hoping that would help.

I did it again, just for good measure, before I opened my eyes and took a few shaky steps over to the chair.

I'd been expecting to see my own clothes from last night there, but instead there was a dark green t-shirt, a pair of grey joggers, socks, and a clean pair of boxers. Since none of them were mine, that obviously made them Spencer's, and that made my head spin before a single thought popped my excitement like a balloon.

I didn't think any of it was going to fit me.

Spencer wasn't that much taller than me, and although he had fairly muscular shoulders, he was lean and fit. He'd been into sport for as long as I'd known him, and although his dreams of a sporting career had ended devastatingly early, he still had an athlete's body.

Me on the other hand…

I was tall, but I was also soft and round. I had a belly; a furry, soft chest; and thick thighs that I fucking loved. It hadn't always been the body I wanted, but it was the one

I'd grown to love over the years. It was strong as well from spending hours in the swimming pool, the one form of exercise, apart from long walks, that I'd always adored. My dad had taught me to swim before I could walk, and I'd always found the pool to be a place of utter calm and peace, where I could reset my thoughts and focus on nothing but the kick of my legs and the swoop of my arms.

It was the place I went to escape everything else and just be.

Being the quiet, chubby, gay guy had always made me feel out of place despite the fact that all my friends were both queer and incredibly loving. In hindsight, any issues I had were largely down to the toxic male body image that had been continuously pushed by the media throughout my childhood, and some of the queer men I'd met at university had embodied the worst of those issues.

The rampant fatphobia I'd been exposed to had been horrifying and had left me sobbing down the phone to Alex on more than one occasion.

And then one morning, after spending an hour in the local swimming pool, I'd finally decided to say fuck it to other people's opinions and live for myself.

Which had sounded easy on paper but had been a lot harder in reality. But it was something I still tried to live by, even if I didn't always believe it.

I picked up the t-shirt, which was worn and buttery soft and smelt like Spencer—something warm and gentle like being embraced by a summer breeze fragranced with lavender and lemons. It fell open in my hands, and I realised it was larger than I thought. When I pulled it on, it clung to my skin, but it wasn't too tight or short.

All it did was fill my senses with the scent of Spencer.

The socks were fine since they were just socks, but the boxers were tighter than I would have normally worn, literally showing every curve and vein on my dick and balls. Luckily, the oversized joggers were looser, so I wasn't going to spend the whole morning trying to cover my crotch. I didn't want Spencer to think I was deliberately trying to force my cock in his face, especially if I'd rambled at him last night about how much I wanted to fuck him.

I scrubbed my face again and sighed. I knew there was no option left now except to go downstairs, especially since Spencer had probably heard me moving around. If I stayed up here much longer, I could see him forming a search party.

"Come on," I said to myself. "It won't be that bad."

Alex had always said I was a happy, sleepy drunk, so I crossed all my fingers and toes that that was as far as I'd gotten last night.

Then I pulled open the door and made my way down the stairs.

CHAPTER TWO

Spencer

I HEARD the sound of someone walking around on the top floor, and I grinned to myself as I finished refilling the kettle. Tea, bacon sandwiches, and orange juice were always the best way to cure a hangover, no matter how deep it had sunk its claws in.

And given what Noah had been like last night, I guessed his head was going to be really sore this morning.

I flicked the kettle on and began pulling things out of the fridge to set on the island in the middle of the kitchen, resisting the temptation to put music on like I usually did in the morning. I didn't think Noah's head would appreciate drum and bass with a hangover.

Noah's footsteps were tentative on the stairs, and I wondered if he felt dizzy at all. I grabbed a glass out of the cupboard and filled it with cold water from the fridge, setting it on the island so he'd be able to see it when he came in. I heard him reach the ground floor and hoped the noise would tell him where he needed to go since I didn't think Noah had been here before.

"Morning," he said as he trudged into the kitchen. I stopped, a pack of bacon still in my hands, to give him a smile and a once-over. He looked pale with dark circles around his eyes, and his brown hair was stuck up at odd angles. I cursed because I should have left him a hairbrush and a towel for the shower. He wasn't swaying, though, and he didn't look two seconds from throwing up, so that was a good start.

He'd found my clothes, and I liked the way the dark green t-shirt looked on him. It definitely suited him more than me. It was a bit more fitted than some of the shirts Noah usually wore, but I thought it looked great. Noah always looked good to me, but there was something about seeing him in my clothes that made me extra happy. I didn't know why.

It was probably a protective instinct or something. I'd known Noah for years, ever since my little brother Alex had sat next to him at primary school, and I'd always looked out for him. Even if he didn't need it because Alex was like a sharp, scrappy terrier and always ready to pick a fight.

Noah had always been a sweet guy, though, and I didn't want him to get hurt.

"Hey," I said, giving Noah my brightest smile. "You're awake. How're you feeling?"

"Er, I think we'll go with alive," he said with a dark chuckle.

I pointed at the water, then swapped the pack of bacon

in my hands for a carton of orange juice. "Drink that, and I'll get you some juice. I'm going to make you some breakfast too."

"Oh, you don't have to do that."

"It's fine," I said with a wave of my hand. "You've gotta eat something. Especially after last night."

Noah groaned and his face tinted, giving it the first flush of colour I'd seen. "I'm sorry. I have no idea what happened last night, and I'm so sorry for whatever I said or did."

I frowned. Had I missed something? "What do you mean?"

"Er, I just thought… well, considering I was so drunk, I must have said something inappropriate," Noah said, fumbling over the words before reaching for the glass of water and downing it.

I thought back to the previous evening, racking my brain to see if I could think of anything. "No, you didn't. You had two of Laurie's daiquiris, which he put, like, two bottles of rum into, and you were getting pretty drunk, so Alex got you some water and food. Then you felt sick, so I took you to the toilet." I decided to leave out the part where I'd carried him, bridal style, to the downstairs toilet. Noah seemed embarrassed enough, and I didn't want to make him feel worse.

"I remember the drinks," Noah said quietly, taking the glass of orange juice I handed him. I took the water glass in return and refilled it. Noah was going to need to stay hydrated today. "And a little bit of the food. I think you were talking to me at one point too."

"See? It wasn't so bad."

"Weren't you…" Noah grimaced and shook his head. "Were you supposed to be working today? I vaguely remember something about you having to open this morning."

Now it was my turn to be embarrassed. Luckily, Noah was too busy looking down at his glass of juice to notice.

Noah was right. Technically, I was supposed to have been helping open Novel Tea, the book-themed coffee shop I ran with Alex, this morning. It was why I'd left Lane and Oliver's early last night. But with Noah being wasted, I hadn't wanted to leave him alone. Alex had also been hammered, so I couldn't ask him to look after Noah or take the early shift, even though I knew he'd have done both with no hesitation. He'd just have grumbled constantly about it for months, but that was nothing new.

I loved my brother, but he really needed to look on the bright side of life sometimes.

"Er, yeah," I said. "But it's fine. You weren't well, and I didn't want to leave you to wake up somewhere strange, so I got Mina to cover for me. I mean, technically she was going to be in anyway, but she said she'd be fine on her own until Cleo started at ten."

"Oh God. I'm so sorry. You could have just taken me back to mine and left me there. Or I could have stayed at Lane's."

I shook my head and pulled a frying pan off the hanging rack above the oven. "Nah, man, it's fine. Seriously."

Noah scrubbed his face with his hands. "It's really not."

"Yeah, seriously, it is." I grinned at him. "What are

friends for if you can't come and crash at their place when you're wasted?"

Noah hummed. "I suppose. But you didn't have to let me have your bed or give me your clothes."

"What else was I meant to do? Leave you on the sofa?" I stared at him. I supposed I could have done, but then I'd have spent the whole night worrying he was uncomfortable. At least in my bed, he could sleep off the alcohol in comfort with a bathroom nearby, and giving him clean clothes was just a basic decency thing.

My parents would have been horrified if I'd just dumped Noah. Both of them had raised me to be a good person, and I tried to always do my best.

"That's what most people would have done," Noah said, then he smiled again and took a sip of his orange juice. "Sorry, I shouldn't be picking at you. It was really nice of you to take care of me. I really appreciate it. I'm just horribly embarrassed. I can't remember the last time I was that drunk."

"Don't sweat it." I put the frying pan on the hob and flicked on the burner, digging a pair of tongs out of a nearby drawer. "And you were very easy to deal with. Mostly just like sleepy and telling me random chemistry facts. Like, er…" I searched around in my brain and tried to remember one. Science had never been my strong point, and I was worried that I'd get whatever I was about to say wrong. "Something about the only letter not on the periodic table is J?"

"Jesus Christ," Noah said. "I was chemistry drunk. That's new."

I chuckled. "It was fun. You sang a little song too."

Noah was bright red now, but he was smiling, and I hoped he wasn't that upset by me telling him what had happened. "Okay," he said. "I am absolutely swearing you to secrecy about the singing. I can't believe I did that."

"It was cute." I began humming the tune to the element song Noah had been singing. I decided I wouldn't tell him that he'd tried to teach me or that he'd kept stopping and frowning and saying he'd gone wrong before going back to the beginning and starting again.

It had been nice seeing that side to Noah because he was usually so quiet and serious. I wanted to see him let loose more often, just without Laurie's daiquiris.

"I'm not sure I believe that," Noah said. "But I'm not going to argue with you." He took another sip of his orange juice while I put bacon into the pan.

"You okay with bacon sandwiches?" I asked. "You've gotta line your stomach. I've got some, like, brie or some avocado if you want those too."

"Just bacon is fine, thanks."

"Sure?" Now I'd thought about it, adding avocado and brie sounded lush. I was totally doing that to mine. Usually, I'd have had breakfast hours ago, but I'd wanted to wait for Noah so all I'd had was some fruit and a yoghurt.

Noah thought about it for a second. "Actually… the brie does sound good."

"Nice!" I walked over to the fridge to dig out the cheese. "Do you want avocado too?"

"If you're offering, then yes, please."

"Wouldn't tell you it was an option if you couldn't have

it," I said, slightly confused by Noah's line of thinking. He'd always been very polite, so maybe it was just part of that. I grabbed an avocado out of the little wire basket on my windowsill and began to slice it open while keeping an eye on the bacon.

Noah and I lapsed into comfortable silence for a few minutes before he said, "I don't think I've been to your house before."

"I don't think you have either. Usually, we just hang out at the pub or yours. I should have everyone over at some point. I don't know why I haven't."

Maybe it was because despite the fact that I hung out with Alex, Noah, and their friends every week, I still sometimes felt like an outsider. Noah, Alex, Lane, and his boyfriend Oliver had known each other for donkey's years, and I'd always just been Alex's big brother to them.

The other members of our group were newer additions, and although I'd known Will at school and through playing football together as teenagers, he was better friends with Lane than me. Laurie and Theo were really fun to hang out with, but it had always felt like they came as a pair and never really wanted anyone else, even though they always hung out with us. I'd been to their flat a couple of times to chill and game with Theo, but I still wouldn't have called them my best mates.

I didn't really know if I had anyone who fit that category these days.

I was just the one on the edge of everyone else's friendships.

"You don't have to," Noah said. "I didn't mean for

that to sound like I'm trying to score an invitation. Besides, we're not exactly a quiet bunch, and there are a lot of us these days, and you probably don't want us disturbing your peace." He grinned at me, then looked around the kitchen again. "I like how bright your house is. It's fun."

I chuckled. "Alex says it looks like a kid's funhouse."

I'd always loved bright, bold colours, but I'd never been allowed anything more than blue or cream on my walls as a kid. When I'd moved back to Heather Bay after my professional footballing career had ended prematurely, I'd bought my house and decided to make it somewhere I'd be happy. I'd been in a major funk at the time, and decorating the house had become a form of therapy.

My bedroom was a warm yellow that made me think of the sun. My bathroom was jungle themed with plenty of plants and zebra print along with a flamingo shower curtain. My living room was orange, white, and blue. And my kitchen was pink with teal accents that my mum had ungraciously described as looking like something out of Barbie's dreamhouse.

I loved that comparison, though, and had gone out and bought a metallic, raspberry-pink stand mixer just to spite her. I loved my mum, but she could be pretty set in her ways sometimes.

"Well, luckily, Alex doesn't have to live here," Noah said. "It's your house, and I like it."

"Even the pink kitchen?" I asked, unsure why I suddenly wanted to know what he thought.

"Especially the pink kitchen." He smiled at me. It was a

sincere gesture, and for some reason, it made my stomach flip.

"Thanks."

There was another pause, and I didn't know what to say, which surprised me because I'd never had that happen before. I kept slicing the avocado and hoped something would come to me, but it was like my brain was still loading and stuck on that spinning wheel.

"Can I give you a hand with anything?" Noah asked.

"Maybe grab some plates out of that cupboard? We're nearly there. I've just gotta butter the bread."

"I can do that," Noah said as he retrieved some teal-and-white plates. "Where are your knives? And the bread. Hmm, I'm really not being that helpful, am I?"

I chuckled, the sound filling the room. I'd never had a morning like this before, but it felt like there was sunshine inside my kitchen. I didn't know if it was because I had someone here with me or if it was because that someone was Noah, but either way, it was a feeling I wouldn't forget in a hurry.

CHAPTER THREE

Noah

HAVING breakfast with Spencer wasn't nearly as awkward as I thought it would be. Instead, it was fun and cosy, and despite my initial thoughts that food would make me feel worse, the bacon, brie, and avocado sandwich on thick-sliced white bread Spencer made me lessened my nausea considerably.

I'd have happily stayed there all day with him, talking about everything and nothing in his charming, quirky little house and trying not to blush when he recounted some of the chemistry facts I'd apparently spewed at him last night.

But unfortunately, time didn't work like that.

It was closing in on noon when we'd finished eating, and Spencer had to get to Novel Tea to help Mina while I had the delightful prospect of marking a stack of my year nines' books ahead of me.

Spencer walked me down the road until we had to go in

opposite directions, and I found myself standing on the street watching him until he disappeared from view. I knew it was stupid to still have a crush on him after all these years when I logically knew nothing was ever going to happen between us, but I was too hungover to care.

Spending the morning with Spencer had only added fuel to the fire of my intense longing, especially now that I knew what his bed smelt like and how good he was at making enormous breakfast sandwiches. I'd seen the sunny smile on his face when I'd come downstairs, and if my head hadn't still been pounding, I'd have sworn I saw a pleased spark in his eyes when he realised I was wearing his clothes.

That sort of thing didn't have a friendly explanation, but it also didn't make sense. Spencer was, to the extent of our collective knowledge, straight.

I shook my head and stuffed my hands into the front pocket of the oversized Greenwich Athletic hoodie Spencer had lent me to walk home in. The early-October wind coming off the bay was bitter despite the blue skies and autumn sunshine overhead. In normal circumstances, it was the sort of weather that would make me want to wrap up warm and go for a brisk walk along the beach. But currently, the idea made me shudder, and I wanted nothing more than to lie on the sofa all afternoon and take a nap.

It didn't take me long to walk back to the flat I shared with Alex. We lived in a tall, Victorian townhouse that had once been just one residence but had been bought and split into two double-level flats some time ago. We lived on the top two floors, which gave us a nice view out over the street below and, if you looked through the right window, all the way down to the sea.

Alex was already on the sofa when I arrived, half-asleep with an old action movie playing on the TV.

"There you are," he said, glancing across at me with a scowl. "You're alive, then?"

"Just about." I walked around the sofa and pushed his legs off the end so I could flop down. Alex put his legs in my lap, his grey eyes roaming over me. He was buried in an old Metallica hoodie and a holey pair of black joggers, looking not much worse for wear apart from the dark circles around his eyes, but that might just have been where he hadn't taken his eyeliner off properly.

"You look fucking terrible. And is that Spencer's hoodie?"

"Er, yeah. He took me back to his last night to crash, then made me breakfast this morning," I said.

I'd never told Alex how much I fancied his brother, even though he was my best friend. I'd always thought it was a line I shouldn't cross, and I knew Alex would just tell me it was pointless because Spencer didn't like men. I loved Alex to a fault, but he wasn't tactful. He possessed a certain level of realism that came across as blunt and uncaring, but underneath, he was a man who cared incredibly deeply. He just didn't let many people see it for reasons I still hadn't figured out.

"Why didn't he bring you back here?" Alex asked. "Seems bloody stupid to take you all the way back to his when we're closer to Lane's."

"He didn't want to leave me alone and wasn't sure

when you'd be back." I smiled to myself at Spencer's slightly flawed but sweet logic.

Alex sighed. "He's a bloody banana. Has he gone to work now, then?"

"Yeah, he's gone to help Mina."

Alex nodded but didn't say anything. Sometimes it was hard to believe he and Spencer, with their opposite personalities and constant bickering, ran one of Heather Bay's most successful independent coffee shops, but their differences seemed to be the reason it worked.

"Have you got marking to do?" Alex asked as something exploded on-screen. I realised he was watching *Predator* when Arnold Schwarzenegger appeared on-screen and screamed about the chopper.

"Yeah." I rubbed my face because the prospect wasn't a fun one, but it had to be done. I loved teaching, but the sheer volume of admin and paperwork that went with it was hell.

Alex nudged me with his foot. "Go and get it then. Or you'll sit there all fucking afternoon, then panic later when it's not done."

I rolled my eyes and pushed his legs off me again. "Are you going to help?"

"No, I'm not a bloody teacher." He grinned at me. "But I'll make you some tea. Will that help?"

"It would be a lifesaver."

Alex swung himself off the sofa and sloped off to the kitchen. "Yeah, yeah. I'm a fucking miracle maker."

. . .

I felt human again by Monday morning as I took my seat in the staff room for the start of the weekly briefing. There were already quite a few people milling around despite the early hour, and someone had had the foresight to leave a large packet of chocolate biscuits open on the coffee table.

Heather Bay had two secondary schools—Hareford Grammar and St. Robert's—because although the town was small, it served a lot of the local villages. Neither school was massive, both having just under nine hundred students aged eleven to eighteen, although we shared a Sixth Form, so the last two years could choose where they wanted to have classes unless they wanted to go down to Scarborough College.

My friends and I had all gone to St. Robert's, which had just been the local comprehensive, but somehow, I'd ended up teaching at Hareford Grammar. Maybe it was because I didn't think I'd be able to look some of my old teachers in the eye considering some of my friends' antics.

Both Lane and Alex had been troublemakers despite mine and Oliver's attempts to keep them in line. They'd both mellowed out by the end, which had helped, but I was pretty sure the four of us had gained a reputation.

"Morning, Noah," said Katie, one of my fellow science teachers, as she sat down next to me, clutching an enormous mug of coffee. "Good weekend?"

"Not too bad," I said, taking a sip of the tea I'd made as soon as I'd arrived. "Just went to a housewarming for some friends. What about you?"

"Napped, read, and played endless hours of *Animal Crossing*." She grinned at me. "It was awesome."

I chuckled. Katie and I had started at the same time, and we'd become good friends over the years. "You've got year seven first this morning, right?" I asked as more people filed in and the room filled with the low hum of chatter.

"Yeah," Katie said. "I've got 7C. They're actually not too bad. Still in that period where they're not quite used to being here so they're a bit quieter." She sighed. "They'll be totally different in three weeks after half-term."

I nodded and opened my mouth to reply when Helen Rice, the headteacher, bustled in. "Morning, all," she said. "Everyone all right?" There was a murmur of assent and a few actual answers. Helen chuckled. "Nice and awake then I see. Don't worry, just a brief one this morning."

She rolled quickly through the briefing for the week, listing off a few memos and events as well as a few notes about administrative points. I listened quietly, making a mental note of everything that applied to me. As the briefing began to wind down, Helen grinned and looked towards where Katie and I and a few of the other science staff had gathered.

"Don't forget that the Friday before half-term—that's *next* Friday, not this one—is the science department's turn to do the bake-off," Helen said. I felt my heart sink like a stone.

The bake-offs were supposed to be a fun staff engagement initiative, where every month a different department would run a little baking competition in the staff room. The entries were judged blind by the rest of the staff, and the winners of each month went forward to a final that we ran in the summer. Every teacher from each department was expected to bring something when it was their turn, and some people got quite competitive about it.

I, on the other hand, hated the staff bake-offs. I couldn't bake for toffee and found the whole debacle to be a stress-inducing nightmare.

They'd run the bake-offs for the past three years, and every year I'd come last in science's month.

Baking was apparently meant to be about chemistry, something that should have come easy to me considering I was a chemist, but I'd never managed to get it right. Last year, I'd just ended up getting two boxes of brownie mix and making those, and even following the instructions, I'd still managed to burn the edges. Alex had taken pity on me and helped me make them presentable. Katie had sweetly said it was my most edible entry yet, but that hadn't done much to raise my spirits.

Although, I had noticed that even though the brownies hadn't been that good, there hadn't been many left. Free food was free food, no matter how edible it was.

"So," said Katie as we left the staff room and headed through the packed corridors to the science block at the other end of the building. "What are you going to make this year?"

"I have no clue," I said, pulling open a door and nearly running smack bang into one of my year eights. "Whoops. Sorry, Melissa."

"Just get a box mix again," Katie said. "And take it out like five minutes before you think you need to. You were nearly there with your brownies last year. Just get them again and chuck some extra butter and chocolate chips in or something."

"Yeah, I'll probably just do that." I sighed. Baking some brownies should not fill me with so much dread. If I was happy to demonstrate the effects of alkali metals in water or let my year twelves make esters, then I should be able to make some bloody chocolate brownies.

I said goodbye to Katie and headed towards my classroom, where my form would be waiting for registration. As I did, I wondered if there was a way I could bribe Alex to make them for me, although he didn't do a lot of baking for Novel Tea.

That was Mina.

And Spencer…

CHAPTER FOUR

Spencer

Rain lashed against the window of Novel Tea as I carefully lined up the day's array of cakes, brownies, buns, and pastries in the display counter, grinning to myself as I adjusted the super cute ghost cupcakes I'd made so they faced outwards.

Mina and I had been experimenting with Halloween designs for our bakes for the last few weeks, and I loved making the little ghosts out of marshmallow icing and piping little faces onto them in chocolate.

Baking was something I'd only really started getting into this year when our awesome baker in residence, Mina, had offered to teach me one morning. I'd been feeling blue, and she'd wanted to cheer me up, so she'd handed me a piping bag and showed me how to ice cupcakes. They hadn't been great, but I'd loved the feeling of calm I got from practising.

After that, I'd wanted to learn more, and Mina had been more than happy for me to give her a hand. The coffee shop was getting busier by the day, and she was struggling to do everything by herself. It made sense for me to step in and help out rather than leaving her to sink, and Alex had been happy to hire another part-time staff member to work the counter in my place.

"Okay, little buddies," I said, lining up the last of the cupcakes. "You look awesome. Go be scary and delicious."

I grinned and stood up, feeling my ankle twinge from being fixed in place too long. It didn't happen very often, but it was a niggling reminder that my life could've been very different from serving coffee and cake.

I'd been signed by the London based Premier League club, Greenwich Athletic, when I was seventeen, and it was literally my dream come true. I'd moved to London and worked my butt off on the youth team, determined to make it in the game I loved. But it wasn't meant to be. I'd been twenty-one and on loan to a club in Norwich when I'd broken my ankle in a freak accident during a game—the result of a bad tackle gone wrong. I'd had two surgeries on it and done months of physio, only for the club doctor to sit me down with the manager and tell me I wasn't going to play again.

Or, at least, I could, but there was like a ninety-five percent chance I'd do myself an incredible amount of permanent damage.

The club wasn't willing to take the risk, and I'd been forced to retire before I'd even begun my career.

Afterwards, I'd come back to Heather Bay and had been

drifting along ever since. I was mostly pretty happy with my life, but sometimes I couldn't stop myself from wondering what things could have been like if the accident hadn't happened. I knew it wasn't the healthiest coping mechanism, but I still hadn't stopped dreaming.

"How're we looking out there?" Mina asked, appearing in the kitchen door in her customary Novel Tea apron, her dark hair swept up into two buns that made her look like Princess Leia.

"Looking good!" I gave her a thumbs up and began to start prepping the coffee machine. "We can put the sandwiches out in a bit. I don't know if we'll get a lot of people in this morning."

I glanced out at the dark, deserted street where rain was still hammering against the window. We opened at eight every morning during the week so we could catch people on their way to work, but I didn't think anyone would want to stop today.

"I'll get you a tray now," Mina said. "Just in case."

"Sounds great." I bent down to retrieve a couple of bags of beans from under the counter to pour into the top of the machine. As I did, I heard the sound of the bell above the door ringing and the door sweeping open, intensifying the sound of the storm outside. I stood, bags of beans in hand, wondering who on earth wanted to be out this morning.

And saw Noah.

My face split into a grin, my heart skipping at the sight of him. He was wearing a dark raincoat with the hood up over his suit and a large backpack slung over his shoulders. He had a large, orange umbrella tucked under his arm. I guessed the wind was too strong for him to use it without it getting turned inside out.

Whenever I saw that happening, I always thought of the old Disney film, *Mary Poppins*, where all the nannies get blown away in the magical wind. I couldn't imagine Noah getting blown away, though, because there was something about him that just seemed so solid. It made a feeling of warmth spread through my chest that didn't really make sense. But I didn't want to question it because it felt good.

"Noah! Hey, I didn't expect to see you this morning. Especially in this rain," I said. Noah sometimes stopped by to get a drink on his way to school, but that was normally when Alex was opening.

"I didn't think it was that bad when I left." He chuckled softly and lowered his hood. "I think it's getting worse."

"That sucks, man. I was hoping it would be nice this afternoon so I could go running."

"Looks like you'll have to hit the gym instead," Noah said. "Unless you fancy getting drenched."

I shrugged. "Probably not. It'll just make my house smell like wet dog." Noah laughed, and I grinned. His laughter kind of reminded me of the feeling I got when I drank hot chocolate with Baileys in it—rich and comforting. I didn't know why I'd only just noticed. "What can I get for you?"

Noah walked towards the counter, peering at the menu written across the large chalkboard on the wall behind it. He left wet footprints on the wooden floor behind him.

"Something warming," he said. "Is it too early for hot chocolate?"

I scoffed. "It's *never* too early for hot chocolate. I think, like, the French have it for breakfast, so you're totally fine having it now. Which one do you want?"

We'd expanded our hot chocolate range over the last year after Alex had seen a place on Instagram offering a whole hot chocolate menu with about twenty different options. Ours wasn't quite that big, but we did have six solid choices, plus two rotating seasonal options.

They'd turned out to be pretty popular, especially with our regulars who weren't fans of tea or coffee or wanted a delicious caffeine-free option.

"What is the pumpkin spice one like?" Noah asked with a quizzical expression. "I've heard of pumpkin spice lattes but not hot chocolate."

"It's pretty good," I said. "It's not my favourite, but it's nice. It's like the American pumpkin pie spice mix—cinnamon and cloves and nutmeg—mixed with the chocolate. If you like spiced stuff, you'll probably like it."

"Hmm, okay." Noah considered for a second then smiled. "Can I tell you a secret?"

"Sure."

"When I first heard about pumpkin spice stuff, I thought it was actual pumpkin." His face flushed, and I grinned.

"Dude, me too! I was so confused because I didn't know why anyone would want a pumpkin-flavoured drink." I grimaced. "Pumpkin is gross. My mum used to make pumpkin soup every year, and I hated it."

"I'm glad I'm not the only one," Noah said. "Okay, which one would you recommend?"

I thought for a second, trying to remember what I could

about Noah. I liked making suggestions and helping my customers decide on their order, but it felt like there was more pressure this time. I really wanted Noah to enjoy what I suggested. "I really like the chocolate orange one," I said. "And the salted caramel one is lush, but it's pretty sweet. The mint is awesome too. It kinda tastes like those After Eight chocolates."

"I'll try the chocolate orange one, then, please," Noah said with this soft smile that made me feel like I'd had another shot of Baileys.

"Awesome. I'll do that now for you. Do you want any cakes or anything? Mina's just doing the sandwiches if you want to get something for lunch."

Noah thought for a second and glanced at the cabinet while I pulled out a large takeaway cup and grabbed everything I'd need for his drink. I heard him chuckle and saw he was looking at the ghosts. "These are cute."

"Right? I think they're my favourite of our Halloween range," I said. "I made them this morning if you want one."

"I'd love that. Thanks."

There was a moment of quiet between us while I frothed the milk and mixed it with the rich chocolate powder we used. We'd modified this batch to make it chocolate orange flavoured and the smell was making my mouth water. I grabbed a new Terry's Chocolate Orange and smacked it against the counter, hoping it would break up inside the wrapper.

"Can I ask you something?" Noah asked. He was still looking at the cakes.

"Yeah, what's up?"

"Are the cupcakes difficult to make? We've got the science department bake-off next week, and I've got to attempt to make something again. I'm trying to find something simple."

"They're pretty easy," I said, unwrapping the chocolate orange, pleased to see it had split into segments. "The most difficult part is probably the marshmallow icing since you've gotta soft boil the sugar."

Noah laughed. "When you're me, everything is difficult. Everyone tells me baking is a science, so I should find it easy, but it's one skill that utterly eludes me."

"Dude, no. Baking is an art. Yeah, you have to follow the recipe exactly if you want it to work, but it's more than that." I tried to think of a way to put my feelings into words, but I couldn't explain it. I didn't know how to tell Noah that you had to let yourself relax and feel it in your soul. He probably wouldn't believe me anyway.

"It's the *more* part I struggle with. I can follow recipes, but they're never right. I'm sure it's me." He shook his head. "Boxed brownies it is, and if I'm very lucky, Alex will take pity on me and help."

"I mean, I can help you if you want," I said. "I'm not like the world's best baker, but I'm pretty decent. I can teach you. Or at least help you make something for school."

"Oh." Noah's face flushed again, but I didn't know why. Was it hot in here or something? "You don't have to do that. I can't ask you to do that."

"I'm offering," I said. "It's not like you're demanding my help. You're my friend, and that's what friends do."

"Are you sure?"

"Yeah, I'm sure! Let me teach you how to make cupcakes. We can just do simple ones. It'll be fun!"

"Okay then, that would be great. Thanks, Spencer."

"You're welcome. Just drop me a message and let me know when you can come round. We can use my kitchen because I've got everything we'll need. Did you say it was for next week?" I was already thinking about what we could make that would be a good starter recipe for Noah to get his head around. Mina had started me with basic vanilla cupcakes, so I'd probably do the same. Although that might be kind of boring for the school bake-off.

Maybe we'd start with chocolate instead. That was usually a pretty good shout.

Noah nodded. "The bake-off is next Friday, the day before half-term. So at least if I totally suck, I'll have a week to wallow in self-pity before I have to go back to school."

"If I'm teaching you to make them, they're definitely not going to suck." I grabbed the silver whipped cream dispenser out of one of the under-counter fridges and began to load up Noah's hot chocolate. The whole thing looked amazing, and I was tempted to make one for myself.

"If you say so," Noah said. "I trust you."

"As you should." I grinned and stuck a few chocolate orange segments into the cream, suddenly wondering how I was going to get the lid on. I'd been a little ambitious with the amount of cream I'd used.

But it was Noah, and I didn't want to be stingy. I grabbed a lid and began trying to carefully squish everything down while Noah watched. Some of the cream dribbled down the side, and I sighed. I was always making a mess.

Eventually, I got it clipped on, and then I grabbed a couple of extra pieces of chocolate orange and rested them on top of the lid.

Just because I could.

CHAPTER FIVE

Noah

Spending my Thursday night at Spencer's wasn't quite what I'd had planned, but he'd insisted we start sooner rather than later in case I needed a couple of rounds of practice before the bake-off.

I didn't want to tell him a couple of rounds was optimistic. I still wasn't convinced I could be taught.

His offer was sweet, though. When I'd asked about the cupcakes, I'd been hoping for a couple of tips or even a basic recipe if he felt generous, not an offer of private baking lessons. My mind still hadn't quite wrapped itself around the fact that I was going to be alone with Spencer in his house, and even though I knew he was just being friendly, an idle part of my brain couldn't help but wonder if *maybe* it meant something more.

It didn't. But that didn't stop me from dreaming.

Like I Wished

I knocked on the bright yellow door of Spencer's beautiful townhouse and stepped back, digging my hands into my pockets. Thankfully, the rain from yesterday had let up, but the bitter wind that had been lingering all week still refused to budge.

I heard footsteps on the other side before the door swung open, spilling warmth and light into the darkening street. Spencer was bathed in light, dressed in a t-shirt and jeans with bare feet on the wooden floor. His shoulder-length blond hair was pulled back into its typical loose bun, and there was a bright smile on his beautiful mouth.

Spencer had always been gorgeous, dressed up or down, but there was something about seeing him like that —so casual and relaxed—that made my stomach twist.

"Hey! You made it," he said, moving back and waving me in. "Come on in. I've got us all set up in the kitchen."

"Thanks so much for doing this," I said as I stepped inside and kicked off my shoes. "I really appreciate it."

"No worries. It's going to be awesome. Just follow me."

Spencer walked down the short corridor towards the back of the house, where the Barbie kitchen was located. I'd meant what I'd said to him last weekend—I loved how bright and vibrant his house was. It felt like such a clear reflection of Spencer's personality—from the sunshine vibe of his bedroom, to the brightness of his kitchen, right down to the flamingo pots on the bathroom windowsill that held large, tropical plants.

The house was already filled with the smell of something baking, and when I entered the kitchen, I saw two trays of cinnamon buns sitting on the side, steam curling off them as they cooled.

"Sorry about the mess," Spencer said, even though there was very little mess to be seen. The counters were all wiped clean, and there were various bowls and beaters drying on the drainer beside the sink. His metallic, raspberry-coloured stand mixer stood proudly on the side like some shining beacon to the baking gods. "I was just testing out a couple of different bun recipes for the winter. Like a couple of Christmas specials."

"What flavours are you testing?" I asked, pulling a notebook out of my backpack before setting the bag down in a corner.

"Spiced orange and gingerbread. They should be cool in a bit so you can test them with me and let me know what you think."

"I'm not sure how much help I'll be because they both sound delicious."

"Nah, you'll be perfect. I want, like, a general consumer's opinion because Mina and I can sometimes be a bit picky."

"Surely that's a good thing, though?"

"Yeah, I guess, but we don't want to get stuck on the fence because we can't decide if they're good or not." He grinned. On anyone else it would have looked cocky, but on Spencer it just looked charming. "Although, I mean, they're ours, so they're not gonna be totally shit or something, but you know what I mean."

"I do, and I agree, they're never going to be shit. Mostly because my baking will *always* be worse," I said.

"Dude, stop putting yourself down," Spencer said. "You're gonna be awesome!"

"If I am, then you can take all the credit," I said. "So, where do we start?"

Spencer handed me a black apron, then showed me the recipe we were going to use. "They're just simple chocolate cupcakes, so you can't really go far wrong. I picked our basic recipe too, so you don't have to separate and beat egg whites or something."

"That's a thing? For cupcakes?" I stared at him.

"Yeah, Mina's got this really fancy cupcake book, and a couple of the ones in there are, like, blow your mind complex," Spencer said with a nod. "But you don't need to worry about that."

"Okay, this sounds far simpler in comparison," I said, suddenly glad I wasn't being asked to do anything like that. I felt more confident about pulling a rabbit out of a hat than doing any kind of whisked egg-white cupcake concoction.

"See? You've got this." Spencer clapped me on the shoulder and beamed at me. His belief in me was almost infectious, and I started to wonder whether making cupcakes really wasn't beyond the bounds of possibility.

Spencer gave me two cupcake trays to line with colourful paper cases before presenting me with two bowls and a set of scales. He set them on the kitchen island and watched me measure out and sift flour, cocoa powder, and a pinch of salt into one bowl and caster sugar and softened butter into the large bowl of the stand mixer. Then he showed me how to clip it into place and switch the mixer on.

"You can do it by hand or with one of those little hand mixers, but since I have Betty, it would be a crime not to ask her to do it."

"Betty?" I asked, raising an eyebrow. "You named the mixer?"

Spencer flushed, and his shoulders had gone tense. "Yeah. Is there a problem with that?"

"No! I think it's cute. But why Betty?"

"I thought it was cute too," he said. "And it just kind of fit. So she's Betty. And she's a legit lifesaver. I couldn't live without her."

"I think she's wonderful," I said, peering down into the bowl. "How much longer do you think?"

Spencer leant across me and glanced into the bowl, his shoulder brushing against mine. "Definitely another few minutes. You want to make sure they're properly combined, or it can end up grainy, and it'll make your cakes dense. It's gotta be light and fluffy."

I nodded and tried not to think about the brush of his shoulder. I was too old to lose myself in daydreams and fantasies from one accidental touch. Spencer wasn't suddenly going to magically see me in another light and swoop me up in his arms. We were friends, and that was it.

While the butter and sugar creamed, I combined an egg, some milk, and a splash of vanilla extract in a jug. I'd not used milk in baking before, but Spencer explained it was good for ensuring the cupcakes stayed soft and moist while also enhancing the flavour. It made sense, and I made a little note in my notebook to remind myself for the future.

I'd decided I'd write down as many tips and tricks as possible to help myself out next time I ventured into the land of baking.

"Okay, now you've gotta slowly add the egg and milk mix, then the flour," Spencer said. I reached for the jug and went to pour it straight into the bowl, but Spencer reached out and gently gripped my wrist. His hand was warm against my skin as he slowly guided me. "Gently," he said. "Gotta do it slowly, a little bit at a time."

"Doesn't the recipe say to add it all at once?" I asked, trying to keep my racing heart in check. Why did this moment suddenly feel so intimate?

"It does." Spencer's voice was soft and understanding. He stepped slightly closer to me, and I felt heat radiating off him. "But what you actually want to do is add a little bit of the milk, then a little bit of the flour, then milk again until it's all combined. Otherwise you risk it splitting."

"Oh, that makes sense."

Spencer didn't let go of me until he decided enough milk had been added, and then he drew my hand back. "Good. Now the flour mix. You want, like, a third of it."

I nodded and gently added the flour. Betty mixed everything carefully, and it was nice to see everything starting to come together. I glanced at Spencer, and he smiled at me in approval. I couldn't stop myself from grinning as I added the rest of the ingredients in turn.

"That's perfect," Spencer said. "You don't want to over mix it, or you'll knock all the air out of it, so I think we're nearly done."

"That was both easier and more complex than I expected," I confessed as Spencer switched Betty off and carefully lifted the arm. He unclipped the beater and tapped it against the edge of the bowl to dislodge some of the mixture that was clinging to it.

"You did great, and these are going to taste amazing." Spencer ran his finger along the beater to collect some of the mix on his finger. He lifted his finger to his mouth and licked the chocolate batter off his skin while I stood staring, utterly transfixed.

My cock stirred in my jeans, and I was glad I could lean against the side of the island and hide my crotch from view. If Spencer noticed, it would lead to a very awkward conversation I'd rather avoid.

Spencer held the beater out to me. "It's really good. You want to try some?"

"Thanks," I said, taking it from him. When I was a kid, my mum would let me clean the bowl of any cakes she made, but I didn't think it was appropriate to start licking Spencer's beater in the middle of his kitchen.

I suddenly imagined showing Spencer all the things I could do with my tongue and groaned internally because those were not the sort of thoughts I should have been having.

I ran my finger across the beater, then sucked the mixture off, hoping I was doing it in a graceful, nonsexy manner. The batter tasted amazing, and I made a little happy noise. Spencer chuckled.

"Good?"

"So good! This is amazing."

"If you think it's good now, just wait until they're cooked." He handed me an ice cream scoop, and I raised an eyebrow.

"Did I miss something?"

"Nah, it's for adding the mixture to the cake cases. Works so much better than a regular spoon or trying to pour it in."

"That actually makes a lot of sense," I said, lining up the two trays and starting to scoop the cupcake mixture into them. Spencer watched, and when I'd finished, he showed me how to give the trays a little wiggle so the batter flattened out, allowing them to bake more evenly.

"And now, these delicious little dudes are going into the oven." Spencer lifted one tray and bent down to slide it into the oven underneath the hob. "They'll need about twenty minutes, but we'll test them to see if they're done." I passed him the other tray and watched him slide it onto the second shelf. "While they cook, we can clean up and try some of the cinnamon buns. Are you okay to have them without icing? I meant to make some earlier, but I ran out of time. I can do some now if you want, though. I probably should so we get the full bun experience."

"I was going to say I was fine without it, but now I feel like I need the full bun experience too," I said, almost teasingly. "Will it take long to make?"

"Not really. I can do it in, like, fifteen minutes, maybe twenty."

"I can clean up while you do." I collected the various

bowls and moved them over to the large sink on the far wall. "Do you need any of these now?"

"I could do with Betty's," Spencer said, a soft smile on his face. "I really need to get a second one for times like this, but I keep forgetting."

"That's okay. It'll only take me two minutes to wash."

I turned on the tap and quickly cleaned and dried the mixing bowl while Spencer assembled what he needed for the icing. We lapsed into comfortable silence as Betty whirred and the dishes clinked in the sink. It was one of those calm, domestic moments I'd never really experienced before. Alex and I were always chatting, and if not, he usually had music playing to fill the quiet.

Alex didn't like silence that much.

"Okay, I think I'm done," Spencer said as I slotted the last of the clean dishes that had been drying on the rack into the cupboard. I'd had to move them to make space for the new bowls, and it seemed silly to leave them sitting there when I could easily put them away. "First, though, we'll check these cakes."

He grabbed a small skewer out of a drawer, then noted my confusion. "It's to test the cakes to see if they're cooked all the way through. If they are, the skewer will come out clean. It's not, like, the most scientific method, but it works."

Spencer opened the oven and grabbed some tea towels to lift the two trays of cupcakes out. I stared, mouth half-open, because they actually looked pretty decent. They weren't completely smooth and even—a couple of them had sprouted mountainous peaks in the middle and one had erupted over one side of the case—but they were a damn sight better than anything I'd made before.

"Oh my God!" I exclaimed. "They look like cakes."

"They look awesome," Spencer said, carefully putting the trays onto the hob before shutting the oven door. He handed me a skewer. "Okay, time to test. Just gently push it into the middle, then we can see how they look." He gently pressed a finger to the top of one of them, nodding as it sprang back. "See that? That's a good sign too. And they're not making a hissing or bubbling noise either."

I held my breath as I pushed the skewer into the cake and pulled it out. The shining metal was clean with one or two crumbs sticking to the end. I turned to Spencer, my face split from ear to ear in the biggest smile I'd ever worn. "They're cooked. I did it!"

"Yeah, you did!" He held out his hand for a high five, and the slap of skin echoed around the kitchen. "I knew you could."

"Only because you helped me do everything."

"Hey, everyone needs help at first," he said. "And I'll help you next week too when you make them for school. And if you want, you can always come round again at the weekend, and I'll show you how to ice things. I don't know if we'll get time tonight."

"Are you sure?"

"Yeah, positive. Come round Saturday afternoon. Like three-ish. I'll bring some plain cakes back from work, and we can practice on them."

"Okay," I said, giving him a little nod and trying not to

get swept off my feet by the idea of coming back here. "That sounds great. Thank you."

Spencer waved his hand and shook his head like giving up his precious free time to help me wasn't a big deal. "No worries. Now, did you want to test one of the buns?"

CHAPTER SIX

Spencer

My Friday morning workouts with my small group of gym friends were one of the highlights of my week, so I couldn't understand why I was so distracted that morning. I'd nearly tripped over my own feet during our warm-up, and now I kept finding myself staring off into space when I was supposed to be squatting.

"Spencer? You all right, mate?" Sean asked, frowning at me from his spot next to me where he was doing glute kickbacks, a cuff around his ankle so he could use the cable and weights to add more resistance.

Sean was short and muscular, the sort of guy who could probably pick me up and throw me over his shoulder without thinking about it. He was the one I'd known the longest out of my mates here, after we'd gotten chatting not long after I'd moved back. My doctor and physio had both sent me away with a long list of exercises and the assurance that gentle work-outs and building muscle would be good for me and help with my recovery.

Sean had been on the floor next to me and seen my Greenwich t-shirt, which I couldn't bring myself to part with, and started chatting to me. Our friendship had gone from there. We didn't hang out much outside the gym, but I still considered us close.

"Yeah," I said, racking the squat bar. "I'm fine, why?"

"I don't know. You just seem a bit all over today." He nodded at the bar. "That's lighter than usual, right? Something wrong with your ankle?"

"No, it's not that." I shook my head, pleased and irritated that Sean had noticed. I'd have talked to him if I'd known what the problem was, but I had no idea what was throwing me out of whack. I thought back over the past few days, trying to think about what had happened.

Work had been pretty busy but nothing more than normal. I'd made a toffee apple cake with Mina's supervision and had my first successful attempt at making caramel shards. That had been pretty sweet. But I didn't think that was the issue because that had been an awesome, exciting thing, and right now, I just felt… confused and drifting. Like an abandoned dinghy on the water.

There was something causing it. I just couldn't think what.

"Girlfriend?" Sean asked. "Did you and Natalie go on another date or something?"

"No, that's definitely over." Natalie was a girl from the gym I'd had a brief thing with in September, but it had fizzled out pretty quickly when we realised there was zero chemistry between us.

Sean frowned, and I wished he'd let it drop. But that wasn't going to happen when Sean's boyfriend, Chris, and our mutual friend, Andrew, came strolling over, having abandoned whatever they were doing when they saw Sean and me talking.

"You guys okay?" Chris asked. He was built like a tank with the squishy heart of a teddy bear. I hadn't realised when I first met them that Sean and Chris were together, but they'd opened up to me after they'd seen me in the Sleeping Goose, one of the local pubs, which was the closest thing Heather Bay had to a dedicated queer space, and realised I was a safe person.

It had probably helped that I'd been with Noah and company, including Theo, who had told me his mission in life was to be a walking beacon of queer, femme-boy energy.

"Spencer's not feeling great," Sean said.

"Is it your ankle?" Andrew asked. He was a chilled nerd who spent his weekends doing zombie runs, organising Dungeons and Dragons sessions, and hiking for miles across the Yorkshire moors with his golden retriever, Harley.

"No," I said. "My ankle's fine."

"Have you got a cold or something?" Chris asked. "You're looking a little… I don't know… pale. Tired too."

"I don't think it's a cold." I shrugged. "I don't know what it is. I'm just feeling a little off today. It happens."

The others nodded. "You want to talk about it?" Andrew asked. "You know we're here for you."

"I don't think there's much to talk about. I don't even know what's wrong," I said, looking around the gym. "Maybe we can just do a bit more? I think just doing something will help my brain switch off."

"Of course," Chris said, slapping me on the shoulder. "You wanna do some walking lunges with me?"

"Sure, sounds good."

Chris and I found a clear space and grabbed some weights before making a start. I tried to focus on putting one foot in front of the other, keeping my posture upright and dipping my back knee as close to the floor as I could. It helped, but I was still wobbly and unfocused. I didn't know what was distracting me, but it was starting to become a problem.

At the end, I grabbed my water bottle and took a long drink, trying to clear my head. Across the gym, I saw a younger guy in a loose tank top and small shorts doing hip thrusts with a barbell. I stopped to watch him for a second, my gaze lingering on the muscles in his thighs and the way his butt squeezed when he raised his hips. He had pretty good form.

The guy saw me looking and grinned, and I turned away. I didn't want him to think I was staring. Which I wasn't. I was just... looking at his form. Because that was a totally normal thing to do. I did it all the time.

I went back to my lunges with Chris, forcing my brain to focus. Except... when I glanced out the long windows on one side of the gym, I noticed it was raining again.

And I started thinking about Noah and his orange umbrella. I hoped he didn't get wet again today. It couldn't have been fun turning up at school all soaked through on Wednesday, but I hoped the cupcake had cheered him up.

I'd forgotten to ask last night because I'd been so focused on helping him. Noah had looked so happy when he'd seen how the cupcakes had come out, and it had made me feel warm and fuzzy again, like I had on Wednesday. Only more intense.

Noah had insisted he couldn't bake, and that it was going to be a disaster, but the cakes he'd made had been awesome. I'd originally thought I'd have time to teach him how to ice them, but then we'd gotten distracted by tasting the cinnamon buns, and I hadn't wanted to rush.

And I kind of wanted him to come back too. I hadn't wanted it to be just a one-time thing. So I'd put off teaching him how to ice them just so it didn't have to be.

I didn't know if that was sneaky, or weird, or whether it was just being helpful and friendly. It felt like it was more than that, but again, I didn't know why. Noah was my friend, and I liked hanging out with him. He was cute too.

Not cute in a wanting to date him way but cute as in friendly cute. Except I didn't even think that was a thing. And now that I'd thought about Noah not being cute in a dating kind of way, there was a voice inside my head asking why not. Noah *was* cute. I couldn't deny that.

And just because I was straight didn't mean I couldn't think guys were cute.

"Spencer?" Chris's voice jerked me from my thoughts,

and I spun to look at him. He frowned. "You sure you're all right?"

"I don't know," I said. I sighed and went to rack the dumbbells I'd been holding. "Can I ask you a question? Like a personal question?"

"Yeah, anything." Chris and I stepped to one side so we weren't in anyone's way. But now I didn't even know what question to ask. *I've been hanging out with a friend, and it makes me feel all fuzzy. What does that mean?* No, that wouldn't work.

Except now that I thought about it, that was kind of the issue. I'd never felt that way about any of my other friends when I'd hung out with them before. The only time I'd felt like that was around some of my ex-girlfriends.

"So, er, you're bi, right? Like you like people of all genders?" It probably wasn't the best question to open with, but I'd said it now, and I couldn't take it back.

"Yeah, I am," Chris said, giving me an encouraging smile.

"Okay, so, like, how did you know that? How did you know you liked more than girls? If you even started liking girls first, that is. I mean, how did you know you felt the same about lots of people?" I asked. I didn't know why I was flustered or even why I was asking Chris. Several of my other friends were bi or queer; they could've helped me. I should have asked Theo. He always seemed good with this stuff.

But if I asked Theo, then Laurie would probably be there too, and although I didn't mind Laurie knowing, it kind of felt like it would be two against one.

Chris looked at me for a second like he was trying to figure something out, then he said, "I was twelve, maybe thirteen, and I'd had crushes on girls at school, so I knew I liked them. But then I was watching some of *Avatar: The Last Airbender*, and I thought that Katara was cute, but Zuko was cuter. I always said they should have ended up together, but later, I realised it was because of more reasons that I thought they'd be the better couple. It was because I wanted to be with Zuko." He grinned. "Sorry. I guess that sounds kinda weird. I had the same sort of feelings when I watched *Pirates of the Caribbean* too. Elizabeth was hot, but Will was also hot. It took me a while to get there, but then I realised I liked guys just as much, and that was it. Does that help?"

I nodded because it did a little. Knowing that he'd felt the same way about guys as he did girls made it sound pretty simple. But it also threw up another massive question. If I felt the same way around Noah as I had with my ex-girlfriends, did that mean I liked guys too?

I'd never even thought about that before.

Which was weird because ninety percent of my friends were queer, but I'd never really sat down and thought about whether I might be too. I'd just kind of assumed that I was straight because I'd only ever had girlfriends.

Huh. Maybe I had some thinking to do?

"Yeah," I said. "That helps. Thanks."

"No worries," Chris said. "And if you wanna talk about it some more, I'm here."

"Thanks. I think I need to go and do some thinking, though."

"Did you... meet someone?" Chris seemed unsure if he should have asked, and I shrugged.

"I don't know. Maybe? I just... I've been hanging out with this guy a little more, and I don't know... Everything felt nice. Maybe I'm just thinking too much into it."

Chris nodded, and I saw his lips twitch. "You don't have to figure everything out right this second. If you like hanging out with him, keep hanging out with him and see how you feel. And then if you want more, you can ask him. Do you think he'd want that with you?"

I thought for a second. I knew Noah was gay, but did that mean he'd want anything to do with me? I had no idea. He was Alex's best friend, and that would make things more complicated, but on the other hand, he was an adult. I wasn't going to make decisions for him.

"I don't know," I said. "Maybe? I know he's gay, but that doesn't mean he'd automatically want me."

But as I looked at the rain outside, I got the sneaking sensation that I'd be disappointed if he said no.

"All you can do is ask," Chris said. He picked his water bottle up off the floor. "By the way, I wanted to ask you something. It's sports related this time."

"Er, sure."

"Me, Sean, and Andrew were looking at joining that five-a-side football league they run at the leisure centre. I wondered if you'd be up for joining us. I know you haven't played in a while, but it would just be for fun. They're starting a new season at the end of November, and registration for teams closes at the end of October."

Chris's words stunned me. The last thing I'd expected

him to bring up was football, especially after what we'd just been talking about, but maybe it was his way of showing me that nothing was going to change between us. I didn't know what to say, though.

I hadn't played since my forced retirement over ten years ago. At first, it was because I couldn't and then because it was too painful to even consider picking up a ball. My heart had ached every time I'd thought about it, anger and grief bubbling inside me like a lethal combination of fizzy pop and popping candy.

Football had been my life, and giving it up had taken everything out of me. I'd never wanted to feel that pain again, but maybe shutting it off completely had done as much bad as it had good. Instead of processing my feelings, I'd just bottled them up and decided to chuck the source of the problem into the sea, hoping it would float away on the tide of my memories.

But emotions didn't work like that.

Chris was still looking at me, waiting for my answer. My first reaction was to say no and tell him I couldn't risk it. My doctors had told me not to play again, and I'd stuck to that. They'd meant high-level stuff, though. A casual kick about with my mates probably didn't count. But I didn't have to tell Chris that.

But another part of me, a quiet voice that I'd suppressed for so long that I'd forgotten what it sounded like, whispered that I should say yes. I still loved football, and while my sporting dreams weren't ever going to come true, that didn't mean I had to punish myself for the rest of my life.

The two answers were at war with each other, both

firing shots across my heart, and I didn't know which one I wanted to win.

"Can I think about it?" I asked finally. "I've not played in a while, and I'm not sure I can."

"No worries," Chris said, clapping me on the shoulder. "Just let me know. Also, if you can think of anyone else who might be up for it, let me know. We're not going to go proper hard. It's just going to be for fun. Let off a bit of steam and have a kick about."

"Cool," I said. "Will do."

I glanced out the gym window again, feeling like someone had put all my emotions into a blender and turned it on full.

CHAPTER SEVEN

Noah

"Got any plans for the weekend?" Oliver asked as we carried two trays of drinks over to the two tables in the corner of the Sleeping Goose our friends were all grouped around. We'd managed to get the corner nearest the roaring fire that was chucking out heat and keeping the edges of the late-autumn chill away. The pub was packed with people, and there was a loud background hum of chatter and laughter, so I had to raise my voice to make sure Oliver heard me.

"Not really," I said. "I'm aiming for a quieter one than last weekend."

Oliver grimaced. "How're you feeling? Did you have a horrible hangover?"

"Much better now, but it wasn't pleasant when I woke up on Sunday." We reached the table and began to hand out the drinks. It was a bit of a squish getting all of us in the corner, but we didn't have any other option since it was too cold and wet to sit in the garden. That would be off the table until next April at the earliest. I didn't mind too much, though, because this was my favourite time of year, especially because it didn't come with a side of sunburn and sweating to death in my suit while trying to teach.

Oliver slid onto one of the benches next to his boyfriend, Lane, and I took the seat on the end next to him. The opposite side of our table was occupied by Will and Alex, who were deep in conversation with Lane. On Lane's other side, Theo and Laurie were chatting to Spencer. I felt a pull in my chest, wanting to go down and talk to him, but it felt rude abandoning Oliver just because I wanted to see Spencer again.

"I'm sorry," Oliver said. "I feel bad. You were our guest."

"Why? You didn't hold me down and pour the daiquiris down my throat," I said with a self-deprecating smile. "I should have stopped after one. I didn't realise how strong they were."

"Yeah, we're not letting Laurie make the drinks again." Oliver shook his head and grinned. I glanced down the table at our resident goth, who was bundled up in several thick, black jumpers, his dark hair tied up in a long ponytail. Beside him, Theo was wearing a bright pink, knitted jumper with his nails painted a similar colour.

The pair of them always made me laugh because they were such opposites to look at, and people often made the assumption that Theo was more a soft, fluffy-bunny type of person while Laurie was some sort of vampire in disguise.

And although Laurie owned and operated a funeral business, it was actually Theo who worked with the bodies.

Apparently, he found it soothing because the dead weren't argumentative or demanding.

"What about you?" I asked. "Any big plans?"

"None whatsoever," Oliver said. "I'm probably just going to spend it reading and ordering more books for the library. Maybe go and have a dig round the second-hand bookshop in town and see what I can find."

"Oh, the one down on Westgate?"

"There's one there too?" Oliver asked, his eyes lighting up like he'd just discovered the location of some lost treasure. "I was thinking about the one just off the front."

"That one is good, but the one on Westgate often has better stuff. It gets fewer people because it's tiny and full to the brim, so you have to sort through, but I've heard of people finding absolute gems."

"Okay, I'm going there."

"Going where?" Lane asked, turning to face Oliver.

"To the bookshop on Westgate tomorrow. Noah said I should check it out," Oliver said. Lane looked past him and raised an eyebrow at me, but there was a fond smile playing across his lips.

"Really, Noah? Why would you tell him about that?" Lane asked.

"Honestly, I thought he already knew," I said, reaching for my Coke and taking a sip. "I mean, he used to live here. It's been there for years."

Lane, Oliver, Alex, and I had all grown up in Heather Bay, but Oliver had only moved back to town recently after being away for nine years. Still, things in Heather Bay hadn't changed that much. And the bookshop on Westgate was one of those places that seemed to have been there forever and would continue to linger long after everything else. If this had been a fantasy novel, it was the sort of place that would be run by an ancient wizard with a very long beard and small glasses.

"I'd forgotten about it!" Oliver exclaimed. He grinned at Lane. "Come on, my library is *barely* half-full. I need more books."

"Fine," Lane said, leaning over to give his boyfriend a kiss. "But I'm not carrying anything."

"Of course not. I'm taking the van."

I smiled and took another drink of my Coke. The pair of them were very cute together. They always had been, even as teenagers, but there was a new depth to their relationship now. This time round it had gained another level of understanding and emotional maturity. Their love was deeper, and there was no question that it was going to last.

Lane had convinced Oliver to move back, and that was something none of us had expected to happen. He'd even built him a library in their cottage too—with a proper old-fashioned ladder on runners. If that wasn't a grand gesture of love, I didn't know what was.

Sometimes, when it was late at night and I was alone, I felt the deep gnaw of jealousy in my chest over their relationship. I would give anything to have what they had.

I'd just never managed to find anyone who cared about me as much as I cared about them. My track record with men was not particularly good.

"Sorry we're late," another voice said through the hubbub of chatter. I glanced up to see two more men standing in front of the table—Anders and Bastian, who'd been introduced to us by Oliver and had easily folded themselves into our group of friends. Anders was a fantasy author who worked with Oliver, and Bastian was his partner who'd moved to Heather Bay on a whim just for Anders in another touchingly sweet gesture of love that I tried to ignore.

I didn't want to become that person who got jealous of my friends for having successful relationships, and I certainly didn't want them to know I felt that way.

It was Bastian who'd spoken, and he continued as he unbuttoned his coat. "We were both working and lost track of time."

"You're forgiven," Oliver said as he looked up at them before grinning at Anders. "How's the draft going?"

"I told you he'd ask," Anders said. "You owe me a drink."

"Curses," Bastian said. "I thought he'd forget."

"He's my editor," Anders said dryly. "He's never going to forget about work I owe him."

While they were talking, I glanced down the table and realised this might be my chance to move since there was only one seat at our end and one seat next to Spencer. And I could easily frame it as allowing them to sit together and chat. Plus, I could always say I needed to ask Spencer a question about baking if I needed to. Most people at the table were familiar with my dire baking exploits from previous years, so it wasn't exactly a lie.

I grabbed my drink and went to slide off the bench. "Why don't you two sit here?" I said when there was a momentary lull. "I'll move down to the other end. I need to ask Spencer a question anyway."

"Are you sure?" Anders asked. "I don't want to dislodge you."

"You're absolutely fine," I said, standing up and making sure I'd also grabbed my coat. "You stay here."

"Thanks," Bastian said as we carefully all sidestepped around each other, making sure we didn't bump into anyone else. The pub seemed to have gotten even busier since we'd arrived, and I saw Colin and Soren, the owners, both behind the bar pulling pints and serving endless mugs of their hot cider, which was sitting in a steaming cauldron behind the bar.

I walked down the table and slid into the seat next to Spencer just in time to hear Theo say, "And that is why werewolves are in the basic tier of monster fucking and no higher."

I snorted and set my glass down. "I think I came in at the wrong moment."

"Not really," Theo said. "We were just talking about which monsters are fuckable and why."

"You were talking about that," Laurie said, giving Theo a fond smile. "I think you've scarred Spencer for life."

"Nah, I'm fine," Spencer said. "Theo makes good points." He was so chill about the whole thing I wanted to laugh. Then again, it was the sort of conversation you were liable to get with Theo. "How're you doing?"

"I'm good," I said. "Better now there's only one week

left until half-term." And better for seeing him again, but I left that unsaid. I needed to get my crush in check before it spiralled out of control and I did something I'd regret.

"Are you still up for coming round tomorrow?" Spencer asked. "Say about three? I figured I can show you some simple icing ideas you can use next week. Do you have a piping bag?"

"No," I said. I was surprised he'd mentioned our plans, but then again it wasn't like they were a secret. I just hadn't told anyone except Alex for reasons I couldn't explain. Maybe it was because I wanted to keep Spencer all to myself, even though I knew that nobody was going to gate crash.

"Don't worry. I can lend you one. Or if you want, you can come over on Thursday and make the cakes at mine. I can give you some boxes to take them home in."

"Are you sure?"

"Yeah, it's no problem."

"Okay," I said. "If you're sure. But let me know how much I owe you for the ingredients."

"What are you making?" Theo asked. For a second, I'd forgotten he was there, but now I realised he and Laurie were looking between Spencer and me.

"It's my department's turn to do the staff bake-off next Friday," I said. "Spencer's teaching me how to make cupcakes so I don't come in last again."

"My man keeps saying he's got no baking skills, but that's not true. The ones you made yesterday were great," Spencer said with a grin as he clapped me on the shoulder and squeezed, sending a spark shooting through my body.

"You made cupcakes, but you didn't bring us any?" Theo asked. "How rude."

"I didn't think they'd be that good." I felt my face flush. "Usually, I burn everything, or it's so dense you could use it to knock someone out."

"Don't worry," Theo said. "I forgive you."

"There's nothing to forgive," Laurie said, raising an eyebrow. "Anyway, you made cookies yesterday."

"Shh, don't say that. Now I look rude," Theo said. "Especially because I ate most of them already."

"You did?"

"I was bored, and they were tasty."

I chuckled. "If I have some spare, I'll bring you some round."

"You're the best," Theo said. "What sort of cupcakes are you making?"

We ended up talking about baking for the rest of the evening with the other three sharing a variety of kitchen disaster stories and favourite flavour combinations. Listening to Spencer talk about baking made it clear he was passionate about it, and it was lovely to see. I still remembered the way he'd been when he'd first come back after his injury. He'd still smiled, but it had been hollow like he was just a shell instead of a person.

But over the past few years, I'd slowly seen him come back to life. The baking had been a new addition, something he'd only started this year, but it seemed to have given him a sense of purpose again.

Even Alex had commented on how much happier his brother had seemed over the past six months.

When it was time to leave, we all wrapped up and headed out onto the street. The Sleeping Goose wasn't far from the beach, and I saw the water in the bay rolling in the wind and foaming against the shore. The rain from earlier had steadied into a drizzle, but the wind kept sweeping it into my face.

Spencer stood next to me, and as we said goodbye, he leant down, his breath warm against my skin. "I'll see you tomorrow."

And as he walked away, I touched the skin of my cheek as if I was trying to hold the warmth there for as long as possible.

CHAPTER EIGHT

Spencer

I PACED THE KITCHEN, looking at everything I had laid out on the island. Was it going to be enough? I'd quickly made some cupcakes as soon as I'd gotten home after work, and they were cooling on a rack. I'd pulled out all the ingredients to teach Noah how to make two types of icing: a simple chocolate buttercream and the more complicated marshmallow icing I used for the ghosts.

Since he'd thought they were cute, I kinda wanted to show him how to make them. Plus, they'd look awesome at the bake-off. I knew Noah said he wasn't going to win, but I believed in him, and I was going to do everything I could to help.

The only thing I wouldn't do was make them for him because that would be cheating, and I wasn't down for that. Assisting was one thing; cheating was another. Besides, I wanted Noah to see that he wasn't as bad a baker as he thought, and that wasn't going to happen if I just took over.

There was a knot in my stomach that seemed to tighten every time I looked at the clock on the wall. It was pink, like almost everything else in the kitchen, and although it was kind of old fashioned, I liked having it there. Noah was going to be here any minute, and I'd never been so nervous about hanging out with someone.

Chris had said just to keep hanging out with him and see how I felt, but at this rate, my brain was going to explode from being so on edge. I'd barely been able to think about anything else all day, let alone get anything done.

A sharp knock on the door distracted me, and I practically sprinted towards it, pausing only to check my reflection in the large mirror by the door. I didn't look too bad, and I wasn't going to think about *why* I'd spent twenty minutes choosing the perfect t-shirt and jeans combo for this afternoon.

I pulled open the door to see Noah standing there, wearing a nervous smile and a green hoodie. He had a plastic bag in one hand, and I almost frowned because I'd told him he didn't need to bring anything.

"Hey," he said, holding out the bag. "I washed the clothes you lent me last week. Thanks for letting me borrow them."

I'd almost forgotten about that. "Cheers, you didn't have to."

"What? Wash them or return them?" Noah asked as I took the bag and ushered him inside.

"Er..." I fumbled for a second because it hadn't been my smoothest moment. "Wash them?"

Noah chuckled, and the sound made a million lights light up in my chest. "I wasn't going to bring them back dirty. That would be so weird, especially because you lent me underwear."

"Yeah, I guess," I said, trying to work out why I was suddenly thinking about Noah in my underwear. I had no idea where the thought had come from, but now I couldn't get rid of it. It was like now that I'd acknowledged it, it was getting bigger. "Thanks, though."

"You're welcome."

I gestured for Noah to head to the kitchen and followed him, trying to get my head under control. Except walking behind him meant I got a good look at the way Noah's jeans hugged his butt and thick thighs, and I couldn't stop myself from staring.

I'd always thought it was normal to check out guy's asses at the gym, but now I wasn't so sure.

My confusion ratcheted up another notch.

"How was work this morning?" Noah asked as we entered the kitchen.

"Busy but good. Pretty normal Saturday."

I saw Noah staring at the cakes, a sweet expression of confusion forming on his face. "When did you make cupcakes?"

"When I got back." I shrugged. "I said I'd have some for you to practice on, and it didn't take me long."

"Yeah, but I thought you were going to bring some back from work?" Noah asked.

"We didn't have enough," I said. "Don't sweat it." I really didn't want Noah to worry because it wasn't like it had been a hardship.

For a second, it looked like Noah was going to say something else, but then he smiled and nodded to himself. "Okay. So where do we start?"

I decided to start with the chocolate buttercream, and once I'd handed Noah an apron, I showed him how to mix the room temperature butter with a little hot water so it went even softer before adding the melted dark chocolate.

"A lot of people say you have to do this over a saucepan of water on the hob," I'd said as I helped Noah to break up the chocolate into a bowl. "But you can just as easily do it in the microwave. You've just gotta keep an eye on it."

I'd shown him how to spot when the chocolate was just melted enough that a good beating would break up any remaining lumps and leave it smooth and silky without the risk of burning. It was so much less of a faff, and soon we had a delicious-looking chocolate and butter mixture we could add the icing sugar too.

I grabbed a tea towel off the side and gave it to Noah as he added the last of the sugar to the bowl and lowered Betty's arm. "Put this over the top," I said. "It'll stop the icing sugar going everywhere when you first switch it on."

"That's... I'd never have thought of that," he said, taking the towel from me. His fingers brushed against mine as he did, and a shock shot down my arm so fast and sharp I flinched.

"Sorry. Static shock."

"It's fine." Noah had flushed slightly, but I didn't know

if it was because of the shock, or the fact the kitchen was warm, or something else. He draped the towel over Betty. "Like this?"

"Perfect," I said. My tongue suddenly felt like lead, and my mouth was achingly dry. "Just leave that to talk to itself for a few minutes, then we'll have a look. Do you want a drink or something?"

"Er, just some water would be great. Thanks."

The glass of water didn't help my leaden tongue, but I hadn't thought it would. Instead, I distracted myself by checking the buttercream and showing Noah how to achieve the perfect consistency.

"You don't want it too firm," I said. "Otherwise it's really hard to pipe, but if it's too soft, it just runs everywhere. It's why baking in the summer is a nightmare."

Noah smiled. "It's basic chemistry."

"Yeah, exactly." I nodded and looked at the bowl in front of us. "Right now, this is pretty much good to go. I'm going to chill it for like ten or maybe fifteen minutes so it's easier to work with, but then we can ice some cakes!"

"This is actually simpler than I thought," Noah said as I slid the large, metal bowl onto the shelf in the fridge that I'd cleared and set a timer through the Alexa on the windowsill. "I thought it would be a lot more involved."

"I mean, you can make super complicated buttercream if you want, but I think the simple stuff is just as delicious. Like to me a good, simple vanilla or chocolate buttercream will beat your Italian meringue white chocolate ganache buttercream any day of the week."

"That just sounds over the top," Noah said. "Nice but over the top."

"Exactly. Although, if we get time, I'll teach you how to make the marshmallow icing for the ghosts. It's a bit more complex because we've gotta boil sugar, but I figure since you're a chemist, you'll enjoy it, and it won't freak you out too much. Plus, you'll know not to stick your finger in it."

"Speaking from experience?" Noah asked with a raised eyebrow.

I coughed and looked away. "Maybe. In all fairness, it wasn't deliberate. There was just a bit on the spoon, and I went to push it off with my finger. Luckily, it wasn't boiling boiling, but it still hurt like fuck. Mina made me stand with it under the tap for ages."

"Don't worry. I once had a beaker explode on me because I let it get too hot before I put water in it. Luckily, it was just water instead of acid or something, but that was not fun," Noah said. "I got such a bollocking from my supervisor."

I chuckled. "I think yours is almost worse. Do I have to get more baking injuries now?"

"Definitely not." He unclicked the beater from the mixer and held it out to me. "Want some before I wash this?"

"Always." I ran my finger over the edge and scooped up some of the buttercream. I'd already had some, but where was the fun in home baking if you didn't get to lick the bowl and the beater clean? Otherwise it was just going to go to waste.

I sucked the buttercream off my finger, revelling in the rich, chocolaty taste. I'd happily squirt a whole piping bag of the stuff into my mouth, but then I'd probably feel sick, and we wouldn't have any left to decorate with, so it wasn't going to happen. I realised Noah was staring at me, and I let my finger linger between my lips for a second.

Noah licked his lips. They were a delicate pink colour and looked really soft.

"You should have some too," I said, my words coming out quieter than I'd intended, but to me, they still sounded deafening.

"Sure. Okay." He grinned and lifted the beater to his mouth, flicking out his tongue to lick icing off it. I couldn't tear my eyes away from him as his tongue deftly curled around one of the metal bars.

All I could think about was that Noah had a talented tongue. Then I wondered whether there were other ways he'd know how to use it.

My cock stirred, sending a wave of heat through me accompanied by a flood of panic. Not at the idea of getting hard, but at the idea that Noah might see it and that would be hella fucking embarrassing. How the fuck could I explain that? *Watching you lick up chocolate buttercream was turning me on?* That just sounded creepy.

I didn't want him to stop, though.

A ringing alarm pierced the air as Alexa signalled the end of the timer. Noah froze, his eyes widening like something was wrong.

"Alexa, stop," I said. The alarm stopped. "Sorry, I didn't mean to startle you."

"It's fine," Noah said, walking over to the sink and

putting the beater in the bottom. He sighed. "Sorry, I meant to wash everything up while the icing was setting."

"Don't worry. I can do it later." I opened the fridge and checked the buttercream, taking a moment to let out a deep breath. I needed to get my head back on track before I got carried away and ended up God knew where.

I was in well over my head, and although my feelings didn't exactly scare me, they were confusing because I'd never experienced anything like this before. Not for a guy at least. I'd only ever felt like this for girls. But this felt different, more intense, and I didn't know if it was because it was so new or if it was because it involved Noah, someone I'd known almost all my life.

"How's it looking?" Noah asked.

"Great," I said, grabbing the bowl. "We can start piping now." I put the bowl on the island and grabbed the racks of cupcakes from where I'd left them to cool. I'd made twelve since that would give me a couple to demonstrate on and still leave plenty for Noah to use for practice.

Noah stood on the other side of the island, watching closely as I showed him how to fit the star nozzle I'd chosen into the piping bag and then how to fill it without getting buttercream all over his fingers. His gaze was intense but not in an intimidating way. Instead, it just made my stomach twist and bubble.

"Okay, so what you want to do," I said, grabbing a cupcake to demonstrate, "is start in the middle with a little bit of pressure until you get almost, like, a small flower, and then you want to make a swirl going outwards and let it overlap slightly." I slowly moved the piping bag so Noah could see what I was doing. "Then when you get to the edge, you just slowly release the pressure and almost tuck the end in." I lifted the bag up with a flourish and grinned at him. "And there you have it, a simple, piped rose. It looks proper fancy but is super easy. Everyone will be dead impressed."

"Including me," Noah said with a laugh.

"Come on, you can do it. Watch again." I grabbed another cupcake and repeated the process. "Now you try."

Noah took the bag, his lips setting themselves in a nervous grimace as he reached for a cupcake. I moved around the counter so I could watch him closely, my eyes fixed on his hands as they gripped the piping bag.

"That's it," I said. "Just do it gently."

"Oh God," Noah said, his tongue darting out to lick his lips. "This is a disaster. It looks so squashed."

"It's not that bad." It was a bit squished and lopsided, but it was still recognisable. "Especially for a first attempt. Try again." I picked up another cupcake and placed it in front of him, sliding closer until we were side by side. I felt the heat of his body against mine, which meant I was probably too close, but I didn't care.

I reached out and gently moved his hand. Another spark zipped across my skin, but I couldn't blame this one on static.

There was something going on I couldn't explain.

"How's that one?" Noah asked, turning his head to face me. We were almost nose to nose. I swallowed.

"Perfect."

Noah smiled. "You didn't even look."

I glanced down. "I did that time."

"And?"

"Like I said, it's perfect."

"Okay." There was a moment of silence that stretched out between us. I wondered if I ought to break it, but I didn't know how. "I should do another one," Noah said eventually, tearing his eyes away from mine. "I need the practice."

"Yeah, makes sense," I said. "If you do these, I can teach you how to make the marshmallow if you want?"

"I'd like that."

It was only later, when I was shoving things into the dishwasher, that I wondered if I should have kissed him.

CHAPTER NINE

Spencer

I SHOVED the last of the crockery into the dishwasher and a tablet into the dispenser, hitting the power button as I slammed the door shut. Grabbing my phone and keys off the kitchen counter, I retrieved my hoodie out of the bag of clean washing that Noah had brought me and headed towards the front door.

I needed help to figure out what the fuck was going on in my head and the rest of me, and there was only one person I could think of who'd give it to me straight. And it didn't matter that his best friend slash roommate slash potential boyfriend would also be there too, despite my earlier reservations.

Theo and Laurie were the only people I wanted to turn to because I knew neither of them would judge me, neither of them would try to overcomplicate it, and neither of them would let me hide from my feelings. They were like two members of the Scooby Gang, only instead of solving ghostly mysteries, they'd help me solve the question of what the hell I was going through.

I pulled the hoodie on and stopped dead in my tracks. It smelt like Noah.

Which wasn't surprising since he'd washed it, but what was surprising was the way my body responded to the scent of whatever fabric conditioner he'd used. My pulse quickened like I was sprinting on the treadmill, and there was a tingling sensation racing across my skin. I took a deep breath, allowing the smell to envelop me and not caring if it was weird. It wasn't like there was anyone around to see me.

With my head still spinning, I raced out into the street. It was dark outside, which wasn't a shock considering it was nearly half eight in the evening, but it was easy to follow the road under the warm glow of the streetlights.

It was about a ten-minute walk to my destination, but I ended up jogging most of the way until I reached the red brick building with several large bay windows and Winchester & Sons Funeral Directors written in gold across the grey frontage. The door to the flat was at the back, so I headed around the building to the unassuming black door with a brass knocker shaped like a fox in the middle. There was a little camera with a buzzer underneath it on one side, about head hight. I pressed the button and waited.

"Hello?" Laurie's surprised voice came out of the speaker. "Spencer, is that you? Everything okay?"

"Yeah, maybe. Can I come in? I need to talk to you and Theo."

"Sure. Hang on." A couple of seconds later, I heard the soft thump of footsteps, and then the door swung open to reveal Laurie. He was dressed in a cosy-looking black jumper and joggers with slippers that looked like monster feet. He was still wearing all his rings, but he'd taken off his normal make-up.

"Sorry it's so late," I said as I stepped inside, shutting the door behind me. "I'm, er, kinda having a crisis?"

"You don't sound sure," Laurie said, but he didn't seem annoyed, more intrigued.

"Honestly, I'm not sure of anything right now. But I need to talk to someone, and I figured you and Theo could probably help." I lowered my voice conspiratorially, even though there was nobody else around. "I, er, I don't think I'm straight. And I'm a bit... confused."

Laurie nodded. "Come on. I'll put the kettle on."

I followed him upstairs and into the large sitting room, which had the same kind of vibe as Sherlock's living room. It had similar old-fashioned wallpaper, an old red carpet, and a fireplace in the far wall with bookcases on either side of it, each one overflowing with books and knickknacks. On the wooden mantelpiece above the fire stood two things that had freaked me out the first time I'd seen them: a stuffed raven with a top hat and monocle, named Lord Featherby, and two stuffed mice who were tap dancing.

Laurie had said, with a bemused smile, that they were Theo's.

"Take a seat," Laurie said, gesturing at the squishy leather sofa. "I'll get you a drink." He walked over towards an open doorframe, which I knew led to a kitchen-dining room and beyond that, two bedrooms and a bathroom. I heard Laurie's footsteps recede and then some muffled conversation where he was obviously talking to Theo.

I looked around the living room to the TV in the corner where the screen was paused on an episode of a show I didn't recognise. It was something historical, though, given the way everyone was dressed. Maybe about Vikings. Or pirates. They were definitely on a ship.

I didn't get much of a chance to think about it, though, because two seconds later, there was a thundering of footsteps, and I turned my head just in time to see Theo come flying into the room, dressed in what looked like a *Playboy* bunny outfit, complete with enormous ears nestled into his blond hair.

I stared. Theo didn't notice.

"Are you okay?" he asked, flopping down on the floor in front of me and looking up at me with a penetrating expression. I tried not to meet his eyes. Mostly because that would mean looking at Theo in his bunny suit, and it was making me consider things. Weird things. Like what Noah would look like dressed like that.

"Er, not sure," I said, looking at a spot just behind Theo's head.

"Laurie said you were in distress and needed help. Did something happen?"

"I did not say he was in distress," Laurie said, appearing with a large, old-fashioned biscuit tin and shoving it under my nose. "I said Spencer needed to talk to us about a specific issue he believed we could help with." He shook the biscuit tin. "Have a biscuit. It'll help. In fact, take three."

I picked out a couple of chocolate biscuits as Laurie turned back to Theo and raised his eyebrow. "Did you not want to put some clothes on?"

Theo looked down at himself and laughed. "Oops, I didn't realise how much was showing. Hand me that blanket?" Laurie threw a black fleece blanket at his head, and Theo caught it and draped it over his lap. "Better?"

"Yes," Laurie said with an approving nod. "We can't see your dick now."

"Sorry," Theo said. "Can I have a biscuit?"

"Here." Laurie handed him the tin, which Theo took with a beaming smile. "I'll be back in a minute." He walked back towards the kitchen and there was a moment of silence while I waited for Theo to ask the inevitable question.

"So what did you want to talk about?" His tone was soft, innocent almost, but I could hear the gently prodding note underneath it that told me Theo wasn't going to let me sidestep things. Which was fair enough since I had turned up at his house on a Saturday night without even giving him a heads-up.

"I, er, well…" I'd told Laurie and Chris, so it should have been easy to say it again, but the reality was starting to hit me as I remembered how my body had reacted to seeing Noah licking up buttercream in my kitchen. "I'm… I have… I don't think I'm straight. I think I have a crush… on Noah. And I don't know what to do."

Theo looked at me for a second, and then he nodded and smiled reassuringly. "Don't worry, we've got you. Don't we, Laurie?"

"We do indeed," Laurie said, bringing in a tray laden with three large mugs. He slid it onto a small table next to the sofa and handed me one, which was unsurprisingly black with a pattern of little white stars all over it. He handed Theo a mug patterned with colourful, pixelated hearts before sitting on the sofa next to me with his own cauldron-shaped mug in his hands.

"Thanks for telling us," Theo said earnestly before dunking a chocolate biscuit in his tea. "I'm glad you trust us. Have you told anyone else?"

"Sort of," I said, feeling an overwhelming sense of relief that he wasn't making a big deal out of it. "Just in vague terms to a gym buddy I know is bi."

Theo nodded and then said, "Is this the first time you've ever felt like this about someone who wasn't a girl?"

"I think so? I don't know." I broke one of my biscuits in half and ate a bit, trying to think back. I felt my face flush. "Is it... is it gay to look at other guys at the gym? I always told myself I was checking out their form, but maybe... I think sometimes I stare because they look good."

"First of all," Theo said, "there is no this is *gay*, that is not *gay*. Actions are not gay." Laurie snorted, and Theo giggled. "Okay, so, maybe me sucking dick is gay. As is me getting railed by, like... Anyway, that's not my point. My point is that looking at other guys' asses doesn't make you gay. It's not like a switch. Sexuality is fluid and more like a spectrum than a set of absolutes. Does that make sense?"

"It does. I guess Noah isn't really the first guy I've found attractive," I said, slowly starting to piece things together from my past. "But he's... he's the first man I've ever gotten, like, butterflies around. I feel so nervous around him. Like I'm going to be sick but also like I want to see him all the time. And I... Earlier he came over so I could teach him how to make icing for cupcakes, and he did this thing, and I..."

"He didn't happen to lick icing off the beater did he?" Laurie asked. I turned to him, and I knew my confusion was written across my face.

"Yeah. How did you know?"

Laurie gave me a little smile and sipped his tea. "Just a hunch."

"Yeah," Theo said sagely. "That'll do it. Did you get hard?"

"Theo!" Laurie exclaimed while my face flamed.

"What? There's no point dancing around it. And looking at Spencer's face, I think I just hit the nail on the head."

"I know, but there's no need to be so crass about it."

"Really?" Theo shot him a withering look. "It's me."

I chuckled because they were so funny together—like some old married couple. Nobody really knew whether they were together or not, and now it felt rude to ask. I'd just thought they were really good friends for like the first year until Alex had mentioned something about it. I wasn't really sure what that said about me.

"Um, I..." I swallowed. I knew I could trust these two. They weren't the sort to plaster my secrets all over Twitter. "Yeah, I did. But it was more than that. I really wanted to kiss him. And I've never wanted that with a man before. I nearly did too."

"What stopped you?" Laurie asked, and I shrugged.

"I don't know. I wasn't sure if Noah wanted it too, and I didn't want to make things weird between us. He's my friend, and I really like hanging out with him. I don't want to fuck that up by doing something I can't take back."

"What if you don't fuck it up?" Theo asked. "What if you kiss Noah and he likes it? What if he wants more? Would that change things?"

"No. Why would it?" I wasn't sure what Theo was poking at, but the idea of Noah wanting more didn't bother me. If anything, I couldn't actually imagine it happening because I still couldn't wrap my head around the idea of him wanting me like that.

But if I got the chance, I'd want to do whatever I could to make Noah happy. I'd want to spend hours with him, exploring every inch of his body so I knew just what made him moan. I'd never be satisfied until I'd made him come, whispering my name like a prayer.

Oh…

Yeah, I definitely wasn't straight.

I glanced down and realised Theo was looking at me with a sly smile like he was watching me figure something out that he already knew, like the pieces of the puzzle were clicking into place in real time right before his eyes.

"I really do have a crush on Noah," I said quietly, turning a piece of biscuit over in one hand. "And I really want to be with him. Or at least, I wouldn't mind seeing how things went. Like that doesn't scare me. Not that it would, but… Yeah."

"It's okay," Theo said. "Sexual exploration can be a little daunting if it's your first time, but just talk to Noah.

Healthy communication is important with all your partners no matter their gender. Anyway, this doesn't mean you have to go and jump on him. Just tell him how you feel. Be honest that you like him and you're having feelings and that you'd be open to exploring a relationship with him if it was something he was interested in."

I nodded. Theo made it sound so simple, and maybe it was. But right now, it felt like a massive hurdle to climb. How did I even bring it up in conversation? "I think I can do that. Maybe."

"You don't have to obviously," Laurie said. "But if you do want something with Noah, you are going to have to tell him. You can't expect him to read your mind."

"Exactly," Theo said. "Communication is key!"

I nodded again, repeating the phrase to myself. Then I looked at Theo and asked the question that had been bugging me since I arrived. "Theo, why are you wearing a bunny suit?"

Theo grinned. "I was streaming when you arrived—just playing some *Dawn of Blood*. Anyway, I promised my followers I'd wear the suit if they helped me and a couple of friends raise twenty grand for the LGBT Foundation at an event we did last weekend. We raised nearly thirty, which is why I am now a bunny! I think I look cute, though, don't you? I'm going to wear it again next week when I go to London to film with some friends."

It was an open secret in our group that Theo did amateur porn for fun. Alex was the one who'd found out and asked Laurie about it. He'd apparently just shrugged and said it was Theo's thing. He'd seemed surprised Alex had asked, or maybe he was surprised none of us knew. Anyway, we'd all promised never to watch him—because that was probably weird—and that we'd always support him and be there if he needed anything. We'd never judge him, and we just wanted him to be safe.

"Thirty grand? That's amazing," I said. "And yeah, you look cute. Be safe next week, okay?"

"I will, but thanks." He took a long drink of his tea. "Do you feel better now? Less confused?"

"I feel less confused," I said. "Not sure about better, though. Are the snakes in the stomach normal? What about the feeling sick?"

"It's totally normal," Laurie said. "And I promise, if you talk to him, things will be okay."

"You think?" I asked, wondering if they knew something I didn't.

"I do."

"Okay," I said, unable to stop myself from smiling as I took a sip of my tea.

CHAPTER TEN

Noah

I'D SPENT the start of the week avoiding Spencer. I didn't want to, but after everything that had happened on Saturday, I'd thought it would be good to put some distance between us. I'd seen the way Spencer had looked at me when I'd licked the buttercream off the beater, and it hadn't been anything like I'd expected.

I knew when I'd done it I'd potentially been pushing things. But there had been *something* going on in that kitchen, and I'd just wanted to see what would happen.

I'd been expecting laughter or maybe an eye roll, not Spencer staring at me with heat in his gaze like he'd never seen anything like what I was doing before. It had thrown me because I'd always thought Spencer was straight and had no interest in me beyond being friends. But now…

Now I wasn't sure at all.

After that moment, we'd just carried on with the afternoon, but it felt like things had shifted slightly between us. The way he'd been almost pressed against me as I'd attempted to ice the cupcakes, and later, when he'd brushed against me while we were clearing up, his hand lingering on mine for a moment too long as I passed him icing bags and spatulas… none of them felt like moments between friends. But neither of us had said anything.

It was like we'd unconsciously moved into a state of limbo.

I didn't want to be the one to take the next step, though. That had to come from Spencer, especially if he was figuring something out about himself. I didn't want to push him because there was a good chance it would just make him run in the other direction.

I knew there were plenty of people who went through a process of discovery and exploration about their sexuality in their thirties and beyond, but everyone's journey was different. Some people were bound to find it frightening and push back against it; others were likely just to roll with it and accept it without batting their eyelids.

Given how chilled Spencer was, I'd assumed he'd be part of the latter category if it was indeed something he was experiencing. But I didn't know that for sure. I couldn't exactly read his mind.

So I'd decided that giving him some space was the best option.

Especially because there was a good chance it was all in my mind and my brain was just taking wishful thinking to a whole new level. At least some space would give my imagination a chance to get itself in check and stop conflating innocent touches with some illuminati level of sexual code.

Except it was now Thursday, and I needed to know whether it was still okay for me to use his kitchen that evening. I didn't want to tempt fate and attempt to make cupcakes at home without Betty or Spencer's watchful eye.

As soon as the last bell rang and I'd dismissed my class, I snuck into the science tech room that adjoined my classroom and pulled out my phone. Opening my message thread with Spencer, I tapped out something before I could think better of it.

NOAH *Hey! How's your Thursday? Am I still okay to pop round later and use your kitchen, please? =)*
SPENCER *Sure, no worries! I'll be home about six, so come round any time after that!*
NOAH *Amazing! Thank you! See you later.*

I let out a breath of relief and shoved my phone back into my trouser pocket. That would give me a few hours to go home, do a little work, shower, and try not to think about what this evening might involve.

It was hard to get my mind off it, though. Now that my imagination had gotten a glimpse of the fact that Spencer *might* be interested, it had taken that idea and run with it, completely disregarding the fact that it might not be true. And my attempts to get it in check had been like trying to catch greased weasels with oiled hands.

By the time I got home, all I could think about was the touch of Spencer's hand on my wrist, guiding it slowly, and the way his body had felt next to mine. All I could think about was what it would be like to have Spencer's hand moving mine to where he wanted it, gently leading it up his thighs or down his stomach until I reached his cock.

Would he moan when I touched him? Or would there be nothing but a sharp intake of breath as he waited for more?

I dumped my bag on the sofa, knowing that I really needed to do a last bit of marking before half-term, but my restless mind dragged my thoughts away. There was no way I was in the right frame of mind to do any work, but I still hesitated. I'd always tried to avoid fantasising about Spencer in the past, despite my crush, because it always felt like crossing a line.

Nobody would have known except me, but Spencer was still my best friend's brother, and he was straight. It had felt wrong on some level.

Now, though... Spencer was still Alex's brother, but I was sure he'd shown interest. There was no way he'd have looked at me the way he did otherwise.

Was it so terrible to get myself off thinking about him? Just this once.

It would make this evening easier if I wasn't trying to bake cupcakes with a raging hard-on.

"Fuck it," I muttered to myself, heading for the door out to the tiny landing and the stairs. As I climbed them, I suddenly wondered if Alex was home. I hadn't seen any evidence of him downstairs, but he could be taking a nap or gaming.

I knocked on his door as I passed. "Alex? You in there?"

No response. I knocked again and called his name louder. Still nothing.

That meant I had the flat to myself, and even though I wasn't planning on being loud, there was an extra level of comfort knowing I was alone. Especially since I was planning on jerking off to thoughts of Alex's brother.

Ducking into my room, I quickly shut and locked the door behind me, just in case. My fingers were trembling as I reached for the buttons on my shirt, desperation starting to build under my skin. I pulled my shirt off, cursing as the cuffs caught on my wrists, before unpopping the buttons on my suit trousers and shoving them down my thighs, leaving me in just my underwear.

I headed for my bed, quickly throwing off my boxers before I climbed onto the mattress. My cock was already starting to fill as I thought about taking Spencer to bed. Would he want to take it slowly at first? Or would it be all heat and desperation as we finally gave in to whatever was happening between us? I wouldn't mind either way as long as something happened.

Lying back on the bed, I let out a shaking breath as I let my fingers skim down my chest and across my stomach. I was too wound up to take my time, so a cursory touch of my body would have to do.

"Shit," I gasped out as I wrapped my fingers around my shaft. It was thick and hard in my hand with precum dribbling out of the slit. I slid my thumb across the head, smearing my precum across the skin. I groaned as I slowly started to pump my cock, my hips rocking into my hand as thoughts of Spencer filled my head.

I imagined him lifting my thighs and pressing my legs into my chest as he pressed into me, splitting me open and barely giving me a minute to breathe before he started to fuck me. That was a delicious thought. But then I wondered if he'd wait until I told him to move.

A moan slipped from my lips as I imagined Spencer looking down at me, his face painted with desperation as he waited while his cock was buried deep within me. I wouldn't make him wait forever, just long enough to make him shake with need, stretching out that moment until he was ready to snap.

And then I'd bring his head to mine and let my words brush over his ear as I told him to fuck me and make me scream with pleasure.

A dark voice in my mind whispered that Spencer was probably the sort of person who'd do anything to make his partner happy. That he'd give me whatever I needed and do it without complaint. A shudder ran through me at that idea. I'd never take advantage of him, but just the idea that Spencer would fuck me however I told him had flicked a switch deep inside me I'd only vaguely been aware of.

I'd never been the sort of man to want absolute control in the bedroom, but taking enough to get what I wanted sounded fun as long as Spencer was okay with it.

Although this was a hypothetical scenario, so technically, I could have whatever I wanted.

I gripped my cock tighter, my hips jerking sharply as I tried to find the perfect rhythm. My brain and my body were at odds—one lost in fantasy, the other searching for the familiar. I huffed in frustration as my pleasure rose and fell because I needed to get off, but what I was doing just wasn't working.

Letting go of my cock, I sat up and shuffled across the mattress, reaching down to open the drawer under the bed. Inside was a bottle of lube and a couple of toys I'd acquired over the past few years. I'd never thought they were for me until an ex-boyfriend had convinced me to try some, and while the relationship hadn't lasted, my fondness for toys had.

Grabbing the lube and my favourite dildo, I repositioned myself on the bed in a kneeling position. The dildo was a simple one—thick and flesh coloured with a cup on the base I could use to stick it to a suitable surface. Since my floor was carpeted and my shower was small, I didn't actually have anywhere unless I wanted to ride it on the bathroom floor, but I'd found I could use it perfectly fine on my mattress. It just sometimes required repositioning.

I squirted some lube onto my fingers, quickly opening my hole while stroking my cock. Then I poured more lube onto the dildo and lined it up with my hole, slowly sinking down onto it. I groaned as it entered me, closing my eyes and imagining straddling Spencer's hips. I thought about him resting his hands on my thighs as I took his cock into me, not allowing him to touch my cock or move his body until I was ready.

A shuddering curse rolled off my tongue as I lowered myself down, taking as much of the dildo as I could. It stretched me perfectly, adding just the right amount of burn and giving a new dimension to my fantasy.

"Now," I whispered. "Now I'm going to ride you."

I imagined Spencer whimpering and nodding as I started to move, sliding up and down on the toy faster and faster. I tilted my hips and reached down to adjust the angle, then cried out as the thick head of the dildo immediately rubbed across my prostate. I groaned, jerking my cock as I rode the dildo harder, working the shaft with my hole as waves of pleasure washed over me.

This was what I'd been missing, and now I knew it wouldn't be long before I reached the release I'd been craving.

Another moan filled the room as my balls tightened, my cock hardening in my hand. I was so fucking close, and I felt Spencer's name on my tongue as the fantasy of fucking him consumed me. I fought to keep it back, biting my lip as my orgasm hit me. My body tensed as the delicious feeling of release flooded my body. My hole pulled the dildo deeper into me as my cock shot thick streams of cum across my skin, dripping onto the pillows in front of me and leaving wet marks across the fabric.

"Shit," I said as a deep sense of relaxation pulled at my muscles. It would have been easy to flop down on the bed and stare into space or doze off, still thinking about Spencer and wishing for things that were never going to come true. But that couldn't happen. Not tonight.

Slowly, I eased the dildo out of my ass and dropped it onto the bed beside me. My thighs were starting to cramp, the muscles shaking as I shifted out of my kneeling position and swung my legs off the edge of the bed and onto the floor. I needed to shower and get dressed before Alex came home, and I'd need to change the sheets as well. Just turning them over later wasn't going to work for me.

But I allowed myself to sit there and indulge in my fantasies for just a moment longer.

CHAPTER ELEVEN

Noah

By the time six o'clock rolled around, I was starting to feel nervous, but this time it wasn't over the idea of baking cupcakes.

It felt like tonight was going to be different, although I couldn't put my finger on *why* I thought that. It was just a feeling in my gut like something had drifted in off the wind from the bay. A subtle shift in the air like the desolate calm before a storm, where you knew something was coming, but it was impossible to tell when.

I left Alex on the sofa, telling him I was going to bake with Spencer for tomorrow and not to wait up. He'd raised an eyebrow but said nothing. I didn't know if he suspected something, but that was an issue I could deal with later. First, I had to sort out whatever was happening between me and Spencer, then I could worry about what I needed to tell my best friend. If nothing happened, then Alex wouldn't need to know.

If it did, I could cross that bridge when I got to it.

It was dark when I left the house, and clouds skittered across the sky as I made my way across town towards Spencer's. My feet carried me without any conscious effort while my mind went back and forth about whether the signs I'd convinced myself I'd seen were real or just a figment of my desperate imagination.

Only I would read someone standing close to me or offering me help as akin to a marriage proposal.

I'd always been the sort to fall hard and fast because someone showing interest in me was such a rare thing. Every time it happened, I had a tendency to latch onto them, and it meant I'd pushed more than one man away by coming on too strong.

Maybe Spencer had just been standing next to me so he could keep a close eye on me and make sure I got the frosting right. Maybe he'd stared at me when I'd licked up the icing because he'd been thinking about something else or even dreaming about a beautiful woman doing the same thing and imagining where that would lead.

I shook my head, chasing my thoughts away as I realised I'd arrived at Spencer's front door. I knocked quickly, glancing around while I waited. There was the sound of footsteps on the other side, but this time, when the door opened, I was greeted by a sight that left me speechless.

Spencer was standing there shirtless in just a pair of ratty old shorts while water dripped down his chest. His blond hair hung around his face, still wet from where he'd obviously not long ago climbed out of the shower. Words escaped me. I knew I needed to say something, but my mouth refused to open, let alone move.

"Hey," Spencer said. "Right on time. Come on in!" He stepped back, and my feet carried me over the threshold as I continued to stare at Spencer's broad, well-muscled shoulders. He'd turned around to retrieve a t-shirt from over the banister, and I saw droplets of water clinging to the skin between his shoulder blades. I wanted to reach out and run my fingers across them, connecting them like constellations.

"Sorry," I said, suddenly finding my tongue. "I should have let you know I was on my way or come later."

"It's fine. I got back from the gym later than I meant to." Spencer shrugged on a large, grey t-shirt, and I blinked for the first time since I'd arrived. "Have you eaten yet?"

I shook my head. "No, I was going to get something later."

"Do you want something now? I can make us dinner while you bake."

"Are you sure? I don't want to inconvenience you," I said, not sure why I was trying to discourage Spencer from making me dinner.

"You're not. I wouldn't have offered otherwise." Spencer grinned, and something caught in my chest. I nodded.

"Okay then, that would be lovely."

"Sweet! Probably won't be anything complex, but it shouldn't be too bad."

"I'm sure whatever you make will be delicious," I said

as I followed him towards the familiar warmth of his kitchen. It was becoming one of my favourite places to be.

"Cheers." Spencer headed over to the fridge and gestured at the oven. "Knock yourself out. Oven wants to be about one-sixty for these. You'll want the fan setting too. I'm here if you need anything."

I walked across to turn the oven on, then dug two cupcake tins out of the cupboard next to it, placing them on the counter while I retrieved the science-themed cupcake cases I'd found on Amazon from my bag. I started slotting the paper cases into place, smiling to myself as I did. The pattern was cute with little microscopes and test tubes filled with colourful liquids and DNA double helices as well as some things I thought were supposed to be atoms.

They might not have been scientifically accurate, but they were fun.

"They're cute," Spencer said, appearing beside me to peer over my shoulder. "Very appropriate."

"Thanks. I thought so too."

"Are you okay with salmon? I've got some that needs eating. I was thinking of doing it with some mashed sweet potatoes and some veg."

"That sounds delicious." I looked across at him and saw Spencer smiling. He looked so happy like me just agreeing to have dinner with him had made his day. I didn't want to tell him it had made mine.

"Awesome, I'll do that, then. Do you wanna use the island to prep, and I can use this counter?"

"Sure." I shifted the lined trays out of the way before going to retrieve Betty and the ingredients I'd need. Spencer had told me he'd had plug sockets installed in one end of the island when he'd converted it into his Barbie dream kitchen two years ago because there were never enough sockets in home kitchens. I'd thought about ours and realised he was right.

"How was your day?" Spencer asked as I began to weigh out butter and sugar while he started peeling two enormous sweet potatoes. "Are you looking forward to your break?"

"The day was okay," I said. "A lot of the kids are ready for half-term, so it's difficult to get them to concentrate, even if we still have to get stuff done." I poured the sugar into Betty's mixing bowl on top of the room temperature butter and carefully turned the dial up to start the mixing process. "And yeah, I'm looking forward to the week off, even if I'll still have work to do. I won't have to get up at six every morning, so that's one benefit."

"Yeah, the early mornings are killer. I'm kinda used to them now since on the days I'm baking or opening I'm usually up at four or five, but they were *rough* at first. I was like a freaking zombie for weeks!"

"I'm not surprised," I said with a chuckle. "That sounds like hell."

"Nah, you get used to it. Trick is a good early night. I'm definitely not one of those guys who can manage on like four hours of sleep. I'd be fucking dead in a week. Or like, really, really miserable."

I glanced over at Spencer. "I can't imagine you being miserable, not in that way anyway. Not like Alex if he's tired."

"Oh, man, Alex just gets *mean* when he's tired. He's so cranky," Spencer said as he grabbed a large, sharp-looking knife out of a block and started dicing the potatoes. "Even more so than normal. He's like... like a freaking honey badger. Those suckers are mean, and they don't give a shit. That's Alex when he's tired."

I snorted. "That's the most accurate comparison I've ever heard. I mean, I know he's my best friend, but when he's sleep deprived, I'd quite like to—"

"Throw him into the sea?" Spencer suggested with a cheeky smile. "Trust me, I tried that once. It just made him madder."

"Oh, I remember that," I said. I'd only heard about it second-hand since it had been during the summer holidays, and I'd been on my annual trip to see my grandparents in the South of France. Alex had bitched about it endlessly via text until he'd hit his messaging limit. "I heard about it for days."

"Yeah, it wasn't my best move. I was kind of a dickhead to him, but I thought the water might wake him up."

"I think that's what brother's do, though," I said. "Be kind of dickheads to each other. Although I'm an only child, so my evidence is pretty much just anecdotal." I checked the creaming cupcake mixture and realised it was nearly time to start folding in the flour, cocoa powder, eggs, and milk. I'd already measured everything out in preparation, so it would be easy to move on to the next steps. "Anyway, you get on now, otherwise you definitely wouldn't be running Novel Tea together."

Spencer hummed and nodded. "So, got any plans for

your week off? Apart from working and catching up on sleep?"

"Not really," I said. "I might try to get out for a few walks, but that'll be weather dependent. I should probably go see my parents too since I haven't been over in a while."

My parents still lived just outside Heather Bay in the house I'd grown up in, but I didn't visit as often as I should. It wasn't that I didn't love them; it was just that we didn't always have a lot to talk about. Although, since they'd inherited my grandparents' place in France and now spent a good chunk of the year there, our relationship had improved because I could smile and nod while Mum filled me in on the lives of people I'd never met or barely remembered.

"Cool," Spencer said. There was a nervous edge to his voice like he wanted to say something but couldn't get the words out.

"Are you doing much next week?" I asked, hoping the question might prompt him into action.

"Not really. Just, er, just work and going to the gym. Probably make some more Halloween stuff for the shop, but that's about it."

I turned Betty off and slowly began adding some of the flour mix. I thought that if I didn't look at Spencer, it might help with whatever he was working through. My heart was pounding, and I wasn't sure if it was with excitement, anxiety, or some combination of the two.

"They're, er, they're doing that Fright Night thing up at the Castle next week," Spencer said. "Like with food and ghost tours and stuff. I know a lot of it's for kids, but it could be fun. Do you, er, fancy going? With me? Like, just the two of us?"

"That sounds wonderful. I'd love that."

"Really?" Spencer sounded surprised, and I huffed out a little laugh before beaming at him.

"Yes, really."

"Cool," he said. "Cool, yeah, that's awesome."

"Yeah," I said, trying not to let butterflies burst out of my chest *Alien* style. He still hadn't said it was a date. Even though he'd added "just the two of us", he could have meant just hanging out as friends, and I didn't want to get ahead of myself. "It'll be awesome."

There was a moment's pause while I let some of the flour combine and added a portion of the egg and milk mix to what was starting to resemble cupcake batter.

"I just, er, I…"

I glanced over at Spencer, who was staring down at his pile of sweet potatoes like they might suddenly contain the answer to life and the universe.

"Is everything okay?" I asked gently, wanting nothing more than to walk over to him and put my hand on his shoulder. But I didn't want to crowd him either.

"Yeah, I just… So…" He turned his head to look at me, a quiver of fear lingering in his expression. My heart broke for him, and I wished I could skip through the next moment and tell him everything was just fine.

"I don't think I'm straight," he said quickly. "Like I'm ninety-nine point nine percent convinced I'm bi or maybe pan? I don't know really. But, er, I… I like you, Noah, and I hope that's not weird. I mean, if it is, that's cool, we can just be mates, but I was kinda hoping that this thing to the Castle could be a date? With me? I mean, I guess it would be with me, but yeah… Is that cool?"

"Yeah, that's cool. Very cool." My smile was so big it probably could have been seen from space, but I didn't care. Because I had a date with the man I'd been crushing on for nearly thirteen years.

Happy didn't even begin to describe it.

CHAPTER TWELVE

Spencer

I FLOATED through the whole of Friday, barely paying attention to anything around me, which meant I nearly dropped weights on my foot at least twice. I wouldn't have cared, except broken toes probably would have meant no adventures with Noah at the Castle, and that idea sucked.

Both Sean and Andrew had asked me whether Chris had mentioned the five-a-side thing to me, but I'd managed to shrug it off by saying I hadn't really had a chance to think about it. Which was the truth. All my thoughts for the past week had been wrapped up in Noah.

My mind kept replaying my conversations with him from last night, especially the one where he'd said that going on a date would be cool. Now I couldn't stop thinking about wandering around the grounds of the Castle with him, doing the little pumpkin trail they did for kids and eating toffee apples. Was it weird that I just wanted to hold his hand? I felt like a kid all over again, getting giddy over the idea of holding Kirsty Mayfield's hand and kissing her at the school disco when I was twelve.

Getting the words out and actually telling Noah what I wanted had been one of the hardest things I'd ever done, but his smile had been worth it. It was so pretty, and it just made me want to make him smile all the time.

"Spencer?" Will's voice brought me back to reality, and I realised he'd been asking me a question, but I'd been so lost in thoughts of Noah I'd completely blanked on him.

"Sorry," I said sheepishly. "I missed that."

"What do you want to drink? Lane's getting the first round," Will said, nodding at Lane, who stood on the other side of the table getting orders from Oliver and Alex. We were all in our regular corner of the Sleeping Goose for our Friday-evening catch-up, and although it was nice to see everyone, there was only one person I really wanted to see.

"Er, can I get a Golden Sand please?" I asked as Lane turned towards me. It was one of the pale ales Colin and Soren had on tap from a local brewery and probably my favourite of the ones the brewery had produced. "Is Noah not coming?"

"Alex said he'd be along in a minute," Lane said. "He got held up at school."

I nodded, trying not to look like I cared too much since that would raise suspicion, but I was also desperate to check my phone to see if Noah had messaged me. We'd been chatting back and forth all morning whenever we'd had a spare minute, but I hadn't heard from him since lunch when they were running the bake-off. I really wanted to know how he'd done because the cupcakes had looked awesome when he'd packed them up last night.

"Got any weekend plans?" Will asked. He was a local farmer and had been in the same year as me at school. We'd played football together, and we'd kept in touch when I'd left for London. He was one of the first people who came to visit me when I'd moved home, depressed and drifting with my previously promising football career in tatters.

Will had turned up at the door with a shepherd's pie his mum had made, a case of beer, and said, "This is a bit shit, isn't it?"

He'd been the first person to truly acknowledge how much the whole situation sucked, and I'd just broken down on him, standing in my doorway, sobbing until Will ushered me inside. We'd spent the rest of the night just chilling together, drinking most of the beer and eating the entire shepherd's pie. Will had made me feel human again, but he'd never taken any credit for it. Because to him, that was just what you did for people.

Will was solid and dependable like that, and it had made me appreciate his friendship even more. If anyone ever tried to take advantage of him, I was going to have words because nobody was allowed to fuck over the most loyal and hardworking man to ever set foot in this town.

Now that I thought about it, I'd have to ask him whether he fancied joining Chris and the others since they were looking for someone else. Will worked too hard, and we all thought he needed to get out a bit more, even if he always protested that farming didn't leave time for much else. But a kick about once or twice a week wasn't going to kill him.

"Not really," I said. "Going to make some more Halloween bakes for the shop and maybe try and go out on the moors for a walk. Noah and I might wander up to the Castle for their Halloween week."

I wanted to keep my real intentions about our trip to the Castle vague, but once I'd mentioned it, I wished I hadn't said anything at all. Not that the date with Noah was a big secret, but I wanted to keep it to myself for a little bit. My friends were so nosy, and once it got out we were going on a date, they'd all have questions. And if, for whatever reason, it didn't work out between Noah and me, I didn't want my friends to feel like they had to take sides.

"Sounds fun," Will said. "More fun than mine anyway. We've got to put the rams in with the ewes, and I need to check some of the fencing in the rear fields. I've been meaning to do it for a couple of weeks, but the ground gets so fucking soggy it's hard to work on."

"So you're basically being a sheep pimp this weekend?" I asked with a wry smile.

"Don't be an arse. But yeah, basically."

"Who's being a pimp?" Oliver asked from Will's other side. I leant on the table and looked across at Will, gesturing at him with my hand.

"Will. He's helping sheep get sexy this weekend."

"Jesus Christ, Spencer," Will said, rubbing his face with his hand and giving me a rueful grin. "Can you not?"

"Why?"

"Why is it," Will said, ignoring me, "that this group's conversations always end up being about sex or murder?"

I grinned, remembering the first time Lane had brought Oliver to the pub with us when he'd moved back. I'd thought talking about creepy cellars and murder dungeons would be a good icebreaker—something to distract everyone from asking Oliver awkward questions. It had worked, but nobody had thought it was a good move on my part.

Well, no one except Theo, but considering he was the sort of person who found gruesome podcasts about serial killers soothing, I wasn't going to count his opinion.

"Because sex and murder are the most interesting conversation topics," said Lane as he strolled over with a tray of drinks and set it on the table. "Also, it's us, so why do you expect anything different?"

"True," Will said. He picked up his pint and sighed before taking a long drink like he was casually reevaluating whether being friends with us was worth it.

"Why did you ask anyway?" Lane asked, pulling out the chair opposite Will. "Wait, is it time for you to get the sheep to start shagging again? Do you need to go round and put their harnesses on tomorrow?"

"Why do you have to make it sound so dirty?" Will asked, and I chuckled.

"Again, it's us," said Alex, his head appearing from Oliver's other side. He must have then decided he couldn't see because he stood up and moved around the table so he sat opposite Oliver.

"Harnesses?" Oliver asked. "I think I've missed something."

"Yeah. Every year, Will has to put little harnesses on all the rams with these coloured pads on so he can see who's knocking up who," Alex said. He and Lane were both grinning, and Will was wearing a fond but exasperated expression.

"That makes sense," Oliver said. "Is that why you just see loads of sheep with coloured patches on their bums this time of year?"

"Yeah," Lane said. "Will is helping instigate a sheep orgy."

He winked at Will, who gave him a pointed look and said, "How's the frog?"

I frowned, suddenly confused by the change of subject. "Frog?"

Lane and Oliver groaned and glanced around as if they were checking to see who was nearby. "Theo gave us this stuffed frog for a housewarming present," Oliver said. "It's, er, well… it's…"

"Creepy as fuck," Lane finished. "It's wearing fucking lingerie."

There was a moment of silence, then Will, Alex, and I nodded. "Sounds about right," I said, thinking about the assortment of oddities I'd seen Theo collect over the years. "Have you seen Theo's mice? Or the raven?"

"Yeah," Lane said with a small shudder. "The mice creep me out."

"Are you going to keep it?" Will asked, taking another long drink.

"I think so," Oliver said. "I can't think how to get rid of it, and I don't want to tell Theo I don't like it."

"He's living in the spare room at the moment," Lane said. "And he can stay there."

"Who can stay where?" Noah asked, suddenly appearing through the crowd. He was flushed and rumpled like he'd run to the pub. I couldn't take my eyes off him. The seat opposite me was still empty, and I grinned as Noah flopped into it. Hopefully, when more people arrived, the conversation would drift into several separate ones, and I could chat to Noah by myself.

"Lane's creepy frog can stay in their spare room," Alex said. He shot Lane a teasing smirk. "Do you think it's like a cursed doll? You'll wake up one day and it'll just be in your room?"

"No. And if it does, then you can have it."

"Definitely not," Alex said.

"You should get it a little Halloween costume," I said, suddenly thinking about all those videos I'd seen of people dressing up random knickknacks in their house for various holidays. "Like a little witch's hat or something."

"It's creepy enough by itself," Lane said.

"I don't know. That could be fun," Oliver said. "I could get it a Santa hat for Christmas too!"

"I bet they've got some Halloween craft stalls up at the Castle," Will offered. "You know, with the whole Halloween thing they're doing."

My heart sank, and I silently begged this conversation to deviate. "I bet you could get one online too," I said quickly. "Like on Etsy or something."

"The Castle isn't a bad shout," Oliver said. "Bastian had mentioned maybe going to check out the Fright Night thing since it's his first year living here, and they never ran it when we were kids, so I missed out too."

I glanced at Noah, and although his expression wasn't giving anything away, I saw a glimmer of worry in his eyes. I'd really wanted this to just be an outing for just the two of us, but one wrong word and we'd be going with company.

Oliver looked around at the table, smiling warmly. "Anyone else want to come with us? We're thinking of going on Sunday."

"Didn't you say you and Noah are thinking of going?" Will asked, turning to look at us. I glanced at Noah, wishing I'd kept my mouth shut, but it was too late now because I couldn't deny it. Otherwise, I'd just look like a liar, and Will would twig there was something going on.

"Er, yeah, maybe," I said. "We hadn't figured out the details."

"Why don't we all go together?" Oliver asked. He looked so excited by the idea that I couldn't be mad at him. He didn't know it was supposed to be a date. He was just being friendly, and saying no to him would just look weird because there was no reason for us not to go with them. Unless Noah and I came out and told them we wanted to go together for romantic reasons, but we couldn't just have a side conversation where we agreed on what we wanted to do.

This was becoming too complicated, and it was making my head hurt. I didn't like lying to people, but I also wanted the chance to get to know Noah without all our friends butting in and asking us how things were going or trying to offer advice. Laurie and Theo might know how I felt, but that didn't mean everyone else needed to as well.

I glanced at Noah again, who gave me the tiniest little shrug and nod. It seemed like he was thinking the same as me—we'd been cornered, and there was no escaping the inevitable.

"Yeah, sure," I said. "That sounds fun."

"Awesome," Oliver said. "Alex? Will? Want to come? I'll ask Theo and Laurie when they get here too."

"What about me?" Lane asked, shooting his boyfriend a wry smile. "Don't I get an invite?"

"I just assumed you were coming. Especially because you said they always have fresh doughnuts."

"Fine," Lane said. "I guess I'll come."

"You don't have to," Oliver said. "I'll go with Bastian and send pictures of all the food."

"Nah, you twisted my arm. I've got to see if they've got good doughnuts." Lane grinned and twisted in his chair to look at Noah. "Speaking of food, how'd the bake-off go?"

Noah shrugged and reached into his coat pocket, a small smile starting to creep onto his lips. "Oh, you know, I only went and came second." He produced a little gold star and slid it onto the table. "Also got this."

The star had the words *Most Improved* printed on it, and Noah chuckled. "Had to do a little bit of convincing because a couple of people thought I'd cheated because apparently my baking really was *that* bad in previous years."

"Fucking hell, man. That's awesome," Lane said, clapping him on the shoulder as everyone else offered a variety of enthusiastic congratulations.

"I told you they were good," I said. I wished I could reach over the table and take his hand. Anything to show him just how proud I was.

"Yeah, well, it helps when you have a good teacher," Noah said, giving me a soft smile.

"Looks like all cakes are on you in future," Alex said.

"Definitely not. I'm not that good."

"You at least have to bring us some of these most improved ones," Will said. "Don't worry about the original ones, though. We can use our imaginations."

Noah chuckled. He was still looking at me as the conversation dissolved into cakes and sweets and something else, but I wasn't paying attention.

I was staring at Noah across the table, wishing it didn't feel like an ocean, and imagining what it might feel like to kiss him.

CHAPTER THIRTEEN

Noah

"Okay, where do we want to start?" Oliver asked as we all crowded through the entrance to the Castle grounds, each of us with our hands stamped with a little pumpkin for the Fright Night event.

The grounds of the stately home were packed with families and groups of friends while the Castle itself, which was just an enormous, Gothic house, loomed over us, adding some suitably spooky vibes to the atmosphere despite the clear skies and sunshine.

Everyone had decided to come along, and I tried very hard not to imagine what it would have been like with just Spencer and me instead of ten of us. If I did, I'd probably end up having a childish strop, at least in my head, because I'd just wanted one day alone with Spencer.

Spencer had admitted that he'd mentioned potentially coming to the Castle to Will when he'd asked about his plans for the weekend, but when Oliver had mentioned coming, it had all spiralled out of his control. Spencer had awkwardly said he hadn't mentioned that it was meant to be a date because he didn't want anyone else sticking their noses in, at least to start with, and I had to agree.

I loved my friends more than anything, but most of them tended to get overinvolved, and I wanted us to figure this out together without any of them breathing down our necks. Especially because this was so new to Spencer. I wanted him to have space to work through any fears, doubts, worries, or concerns in private.

If he chose to reach out to people individually for advice, that was one thing. It was another to have all our friends trying to offer their opinions at once.

"Looks like they've got a food market over there," Bastian said, pointing at a collection of stalls on one end of the grounds, where the sizzle and hiss of frying could be heard. The smells wafting from that direction were delicious.

"That sounds good," I said. "We can start there, and if we end up splitting up, it's a good place to regroup as well." I hoped it didn't sound like I wanted to ditch everyone, but I'd also been on enough group outings to know that large parties inevitably split up to go in various directions because everyone wanted to do different things.

"Let's go, then!" Alex waved his hand and began ushering us forward. Even on a blustery autumnal day where the wind nipped at our skin and the sun was bright but distant, he still looked like the epitome of a rock-and-roll icon in his black leather shearling jacket and sunglasses.

Spencer and I followed the group, hoping for a few moments alone, but as soon as Alex realised, he dropped back to walk with us. "I can't believe you two were going to come without me."

"I wasn't sure you'd be interested," I said, trying to downplay the fact that had been my intention. "And I know you've had a busy week. I didn't want to drag you around on your day off."

Alex shrugged. "Yeah, but you know I fucking love Halloween. Do you want to do our usual movie marathon next weekend? I know Halloween's your first Monday back after half-term, so I'm guessing you'd rather just chill than stay up all night."

Alex and I had developed a tradition over the years of binge watching all the *Underworld* movies around Halloween. I wasn't particularly into horror, but those films were more pulp fantasy action-horror than anything else, and they were so ridiculous I couldn't help but love them.

"Maybe we can watch most of them next weekend and save one for Halloween?"

"Okay, but which one?"

I thought for a second. "*Rise of the Lycans*? Just because it's before the main timeline and easiest to watch out of order."

Alex grinned at me. "Is that just because you want to see Michael Sheen shirtless as your reward for going back to work?"

"Maybe," I said, although Alex and I both knew it was the truth. I turned to Spencer on the other side of us, not wanting him to feel left out. "Do you have a favourite of the *Underworld* films?"

He frowned, an expression that always looked so cute on him. "I don't know. I'm not sure I've seen them."

"You have," Alex said. "It's the one with the vampires and werewolves trying to kill each other. You know, the one with Kate Beckinsale in the giant boots and leather trench coat. It's got the pure early noughties gothic aesthetic."

"Oh, yeah, I remember," Spencer said brightly. "I've not seen it in ages, though."

"You should come watch them with us," I said. "It'll be fun. We usually get pizza and make popcorn and just binge."

I glanced at Alex, realising I'd just invited his brother to our sacred Halloween movie night without actually asking him. He raised an eyebrow above the top of his sunglasses, and I saw his lips pinch, which meant he was surprised and maybe annoyed, but he wasn't going to say anything. Not until we got home at least, then he'd probably grumble for a bit, but ultimately, he'd be fine with it. Alex was surprisingly chill under his prickly exterior.

"Sounds fun," Spencer said. "I'll have to check the work schedule, though. If not, maybe you can come round to mine some time and we can watch them? If you don't mind watching them twice in a couple of weeks."

"That sounds great. I'd love that."

I glanced at Alex again, who frowned at me but again didn't say anything. Alex was smart, though, and good at knowing what made people tick. He'd probably have everything figured out by the time we got home. If I didn't get cornered and asked twenty questions over the next few days, I'd be very surprised.

We'd reached the small selection of food stands by that point. They were all arranged in a square around a seating area that had a large, open-sided tent covering it, protecting the tables from any rain. There were enough people there and enough stalls that made it easy enough to split off from the others. Spencer and I had started to wander over to a place selling the most delicious-smelling sausages and burgers, with Alex still in tow, when Laurie had swooped in, looking rather like he'd just stepped out of an *Underworld* movie himself, and politely dragged Alex away to where Theo was waiting.

I raised an eyebrow, suddenly wondering if the pair of them knew something I didn't, but either way, I was grateful for their interruption.

"I'm sorry," Spencer said once we were alone. "I kind of ruined our date."

"Honestly, it's not your fault. They'd probably have found out one way or another." I glanced over to where Theo and Laurie had dragged Alex. "It almost feels like we're going to have to *Mission Impossible* our dates, otherwise Alex is going to get suspicious. And if it's not him, then someone else will find us."

"You said dates," Spencer said, and when I looked up at him, I saw a new blush spreading across his cheeks that had nothing to do with the cold air. "Does that mean you want another one?"

"I'm not sure if this one really counts," I teased. "But

yes, I would. I really like you, Spencer… I, er, I have for a while."

"Really?" He sounded surprised. I wasn't sure I'd ever been that subtle in my pining, but either I was better than I thought, or Spencer was really oblivious.

"Yeah. We won't talk about how long, though, because that's kind of embarrassing."

"Nope. Now I wanna know. You've gotta tell me."

"Since I was like thirteen… You'd have been seventeen." Spencer's eyes widened. "Sorry," I continued. "That probably makes me sound really sad and creepy."

"No, it's cute." He smiled at me, and my chest clenched. "I wish I'd known earlier."

"You do?"

"Yeah." He sidestepped a large family and moved out of their way so he could read the large chalkboard on one side of the stand. "I might only be realising how I feel about guys, but I think it's been there for a while. I just… thought it was normal."

"How do you mean?"

"I mean, like… I always thought things like checking out guys at the gym was a thing everyone did. I told myself I was just looking at their form, even when they were just like stretching or cooling down. And I think I had the same reaction in the cinema as most of the women when Chris Evans stepped out of that machine in *Captain America*—you know, when he first gets the serum and he's all pumped up." He coughed, his cheeks still pink as he tucked a stray strand of hair under the edge of his beanie. "Stuff like that."

"If it helps, it is normal," I said. "And I thought Chris Evans was fit too. I rewatched that scene *so* many times."

"Right? He's so fit and so sweet," Spencer said. "He reminds me of you."

I snorted. "I'm not exactly a ripped superhero."

"I mean, he just seems like such a nice person. Really funny, and sweet, and kind." Spencer turned his head, and I felt his eyes roam over me. A shiver ran across my skin. "Also, I think you're gorgeous, Noah. I can't take my eyes off you."

"But I... I'm... I'm not exactly you." I gestured to him, allowing myself to look at his well-muscled thighs, toned stomach, and strong shoulders. "I can't even remember the last time I set foot in an actual gym."

"So?" Spencer seemed confused by my reaction like he couldn't understand my train of thought.

"I'm not like the sort of man you've been checking out. I'm fat."

"And you're sexy," Spencer said. "I like your body. A lot. And I... I'm hoping one day that I... that we..." He trailed off as a group of small children ran past us with painted faces, each clutching a large bag of candy floss.

It took me a moment to process what Spencer was trying to say, then I felt a grin pull at the corner of my mouth. I stepped closer to him, pretending to be avoiding the frazzled-looking parents following their hopped-up-on-sugar charges.

"Spencer," I said, lowering my voice, "do you want to have sex with me? Is that what you're trying to say?"

It felt quite forward of me, especially considering this

was our first date and Spencer's first time dating a man, but the way he bit his lip and looked at me shyly told me I hadn't missed the mark.

"Yeah, I think so. I've never done anything with a guy before, but I want to… as long as it's with you."

Heat bubbled and twisted in my stomach, and I cursed all the powers above and below that we weren't there alone, and I couldn't just say fuck the rest of the afternoon and take him home to slowly start exploring. But if we left now, someone—Alex most likely—was bound to notice.

"I'd like that too." I prayed that Spencer heard the note of want in my voice. My cock throbbed in my jeans as my mind began to casually remind me of my fantasies from earlier in the week. I pushed the thoughts away, promising to revisit them later when I was at home in bed with the door locked. "And I promise we can just go at your pace. I'll take care of you."

Spencer's smile had a slightly wicked edge that made my body tense in anticipation. "I know. I want to make it good for you too. I want everything."

I swallowed. This really wasn't the place to be having this conversation, but I didn't want to stop.

I wanted to know what everything meant.

CHAPTER FOURTEEN

Spencer

"What does everything mean?" Noah asked quietly.

Standing next to Noah, whispering to each other about sex while pretending to look at the menu for a burger stand was not what I'd thought would happen today. But I was very happy to roll with it.

I hadn't thought sex would come up between us this quickly, mostly because I wasn't sure Noah would be interested while I was still stumbling around in the dark about my sexuality. But apparently, that wasn't something I needed to worry about, and now I really wished we could sneak off somewhere.

Not that I wanted to try anything major while sneaking around a very public place with loads of people, but kissing would be nice. And I really wanted to kiss Noah.

The problem was that my brother had eyes like a hawk, and he'd notice if we disappeared for more than ten minutes, and if I tried kissing Noah there, in the middle of the crowd, then someone was definitely going to see us.

"I don't know if we should talk about that here," I said. We'd been standing still for so long we were starting to get in the way.

Noah sighed. "I guess not. But that doesn't mean the conversation ends here. I still want to talk about it."

"Me too. Do you want to get some food? Then maybe we can find somewhere to sit? Somewhere quiet." There were plenty of benches dotted around the grounds, and if not, I didn't mind getting a wet butt from sitting on the grass as long as we could find somewhere secluded so we could keep talking without being disturbed.

"Yeah, let's do that," Noah said, giving me a smile. "Do you want a burger? Or there's a hog roast over there I think? Or fish and chips…"

"Can we get a hog roast? I haven't had one in ages! Is that okay with you?"

"Sure." We started walking, both of us keeping an eye where everyone else was as we chatted about little things like food and the face painting we'd seen on some of the kids.

I told Noah about the time I'd had my face painted as a tiger when I was about six and had refused to let my mum wash it off at bedtime, saying that tigers didn't take baths. My mum had countered that tigers didn't eat jelly and ice cream either, which I'd been happily devouring an hour earlier. I'd tried to out logic her, but she'd won eventually. Nobody in the world could out argue or out logic my mum.

It didn't take us long to grab two large hog roast rolls

and slide out of the food market into the rest of the grounds. It was still busy but more spread out. I saw a craft marquee and a cluster of stalls as well as a few funfair rides, which was probably where the face painting was, and some stands advertising the pumpkin trail and spooky tours of the house.

Noah and I headed down towards the bottom of the grounds, where there was a drystone wall indicating the edge of the cliff. There was an iron bench there, looking out over the bay where I could see a few fishing boats bobbing about on the water and heading out to sea now that the tide was high.

We sat down next to each other, our legs not quite touching, watching the boats while we ate. They'd added crackling to my box, and it crunched delightfully in my mouth. There was just something about the combination of roast pork, apple sauce, stuffing, and crackling that made me happy. I'd never tried making a full roast dinner at home since it was usually just me, and it felt a bit excessive, but it was making me want to try.

"You know," Noah said, "I think this is a first for me. I don't think I've ever had a conversation about potential sex over hog roast."

I chuckled. "Sounds like you're missing out."

"Have you?"

"Nah. But I did have one with a girl once over hot wings back when I was playing football. She took me to this American place in London, and we had wings and nachos and stuff. They put this sauce on the wings that was so freaking good at first, but then it, like, melted my tongue and set my mouth on fire and everything." I grimaced at the memory. "She was there trying to tell me all these things she wanted to do to me, and I was trying not to cry. It didn't go much further than that."

Noah sorted. "Hopefully this is better than that."

"A million times better," I said. "Unless you've somehow hidden like a billion chillies in the middle of this roll. Then we might have a problem."

"No spicy food for you, then."

"Nope. Well, I can do *some* spicy but not like *that* spicy if you know what I mean," I said. "Definitely not getting extra hot from Nando's any time soon. Man, I haven't had Nando's in ages."

"Oh my God, you are totally a cheeky Nando's person." Noah grinned at me. There was a tiny bit of applesauce clinging to the side of his mouth, and I wanted to reach out and wipe it away. With my tongue.

"What's wrong with a cheeky Nando's? Everyone loves a cheeky Nando's," I said defensively, trying not to think about what Noah's lips would feel like against mine.

"Nothing's wrong with it. It's just… very you, and I like that."

"Thanks?" I wasn't sure whether to be confused or endeared. "You, er… you have something just… there." I pointed at his mouth, and Noah reached up to brush the sauce away. I couldn't stop staring at the spot, though.

"Cheers," he said. "By the way, you still haven't answered my question from earlier."

"About?"

"What does everything mean?"

I felt my face heat, and I glanced back out over the bay. The truth was that I didn't know what it meant because I didn't know where the boundaries were. I didn't think sex with Noah was going to be completely different from the sex I'd had before, but that was just my own assumption. I'd always preferred partners who weren't afraid to take charge and tell me what they wanted, and I'd happily spend hours with my tongue buried between their legs bringing them to orgasm over and over again.

But if Noah's refractory period was anything like mine, then three back-to-back orgasms in the space of twenty minutes was probably *not* going to be a thing.

I had no idea whether I'd enjoy anal, or if I'd prefer to stick with topping because it was what I was used to, or whether I'd be happy with both. A couple of women had fingered me over the years, but I'd never had anything more than a few fingers inside me. I'd always enjoyed that once I'd gotten over the initial weirdness, but I wasn't sure how I felt about taking a whole cock.

Maybe I needed to order a dildo or something and do some research. Would Noah want to help me? Or would that be weird? Was I supposed to just figure this out by myself like I had with everything else sex related over the years?

If push came to shove, I could always ask Theo. He'd be able to help me, and I knew he wouldn't judge. He'd probably just sit me down and help me order stuff.

Noah was still waiting patiently for an answer, and I knew I had to say something. "I don't know," I said, figuring the best thing was to be honest. There was no point lying to him because Noah already knew I'd never been with another guy, so I couldn't exactly pretend I was a gay-sex god.

"That's okay." He didn't sound disappointed, just warm and reassuring. He put his hand on my thigh, and heat shot through me like he'd somehow branded me. I was half expecting to go home and find his handprint on my skin like he'd claimed me. "There's no rush to do anything. We can take this slowly. I'm not going to get bored with you if we don't immediately start having sex."

"I know." The reassurance was nice, though. It felt like there was a different level of expectation here than in my previous relationships, which threw me a little but wasn't unwelcome. "And part of me is super happy to do that so I can figure stuff out, but the rest of me is…" I trailed off, and Noah chuckled, raising an eyebrow at me.

"Super horny?"

"Yeah, pretty much." It hadn't been *that* long since I'd last had sex, but I'd always had a pretty high sex drive, and a month was starting to feel like forever. "And now that I've realised how sexy you are and how much I like you, I can't stop thinking about what it might be like." I shook my head and stuffed the last of my hog roast into my mouth.

"Sorry," I said around my mouthful. "I'm not sure this is great first-date conversation. I should probably be trying to get to know you and stuff instead of talking about how much I wanna fuck you."

"It's not like we don't know each other a little already," Noah said. "And there's no set way this has to go. We're adults, and as long as both of us are happy and consenting, then we can do whatever we want." He glanced around before sliding along the bench and lowering his voice. "And, if I'm being honest, I've been thinking about you too."

"Yeah? What sort of things?" My curiosity had been aroused, and I really wanted to know what Noah wanted. I shifted on the bench, and my cock started to fill in my jeans as I imagined all the possibilities.

"Do you really want to know?"

"Yeah," I said, my voice catching as I spoke. "Please tell me."

Noah lowered his voice even further until it was barely above a whisper, every word ghosting over my skin and making goosebumps appear on my arms. "I thought about you spread out on my bed, your cock all hard and aching for me. I thought about straddling your thighs and sinking down onto you, letting you fill me with your cock until you were buried deep inside me."

"Fuck," I murmured, my hand clenching on my thigh as I desperately tried not to reach for my rapidly hardening dick. "That would be amazing."

"What about if I let you touch my thighs and hold my waist but didn't let you fuck me until I was ready?" Noah asked. "Would you like that?"

"Yeah, I think I would." I licked my lips and nodded. "I'd want to watch you ride me."

Noah let out a soft groan that made my cock jerk. "I'd make you feel so good," he said. "What about if I didn't let you touch my cock or move your hips until I said so?

Would you just be happy to let me ride you? Let me use your cock to get myself off?"

"Shit." My hips gave the tiniest jolt on the bench. "Yeah, I'd be up for that. I like it when people tell me what they want… It gives me something to focus on." I swallowed and licked my lips again, trying to force out words before my brain shut down. "I like making my partner happy, and I love making them come."

"God," Noah said. "You have no idea how much I want to kiss you right now."

I turned to him and let my eyes meet his, feeling pure need soak into my soul. "Do it. I don't care if anyone sees us."

"Are you sure?"

"Yeah, fucking positive." I leant closer. "Kiss me."

"Noah! Spencer!" Alex's booming voice shattered the moment and poured ice-cold water over the burning heat in my veins, shrinking my erection faster than jumping into the sea in February would have. Noah and I turned to see the utter menace that was my little brother strolling towards us. I'd never been so tempted to throw someone off a cliff.

"There you are," he said. "I've been looking all over for you."

"Yeah, we came down here for a bit of fresh air," Noah said, his mouth recovering faster than mine. "It was a little crowded up there."

Alex looked between us but didn't question our excuse. "Okay, well a load of them want to do the pumpkin trail.

Lane and Will are turning it into some sort of competition. Winners get free drinks or something. Come on."

"Do you need us?" I asked, trying desperately not to sound snappy. "My, er, my ankle's a little sore."

Alex raised an eyebrow. "Really?"

"Maybe."

"Yeah, I'm not buying it. You just don't want to enter because you're afraid you're going to lose," Alex said with a smirk. I knew he was trying to get a rise out of me by prodding my competitive side, the one that had never really gone quiet, even after I'd retired.

"I won't lose. It's a trail designed for kids," I said. "How are they going to make it competitive? Tie us together or something?"

"That's an idea," Alex said. "I don't know what they're planning, though. I just said I'd come fetch you. Come on." He patted my shoulder. "You too, Noah. Move your bloody arses, and let's go. I want free drinks."

I stood and sighed, looking sadly at the remains of the moment Noah and I had been enjoying.

"I love your brother," Noah said as we started to traipse back across the grass behind him. "But sometimes I want to kill him."

I laughed. "I think we might need a ticketed system."

"Do you think he knows?" Noah asked.

"I don't know." I shrugged. "But Alex isn't exactly... I don't know. Romantic? He probably thinks we're just avoiding him or something."

I wasn't sure I believed that, though. Alex had always known when I was trying to hide something from him. It was like he had some kind of sixth sense. My only options were to confront him and out myself or wait until he decided to play his hand and start poking me for information.

"By the way," Noah said quietly as we approached the hustle and bustle of the food market again. "I'm going to get that kiss from you. Even if I have to wait."

"Good," I said. "But don't wait too long. Otherwise, I might explode."

Noah snorted, and the pair of us walked back towards our friends, laughing about something we couldn't explain.

CHAPTER FIFTEEN

Spencer

"Okay, what's wrong?" Alex asked, dumping a tray of clean crockery onto the side behind the counter and starting to put cups and saucers away with more ferocity than necessary. "You've had a face like a smacked arse all morning. Is this something to do with yesterday? Are you sulking because you lost?"

"I'm not sulking," I said, trying very hard not to pout. It was late morning on Monday, and I still hadn't forgiven my brother for interrupting me and Noah yesterday.

After we'd ended up being dragged back to join the rest of the group, we'd barely managed to have a moment alone together. Any plans I'd had for suggesting Noah come back to mine had been squashed by Lane and Will suggesting we go to the pub after we left the Castle and then been stomped into the ground by Alex sitting between us.

My money was now definitely on Alex knowing. He was just trying to irritate me into saying something.

"Yeah, you fucking are. You've been right mardy all morning."

"I'm not."

"What are you, then?" Alex asked, his question like a pointy stick he was jabbing between my ribs.

"I'm just… frustrated." I turned to look at the door, wishing I could magically summon a rush of customers to end this conversation. No such luck. The coffee shop was a little busier than usual because of half-term, but we were still half an hour off the lunchtime rush.

Which meant Alex had thirty minutes to prod, poke, and annoy me into talking to him. And my brother wasn't one to give up when he'd fixed his mind on something.

"Why?" Alex asked. "What's frustrating you?"

"Can you just not? Please."

"Why not? Is it something serious?"

"Please, Alex, can you just drop it?" I asked, giving him my best pleading expression. "I don't want to talk about it."

"Is it about Noah?" Alex slotted the last of the saucers into place and gave me a pointed look. "You two didn't just want to get some fresh air yesterday, did you? Which, by the way, is a bloody awful excuse when we're literally standing outside."

I didn't say anything, deciding that if I did, I was more likely to put my foot in it. Instead, I just grabbed a cloth and started wiping down the sides and checking the coffee machine to make sure it was full of beans.

Alex growled. "Proper mature that is, just ignoring me."

I opened my mouth to say... something when the bell above the door tinkled and a group of four mums pushed their way inside. I knew them all pretty well since they came in regularly after one of their baby groups. Their kids were all varying ages, but none of them had started walking yet. One or two of them were starting to happily mush up whatever they could get their chubby hands on and drop it all over the floor, but it was always easy to clean up.

It made me realise we needed to get more kids books for the shelves.

Novel Tea had a whole wall covered in packed bookshelves for our patrons to peruse. They could take a book to read while they had their drinks, and if they really wanted to, they could take it away as long as they left a donation for us to eventually refill the shelves. People could bring books to leave too, and I always liked sorting through the donation boxes to check the quality and content. Anything too battered or questionable was quietly removed.

We didn't want anything racist, sexist, homophobic, transphobic, or containing any other bigoted, nasty things. We also didn't want a million copies of the same book either.

These days, we had a really great selection of every genre, but we probably needed a few more children's books beyond the YA and picture books. I'd have to put a notice in the window asking for donations and ask around for some recommendations to order. I wanted everyone, young and old, to have something to read when they came in.

"Morning," I called, happy to have a distraction. "Lovely day, isn't it? What can I get for you?"

By the time we'd sorted them all out, another few people had joined the queue, and from then on, there was a steady trickle of people filing into the shop for lunch. I thanked every power, big and small, that had fulfilled my wish and allowed me to avoid Alex for a bit longer.

Unfortunately, it wasn't as long as I wanted.

"You know," Alex hissed as he brought out another tray of sandwiches from the kitchen to refill the counter. "I don't mind if there's something going on between you and Noah. And I don't give a fuck if you're bi or pan or still figuring shit out. What I do care about is you hiding it from me. You're my brother, but he's my best friend, and I love him."

"Does that mean you don't love me?" I asked teasingly as I frothed some milk.

"Don't be daft. Of course I do, but he's Noah, and I'll always have his back. And he deserves to be with someone who's going to treat him the way he's always deserved—with love and respect. Now I don't know what the two of you are doing, or if you're even doing anything, but if you're not, then stop bloody faffing about and get on with it. If you like him, then tell him or better yet, show him."

"Is this when I tell you that yesterday was supposed to be our first date," I said, giving him a wry smile. Alex raised an eyebrow at me, tucking the now empty tray under his arm. "That's why we wanted to be left alone."

"You could've bloody well said something. If I'd have known, I'd have covered for you."

I poured milk into the large mugs in front of me, making

little leaves on the top with the milk. I wasn't the best latte artist, but I could do the basics.

"Are you saying you didn't know?" I asked as I put the cups onto a tray ready to take over to the table who'd ordered them.

Alex shrugged. "I had an inkling. I just wanted you to confirm it."

I sighed. "I knew it. That's why you've been so..." I threw my hands up in frustration and grabbed the tray.

"What else was I meant to do?" Alex asked with a note of amusement in his voice as I walked away. I wanted to tell him he could've just asked, then I remembered I'd been avoiding his questions, and if he'd just come out and asked if Noah and I were together, I'd probably have clammed up.

I glanced back over at the counter to see Alex pulling his phone out of the back pocket of his jeans, but I didn't get the chance to think about what that might mean because I had to watch where I was going so I didn't drop coffee and cake all over the floor. As soon as I'd delivered the order, I realised a couple of the other tables needed clearing, which was easy for me to do while I was walking around.

I got so caught up in clearing tables and wiping them down that I didn't pay any attention to who was coming in until a familiar voice said, "Hey, Spencer."

"Noah?" I turned, still holding a cleaning cloth and a bottle of D10. I hadn't expected to see him today. We'd mentioned meeting up during the week but hadn't gotten any further than that.

Noah smiled at me, looking gorgeous as fuck in his cute

knitted jumper and jeans. "Hey, I hope you don't mind me dropping in like this."

"No. Why would I mind?" I frowned. Behind Noah, I saw Alex pretending not to watch us from behind the counter. "Did Alex message you or something?"

"Yeah," Noah said. "He said I needed to get my butt down here as soon as possible. He didn't say why, though."

I sighed, trying not to be exasperated with my interfering baby brother. "He sort of knows about us. That yesterday was supposed to be our first date. I think he's trying to get us to figure our shit out or something."

As if on cue, Alex appeared between us, an unimpressed expression on his face as he beckoned us to follow him towards an empty table in the corner. "Sit down, the pair of you."

We sat.

Alex crouched down between us. "Let's be reight about it. There's obviously something going on between you two, and it's about bloody time if you ask me. Apparently, I fucked up your first date, so to compensate for that, you can have one now. It's not going to be the fanciest date in the world, but it'll be something. And then Spencer can stop moping around for his last hour."

Noah grinned, and it was clear he was trying to bite back his laughter.

"Don't you fucking laugh," Alex said with a grin. "You haven't had to put up with his mardy arse all morning. It's like walking around next to a gigantic kicked puppy."

"I haven't been that bad," I said, folding my arms across

my chest, then unfolding them when I realised it made me look sulky.

"Whatever. I'll get you two some food. Any preferences, or are you happy for me to get you whatever's left?"

"I'm happy with anything," Noah said. He looked over at me and smiled again. "Unless there's a cake you'd recommend?"

"There's a couple of pieces of the toffee apple cake left. That's pretty lush! Oh, and you've gotta try another of the hot chocolates too. Maybe the salted caramel one." The toffee apple cake was one of my favourite seasonal ones that we'd done, and I already knew I was going to be bringing it back every year. It was sweet and sticky with a delicious brown sugar apple sponge and caramel buttercream with hand dipped tiny toffee apples nestled into the icing on top. They'd been a pain in the butt to make, but I'd only broken two and burnt my fingers once, so I considered that a win.

"Then I'll have those, please," Noah said. "And whatever sandwiches you've got left are fine. You know what I like."

"And can I have one of the smoked salmon bagels, please?" I asked. They were my absolute favourite, but there were never any going spare because they usually sold out ridiculously quickly. I was surprised we still had some left, but when I'd glanced at the counter over Noah's shoulder, I'd seen a couple lurking. "And then can I have hot chocolate and toffee apple cake too?"

"Yeah, that's fine. I'll be back in a second." Alex stood

and strolled off towards the counter, talking to Stephen, who'd just arrived for his afternoon shift.

"I'm sorry," I said. "My brother doesn't know how to be subtle."

"No, he doesn't." Noah smiled fondly and chuckled. "But that's okay. He's just doing what he thinks is best. And at least now we don't have to work out how to tell him. I was quite nervous about that. I wasn't sure how he'd take it."

"Me either. I didn't think it would be like a punch-up or anything, but I was worried." I thought for a second, suddenly realising why I'd been so reluctant to talk to Alex. "I thought it was because he's so nosy, but you're his best friend, and I didn't want him to think I was trying to steal you. I didn't want him to hate me."

Noah put his hand on the table, stretching his fingers out to meet mine. "First, it was never going to end in a punch-up. Who does that? Secondly, I understand your fears. I felt the same but the opposite—like I didn't want him to accuse me of stealing his brother or trying to seduce you."

"Did you seduce me?" I asked.

"I don't know. Did I?" Noah smirked and raised an eyebrow, and I knew there was a lot more to him than people usually saw. Noah might have been the quiet, sensible one of our group, but he had layers to him. I just didn't think he let many people see them.

"Definitely," I said. "I think my whole sexual awakening can be summed up by you, plus buttercream, plus a stand-mixer beater. My life will never be the same."

Noah laughed, the sound filling my chest with butterflies. "Seriously?"

"Yeah, seriously. It, er, made me feel things."

Noah hummed like he was storing the information away for later, then said, "So Alex knows. Do you think anyone else does? I get the feeling Laurie and Theo know something just because of the way Laurie swooped in to drag Alex away yesterday."

I coughed and glanced at the shelves to my left, noticing they needed dusting. "They might."

"It's okay. You can tell me. I don't mind if they do."

"Yeah, they do. At least, they know I fancy you. After you came round to mine to make buttercream, I kinda had a bit of a crisis, so I went round to theirs for advice. Laurie made me a cuppa, and we talked about it. They were pretty helpful."

"That's good," Noah said. "I'm glad. It's always good to have people to talk to when you're figuring things out."

"You don't mind?" I'd been nervous to admit it to him in case he'd be mad at me for telling someone else. I wasn't sure why I felt like that, but my family had always been the keep-things-to-yourself type, and maybe that had rubbed off on me.

"Why would I? That's what friends are for. And I'll never mind you talking to your friends if you can't talk to me." He smiled again, and it soothed some of the worry in my stomach. "And you can always talk to me too. I really like you, Spencer, and I know this is new, but I want to see where it goes."

"I do too," I said, squeezing his hand. All the feelings

inside me felt so new and overwhelming but in a good way. There was just something about Noah that made everything make sense. I didn't know how to explain it.

But I wanted to know where these feelings led because I had a sneaking suspicion they were going to take me places I'd never been before.

And that was pretty fucking amazing.

CHAPTER SIXTEEN

Noah

"So you and my brother," Alex said as soon as he walked through the door later that afternoon. I was sitting on the sofa watching some ridiculous action movie I'd found on Netflix. The plot was pretty thin, but it was fun and required little concentration to enjoy. It also didn't hurt that the hero, played by the stunning Henry Lu, was fucking gorgeous.

It was helping take my mind off the fact that I wanted to see Spencer again. Having lunch with him had been amazing, but our time had been limited, and before we'd known it, he'd had to get back to work. Even though he could have taken more time since he was one of the owners, Spencer said he didn't want special treatment, but he'd promised to message me this evening when he got back from the gym.

"Yes?" I said, the word coming out as more of a question because I had no idea where Alex was going with this.

He walked around the sofa and flopped down on the other end, letting out a little sigh as he did. He didn't usually work Mondays, but I knew they had a couple of staff members off for half-term, so Alex had offered to cover because that was what he did. Novel Tea was his baby, and he'd sunk so much time, love, and money into the place over the years. It wasn't just a coffee shop to him; it was something he and Spencer had built together, and Alex would fight bare-knuckled in the street to defend it.

"Do I want to know how?" he asked, a sly smile curling the corner of his lips.

"Honestly, I'm not even sure," I said as I paused the film. Henry Lu was covered in sweat and dirt and just happened to be in a very tight-fitting black t-shirt as he leant out the side of a helicopter, wielding his gun at whatever goons were chasing him. It was one of those scenes that definitely wasn't plausible in reality but was fun in films. "One minute he was teaching me to make cakes, the next he was asking me on a date."

Alex frowned. "Feels like you're missing quite a bit in the middle. How'd you go from making cupcakes to that?"

I thought for second, wondering if it would be weird to tell Alex about the incredible amount of sexual tension and the sparks I'd felt just from brushing Spencer's hand.

"I don't know… We just seemed to click. I think it started when he took me back to his after Lane and Oliver's housewarming. He was so sweet about it all. And then I asked him for help because I knew he could bake, and I wanted to spend more time with him."

"Makes sense," Alex said. "You've been crushing on him for years."

"H-How'd you know?"

"It was obvious." Alex shrugged. "I just wasn't going to say anything in case you thought I was being weird about it. You didn't want to talk about it, so I didn't push."

"Okay," I said, trying to wrap my head around everything. "But I wasn't planning on doing anything. I hope you don't think I seduced your brother or something."

Alex let out a snort of derision. "No offence, but I don't think anyone could seduce Spencer unless he was actively trying to get with them. And even then, the chances are slim. The man is dense. You could've danced naked in front of him, and he wouldn't have realised what you wanted unless he wanted the same thing. I just didn't know Spencer was into guys too. I mean, it kinda makes sense, considering how *literally* everyone else in our friend group is queer, but I wish he'd told me."

"I think…" I started, wondering how much I could say without actively revealing Spencer's secrets. It was hard because it was clear Alex was frustrated with his brother for not telling him and that his frustration came from a place of love, but at the same time, it wasn't my information to share. "He's only just figuring things out for himself. Give him some time. He'll talk to you when he's ready. Or, you know, when you annoy him into telling you."

Alex drew his knees up to his chest. "I just wanted him to tell me. I'm his brother. We've always told each other shit. Even when he annoys the fuck out of me, I still love him. I just want him to be happy. I want you both to be happy."

"I know, and he does too." I nudged him with my foot and smiled at him. Alex returned my smile, but he still looked slightly glum. Like finding out Spencer hadn't told him had thrown him, but he didn't want to admit it. Alex always looked tough, but there was a glass wall around his heart, and a lot of it was stuck together with duct tape. "And thanks. I don't even know where this is going, but I hope… I want it to go well. I like him a lot, and not just in a distant, pining crush way."

Alex nodded. "Good. I've heard liking someone helps if you want to date them. Just do me a favour. Don't tell me all the details about whatever you get up to together. I know we've always talked about that shit in the past, but I really don't need to know what my brother likes in bed. That's a boundary I'm not willing to cross."

I laughed. "I wasn't planning on sharing anyway."

"Thank fuck for that," he said before gesturing at the TV. "What's this?"

"*Red Shadow Rising*. It's that action film with Henry Lu as the government agent who has to save the world from some shadowy agency that wants to bring down world powers. Something like that anyway." I glanced at the screen again, where Henry Lu was still leaning out the side of the helicopter, his dark hair artfully blowing in the wind.

"Nothing special plot-wise, then," Alex said.

"No, but it's fun." I picked up the remote. "Want to keep watching?"

"Sure, why not."

I pressed Play, and the action sequence resumed. "Do you think we'll see much of him when he comes to film that period drama next year?" Henry Lu had been cast in a new regency period drama that was being filmed up at the Castle of all places, and the whole town had been aflutter with gossip since. It was supposed to premier in the summer, and I'd assumed they'd want to start shooting as soon as possible, but there were rumours about a problem with some of the cast and filming schedules. We'd all finally received a letter from the town council that filming would start early next year and that closer to that time we'd get details about applying to be an extra.

It hadn't really appealed to me, but I'd made a mental note about the start date because it would probably cause havoc in town, and my students would be desperately nosy about the whole thing.

"Don't know," Alex said. "Don't care really. I bet he'll be like every other pretty Hollywood asshole and just stay in his trailer. Or if he does come out, it'll be to lord over us. I just want them to get the filming done as soon as possible so everything can go back to normal."

We watched for a few more minutes as Henry continued to pick off the bad guys, who were now chasing him in armoured trucks with rocket launchers because of course they were. Meanwhile, the daring and beautiful heroine, who had been artfully daubed with some dirt so she still looked pretty enough for all the studio executives who didn't want to see women with a hair out of place while saving the world, continued to fly the helicopter towards the nearby coastline, somehow managing to avoid getting them blown up while also handing out snarky one-liners in the process.

"Do you still want to have our movie marathon this week?" Alex asked.

"Of course, why wouldn't I?"

"I thought you wanted to watch them with Spencer." He turned his head to grin at me, and I knew he was only teasing.

"No, I'm going to watch them once with you and once with him."

"Yeah, sure… watch them. Just make sure you go to his. I really don't need to hear the two of you banging or risk seeing him naked on my sofa."

I chuckled and shook my head, but it did make me realise how much I wanted to spend the evening with Spencer.

And how much I didn't want it to involve us just watching a movie.

Later that evening, after Alex and I had made dinner and I'd done a little bit of the marking I had to do over the week, I retreated to my room. I stripped off down to my boxers and flopped down onto my bed, pulling out my phone and scrolling mindlessly through Twitter.

Even after my conversation with Alex and my lunch date with Spencer, I was still struggling to wrap my head around the fact that this was real.

I'd been crushing on Spencer for so long that a small part of me was wondering whether I was trapped in some extended dream and was going to wake up at any moment with a hideous sense of disappointment.

After our conversation at the Castle, I'd lain awake thinking everything through. Spencer had been so earnest about everything that I had to believe he had genuine feelings for me. The way he looked at me stirred up all sorts of emotions in my chest, from affection to longing to lust.

There'd been a quiet, nagging voice in my ear whispering that maybe this was just Spencer experimenting and this whole thing would end up being nothing more than a fling that would leave me heartbroken.

But if that was the case, surely we'd have moved faster than we had? And there'd have been less talk of our feelings and more quick and dirty fucking.

All I could do was hope I was right and that Spencer's feelings for me were real. If it didn't work out because we were incompatible, I'd be able to live with that. If it was just because he was using me, I'd be devastated.

Spencer didn't seem the type, though. I didn't think he'd even consider anything like that.

And if he did, I knew I'd at least have Alex in my corner. Which wouldn't do much, but it would give me a shoulder to cry on.

A notification flashed on the top of the screen, and Spencer's name appeared.

SPENCER *Sorry it's so late! I got chatting with some mates from the gym and then got distracted when I got home. I had so much fun with you at lunch today. Wished it could have lasted longer =(*

NOAH *Me too, but maybe we'll meet up again soon? Hang out just the two of us with no hovering friends or nosy brothers.*
SPENCER *That would be awesome! How about tomorrow? You can come over about six. I'm closing, and we have book club in the afternoon, so I'll definitely be there until later!*
NOAH *I'll be there x*
SPENCER *Awesome! Maybe we can have dinner? And then maybe watch a film? Or pretend to watch one ;)*
NOAH *I think that can be arranged. Maybe this time I'll finally be able to kiss you.*
SPENCER *I hope you'll do more than kiss me.*

I let out a little sigh of anticipation, thoughts of what I could do to Spencer swirling through my imagination and dismissing my earlier worries.

I rolled onto my stomach, slowly grinding my hips into the bed as my cock started to fill. The friction was just enough to make me want more. I wondered what Spencer would do if he saw me like this. If he walked into my bedroom and saw me facedown on the bed, humping the mattress while I thought of him, making myself desperate for more.

NOAH *I hope so too. I don't want to rush you, though. I don't want you to be uncomfortable or do something you'll regret.*
SPENCER *I'm uncomfortable now ;) mostly because I'm thinking about you. Also because I saw this hot as fuck clip on Twitter earlier, and I can't stop thinking about you doing the same thing to me.*

I groaned, thrusting my hips harder against the bed as my mind went wild with ideas. I needed to know what Spencer had been thinking about.

NOAH *Was this the distraction you mentioned?*
SPENCER *Yeah, it was.*
NOAH *Show me.*

I waited, forcing my body to slow the roll of my hips until the friction was barely there. It was sheer torture, and the temptation to just give in to my desires and get myself off as hard and fast as possible was barrelling towards me at speed.

I groaned as two more messages came through—one with a link to Twitter and the second with a picture attached to it.

SPENCER *This is what thinking about you does to me.*

I clicked on it, knowing what it was going to be before it opened. I wasn't disappointed.

"Shit," I muttered to myself as I stared at Spencer's erection. It wasn't the best picture ever taken, but I didn't care. It was as good as the fucking *Mona Lisa* to me.

Spencer's cock was thick and slightly curved, a drop of precum glinting in the low light as it dribbled from his slit onto the swollen, red head. My nose was so close to the screen it was as if I thought enough willpower would make me magically fall through it and into Spencer's lap.

NOAH *Fuck! You have a really nice cock.*
SPENCER *Thanks! Can I see yours?*

My hips bucked forward again at the request. I rolled over and scooted across to the edge of my bed to adjust my bedside lamp, shining the bright bulb onto the mattress. Awkwardly, I slid my boxers down my thighs with one hand, letting my cock spring free and slap against my stomach. I wrapped my hand around it before realising that wasn't going to work for a photo. I felt nerves starting to bubble in my stomach, but I pushed them away. Spencer wanted to see my dick, and he'd already said he thought I was sexy. Seeing my soft belly or my wide thighs wasn't going to put him off.

Twisting my phone in my hand, I pointed it at my dick, taking a couple of shots from a variety of angles. They didn't look as bad as I thought, and I dropped one into the message thread before I lost my nerve.

I stared at the screen, waiting for it to show me that Spencer had read the message. His name appeared at the bottom of the screen, telling me he was typing. I reached for my cock while I waited, trying to imagine what he was going to say. But my brain couldn't focus on anything other than watching his name. He was typing for a very long time.

A voice note appeared on the screen, and my curiosity swelled.

I grabbed my earbuds off my bedside table and slotted them into my ears before I hit Play, just in case Alex was somehow listening through the door.

The note opened with a deep groan that made my cock jump and sent shivers running through me. "Mmm, fuck, Noah. That picture is just... Fuck, it's really hot." Spencer's voice had a low, breathless, needy note running through it. The slap of skin on skin accompanied his words, and I moaned at the realisation that Spencer was jerking off to my cock.

"I'm so hard," he continued. "I wish you were here. I'm so fucking hard for you. I, ugh, I want to kiss you so bad. And I want to know what your cock feels like in my hand. I wanna suck you too. Fuck, I wanna suck your cock so much. I bet you taste so fucking good, Noah. I've never done it before, but I want to make you feel good. Want you to show me what you like so I can make you shoot. And I... Fuck... I want to know what it's like when you blow your load in my mouth. Would you like that? Would you let me suck you?"

"Shit," I groaned, my head rolling back onto the pillow as I arched into my hand, heat shooting down my spine. I wished there was a way just to teleport myself into Spencer's bed so I could make all his words come true. I tapped a button on the bottom of the screen, turning the camera on and pointing my phone at my cock. I held the button down, starting to film myself as I slowly stroked my cock.

"Fuck, Spencer," I said, hoping either my earbuds or my phone would pick up my words. "This is how hard you make me. I want you so fucking much. I bet your mouth would feel so good on me, and you'd look so hot with your lips stretched around my shaft, taking as much as you can.

God, I love how fucking enthusiastic you are. It's so… mmm, it's so hot knowing how much you want me. And yes, I'll show you how to make me come. Then I'll lick my cum off your tongue, slide down your body, and suck you until you shoot. I know you'll taste so good in my mouth, Spencer. Fuck, just thinking about it is getting me so close."

I panted and groaned, releasing my cock. It twitched, desperate for friction, and I didn't know how much longer I'd be able to hold off.

Letting go of the Record button, I hit Send.

CHAPTER SEVENTEEN

Spencer

I WAS two seconds away from exploding as I gripped my dick tightly, my hips thrusting up into thin air as I watched Noah jack his gorgeous cock. His words were sweet and smooth, sliding inside me and making me beg for more. I wanted to come so fucking badly, but I didn't want this to be over.

Or if it was going to be over, I wanted Noah to know what I sounded like when I came.

I was all up for a bit of teasing, especially if it got me what I wanted in the end. Which was Noah with me, spread out across my bed with my head between his thighs and his cock in my throat.

After the gym, I'd ended up doing an Alice in Wonderland down a gay-porn rabbit hole, and now the mental list of things I wanted to try with Noah was overflowing with options. I might not have been interested in some of the really kinky stuff I'd seen, but given how hard I'd gotten watching some guy called Austin Carter use a thick, ridged dildo on this gorgeous, chubby guy before pounding him so hard his partner came untouched, I was more than sure that I was *definitely* bisexual and more than desperate to get naked with Noah.

I watched Noah's video again, trying to work out what I should send in response.

Another voice note would be good, but I wanted to show him what he was doing to me, so instead, I pulled up the video app and hit Record.

"I'm close too... Shit... This is what you do to me, Noah," I said, awkwardly spitting in my hand before starting to jerk my cock again. I groaned at the sudden addition of slickness, a new surge of heat rushing through me. I couldn't remember the last time I'd been so turned on.

"Your voice... your cock... Fuck, I want you so much. Just thinking about you... Shit, I can't wait to touch you tomorrow. I'm not going to be able to keep my hands off you."

I twisted my hand over the head of my dick, then slid my fingers down to my balls, giving them a quick caress before I went back to my shaft. If I had two free hands, I might have tried playing with my hole, but I'd need a stand for my camera for that. The one I sometimes used in the gym would do, but that was in my gym bag, and I wasn't getting up now. Fuck that.

Desire coursed through me. There was so much I

wanted but no time left to experiment. I felt my balls tightening as my body tensed. I was so close, and nothing was going to change that.

My hips jerked, pushing my cock into the tight, slick tunnel of my fist as I thought about fucking up into Noah's ass. That was all it took.

"N-Noah, fuck... I'm... Shit... Gonna come..." I struggled to get the words out between panting breaths as I came, my cum shooting across my skin. I had to move the camera quickly to avoid covering my phone because that would be a nightmare to clean up, but I made sure to keep my cock in the shot. I wanted Noah to see what he was missing and what he'd be getting tomorrow.

Because I already knew I'd be pulling him towards the nearest sofa as soon as he walked through my front door.

When my cock finished twitching, I turned my phone around, hoping my face was still in the frame. I grinned at the camera and shot Noah a cheeky wink. "I can't wait to see you tomorrow."

I lifted my thumb off the screen to stop the recording and hit Send, wondering whether Noah had come already or if he was waiting for me. Was there some sort of sexting etiquette that said I should have waited? Usually, when I'd done this with women, I'd always wanted to make sure they came first because it was gentlemanly, but now... Was it totally different with a man? Had I fucked up somehow?

I didn't know why I was suddenly so worried. I'd never been an overthinker. Alex had always described me as a barely look-before-you-leap person, and I fully admitted to doing things before I'd thought of the consequences, but it had never really blown up in my face, so I'd never felt like this before.

What was it about Noah that made me so nervous? I didn't think it was because he was a guy. That didn't bother me at all. Maybe it had something to do with the fact that I *really* liked him.

Now that I thought about it, every time I started dating someone I really liked, I always felt like a bundle of nerves. Only this time, I'd actually noticed them.

Another voice note came through followed by a couple of pictures. I hit Play on the note while I looked through the pictures. They were all of Noah's perfect-looking cock, spent and covered in cum. I felt a small pang of sadness because I wished I'd been able to see Noah come. Then I brightened because I realised I could see it for myself tomorrow.

"Fucking hell, Spencer," Noah said, his voice thick and breathless. "Fucking warn me next time. I think… Fuck, I think I stopped breathing. God, you look so fucking hot when you come. You sound it too. I wanted to send you another video, but I was too distracted by watching you. Fuck, you're just… You're amazing. You made me come so hard."

I let out a soft chuckle, a pleased glow filling my chest. Another note popped through, shorter this time.

"By the way," Noah said. "Can I keep that video, please? I've never had anyone make me anything like that, and I definitely want to watch it again. But if you want me to delete it, that's not a problem."

I grinned and hit Record. "Yeah, you can keep it. It's

pretty awesome that you like my attempt at amateur porn. I'll have to make you another one. I can get my phone stand out of my gym bag... maybe try playing with my hole..." I tried to keep my voice light and teasing, but as I said it, I knew I wanted to try doing that.

Only not now because I was knackered.

"You'll have to let me know what you want me to try," I continued. "Fuck, I'm exhausted now, though. I... I loved doing that with you. I can't wait to do it with you in person tomorrow."

I sent the voice note, then looked around for something to clean up with. My t-shirt was crumpled up on the floor next to the bed, so I reached down to grab it and used it to mop up most of my cum before it stuck to me. I needed to have a shower anyway. That had been my plan when I'd gotten home, but I'd gotten distracted when I'd sat on the bed for two minutes and strolled off down my Twitter rabbit hole.

It had been fun, though, so I wasn't mad about it.

My phone flashed again, and I grabbed it, assuming it was Noah. But instead, it was a message from Chris.

CHRIS *Hey, mate, sorry to nag, but have you decided whether you wanna join us for 5-a-side? No pressure and don't mind if you say no. We already registered but I just need to know so we can ask around and see if anyone else is interested.*

I stared at the screen, chewing my lip. I'd promised Chris I'd think about it, but I'd kept putting off making a decision. I'd told myself it was because I was so wrapped up in things with Noah, but deep down, I knew it was because I was afraid to consider it.

It shouldn't have been a difficult choice because it wasn't like they were asking me to join the England squad. It was literally just a kick-about league, and even though I hadn't played for years, I'd still probably be better than most people we played against. I had a valid reason to say no as well. It would be easy to say it wasn't worth the risk since some of our opponents would probably make shit tackles. Even if I could outrun most of them…

And it wasn't like we'd be playing for hours. It would be two twenty-five minute halves, and five-a-side allowed rolling substitutions as well, so as long as we got enough people on the team, I could come off whenever I needed to.

But even with all that, I had to consider whether the risk was worth it. The doctors might have told me never to play again, but I hadn't exactly sat down and asked them to lay out in detail what I could and couldn't do. They'd told me to keep exercising, and over the years, my ankle had definitely gotten stronger.

I'd kept up with physio and sports massages too, and at my last appointment, my massage therapist had said it was in better shape than my other leg and ankle, probably because I'd been so dedicated to making sure my muscles were strong enough to support the area.

Deep down, I knew I should probably say no. But I couldn't bring myself to type those two little letters.

Because if I was being really honest with myself, I wanted to play.

There was a part of me—one I'd tried to lock away all

those years ago—that still longed for the feeling of a ball on my foot and the pitch underneath me. As a kid, there was nothing in the world that could've kept me away from football, and giving it up had been the hardest thing I'd ever done.

And now that there was a chance for me to play again, that suppressed voice had come roaring back to life, complete with drums and a megaphone.

I sighed and shook my head. My decision wouldn't exactly change the fate of the world.

It was such a small thing.

But it felt like climbing a mountain.

Discovering I was bisexual had been a piece of cake next to this. I was pretty sure it was supposed to be the other way around.

I knew I couldn't keep putting it off because that wasn't fair to the rest of the guys, but I needed more time.

Spencer *Shit. Sorry. I haven't really thought about it! Can I let you know by the end of the week?*
Chris *Yeah, that's fine! Lemme know Friday morning at the gym =)*

I breathed a sigh of relief, knowing that I'd bought myself a few more days. I wondered whether I should ask Noah about the whole football thing. He'd be able to give a bit more of an outside perspective, and maybe that would help me choose.

Another message from Noah appeared on the screen,

easing the worry that was starting to knot in my chest like an old pair of headphones in my hoodie pocket.

NOAH *I can't wait to see you tomorrow either x*

CHAPTER EIGHTEEN

Noah

"Hey," Spencer said as he welcomed me into his cosy, colourful house for the umpteenth time in as many days. It was starting to feel familiar, even if I'd only really spent time in the kitchen. I wasn't counting waking up in his bed since I could barely remember being there. My overriding recollections from that morning were dizziness, nausea, and the welcoming embrace of a bacon, brie, and avocado sandwich.

And Spencer's smile. That had been the best part.

It had almost been worth the crippling hangover.

"Hey," I said as I stepped inside and pushed the door closed behind me. It clicked shut, but for the first time, Spencer didn't immediately head towards the kitchen. Instead, we stood staring at each other, waiting for someone to move first. "I—"

But whatever I'd been meaning to say was swallowed

up by Spencer's mouth pressed firmly against mine as he closed the distance between us and wrapped his hand around my neck, drawing me deeper into the kiss.

It wasn't the greatest kiss I'd ever had because although Spencer's lips were soft, they were pressed so hard against mine it just felt odd. It felt like Spencer had wavered between tentative and determined and had gone for the latter. But still, Spencer was kissing me, so I couldn't complain too much.

"Shit," he said as he released me. We were still nose to nose, and I could virtually count his eyelashes. "Sorry, that was bad. You're going to think I'm such a shit kisser."

"It's fine," I said, letting one of my hands come up to rest on his chest while the other reached for his waist. "Are you nervous?"

"Yeah…" He huffed out a laugh. "Guess it's really obvious."

"A little, but it's cute. Want to tell me what you're nervous about?"

"Being a shit kisser for one," Spencer said. "Last night was amazing, but today I just kept thinking that I might be really shit at everything in person. Like what if I'm okay at sex with women but not with men? What if I'm just bad at sex with everyone, but nobody's ever told me? I don't want you to be disappointed."

I stroked his chest with my fingers, trying to soothe his worries. His anxiety was almost adorable because I would never have dreamt someone like Spencer would have those worries. But he didn't need to hear that from me. That would just make everything worse because it would be like

I was telling him his fears weren't valid or, even worse, belittling him for having those emotions.

"I won't be," I said. "It's fine to be nervous, especially because this is new for you. But that's what communication is for. If either of us likes something or wants something a little different, we can just say so." I looked up into his beautiful grey eyes. "And we can take it slowly. There's a big difference between jerking off to fantasies and reality."

"Okay… yeah." Spencer nodded. "Can I try again?"

"Yeah."

He drew my lips towards his, slower this time. His touch was almost tentative. His lips brushed against mine, and a little shiver ran across my skin. This kiss was totally different. It was gentle but insistent with a simmering heat underneath that promised so much more.

One kiss melted into another and then another. I let Spencer take the lead, but it was easy to show him what I wanted.

Spencer brushed his tongue against my bottom lip, and I moaned quietly. His tongue slipped inside my mouth to caress mine, and it was like a switch had suddenly been flipped. Spencer's nerves seemed to evaporate, and I felt his confidence growing as he drew me closer until we were pressed together, then slowly walked me backwards until my back hit the front door.

After that, all bets were off.

My hand slipped under the hem of Spencer's t-shirt, finally connecting with his skin in a moment I'd been dreaming about for years, which sounded creepier than I'd imagined. His body was firm against mine, but his skin was soft and bleeding heat into my touch. Spencer let out a muffled gasp as I slid my fingers up his sides and across his abdomen.

Spencer's hand cupped my neck, but his other started to wander down my side. I was happy to let him explore, but I wasn't prepared for the way he went for my stomach, caressing it gently like it was beautiful and something to be revered.

My stomach had always been my least favourite part of my body, and despite my attempts at radical self-acceptance, or at least some kind of body neutrality on the days when I felt like shit, it was still one part of myself I struggled with. It was too round and big and squishy, and I'd never liked the way it stuck out in front of me.

Most of the time, I tried not to care, but there was a reason I tended to avoid close-fitting t-shirts and being shirtless around people I wasn't totally comfortable with. It was why I sometimes preferred having sex in low-lit rooms when I first met someone and carefully chose the position so my belly wouldn't be the thing they focused on.

Or the thing I focused on.

Alex had pointed out, more than once, that men knew what I looked like before we started fucking, and if they didn't find me attractive, they wouldn't be there. I understood his point, even if I sometimes wished he had more tact. But that was my best friend.

And why the fuck was I thinking about him right now while I was making out with his brother?

"You okay?" Spencer asked, and I realised I'd frozen. He

lifted his hands away and took a step back. "What's wrong?"

"Nothing..." It was a horrible lie, and both of us knew it. "I, er... I get a little bit self-conscious about my stomach. I know we wouldn't be doing this if you didn't find me attractive, but I still worry."

Spencer smiled at me and moved closer again, his hand coming to rest on my stomach. "If it helps, I love your body. I think you're sexy as fuck. When you first came back to mine, when you were drunk, I thought you were gorgeous... even though I thought it was just like a friendly thing. And I promise I didn't look that much. Just, like, what was necessary to help you get undressed." He flushed slightly and bit his lip. "And watching that video you sent me... Fuck, I nearly came as soon as I opened it. But I don't want you to feel self-conscious, so is there anything I can do to make it better?"

"Not really, but that helps," I said, surprised at how much his words had affected me. I'd heard them before, but there was something about the way Spencer said them, looking into my eyes with his hand on my stomach that soothed my worries.

It didn't magically undo years of self-consciousness or make me forget my fears—that was never going to happen with the equivalent of a finger snap—but it was a tiny step forward. At least for today.

"I think everyone has things they worry about or don't like about their body. Even me," Spencer said. "And I'm not trying to, like, downplay your emotions or make you feel like they don't matter just because everyone has hang-ups, but what I mean is that everyone has them, so… Fuck, I'm not doing a good job of explaining myself."

"It's okay. I know what you mean." I leant into his touch and kissed him again. "And thank you."

Spencer was trying, and that was all that mattered to me. I still didn't quite believe that he found me as sexy as he said, but that was my issue, not his. I knew Spencer wasn't the type to lie to me just to get me into bed.

"You're welcome."

"Can I ask… What don't you like? I mean, to me you're perfect. Literally perfect," I said as I wrapped my arms around his waist.

"Er, it's weird, but I don't like my feet. I don't know why, but I feel like they're too big, like clown feet. And I wish my butt was bigger. I've tried all the exercises to build muscle there, and it's coming on, but I think I'm doomed to always have more of a pancake butt." A blush spread across Spencer's nose, and I leant up to kiss it.

"I don't think you have a pancake butt at all," I said. "I think it's the perfect size." I slid my hands down the bottom of his back and brought them to rest on his ass. I watched Spencer's face to make sure he wasn't uncomfortable, and then I gently squeezed the firm globes of his butt, trying to keep my own excitement in check. "Definitely perfect."

Spencer swallowed. "Yeah?"

"Yes, I love it."

"Can I…"

"Yes," I said. "Touch me, Spencer, please."

Slowly, Spencer's hands moved down my stomach to rest on my hips before circling around to my ass. His touch was tentative like he still couldn't believe this was happening. I exhaled as he caressed my ass, then squeezed gently, somehow managing to pull me closer.

"Your butt is perfect too," he said.

"Thanks." I smirked at him as a little voice in my head started to whisper filthy ideas. "You're welcome to play with it whenever you want."

"You might regret that," Spencer said, a sly smile crossing his lips. "Or maybe not…"

He kissed me deeply, sliding his tongue into my mouth as his hands gripped my ass. I let out a muffled groan, my cock throbbing in my jeans.

We were still standing in Spencer's hall, and while it was fun to know we'd barely made it beyond the front door, I really wanted to find somewhere softer so I could explore his body more thoroughly.

"Sofa?" I asked, pulling back just enough to make myself heard. "Or bedroom? Or we can stop if you want."

"No stopping," Spencer said. He released my ass and grabbed my hand, pulling me towards his living room with such force that I nearly tripped over my own feet. I laughed because Spencer's eagerness was infectious.

There were lamps on in the living room that gave the whole room a warm glow. The walls were a soothing yellow-orange with bright, white trim. There was a large mirror above a fireplace, and the mantelpiece had three large LEGO dinosaurs arranged across it. The large, squishy-looking sofa and armchair were both deep teal, and I noticed the wall above the sofa had a pretty selection of pictures arranged in white frames.

It was another room that was so utterly Spencer, and I felt so lucky to get insight into his charming, colourful world.

I didn't get much time to look at the details, though, because Spencer was still pulling me towards the sofa. He shoved the orange-and-white throw pillows onto the floor, and the two of us fell onto it.

Spencer was underneath me, spreading his legs around me and wrapping his hand around my neck to pull me in for more desperate kisses.

With every kiss, we became more in sync, the earlier awkwardness evaporating as we slipped into heated exploration. Spencer's hips ground up against me, and I groaned as I felt his hard cock rub against mine. Spencer moaned and thrust up again, desperately seeking more friction. I pressed down against him, giving him something to grind against as my hands worked their way under his t-shirt. I pushed it up as best I could, letting my fingers slide along his skin.

I broke from his mouth to start kissing along his jaw, and Spencer groaned out broken words as he tipped his head back so I could tease my lips down his neck.

"Do you like that?" I asked.

"Y-yeah, I do… Fuck… I want…"

"What do you want?" I asked gently, looking down at the beautiful man spread out beneath me, who seemed at a complete loss for words.

"I don't know." He tilted his head to grin up at me. "Everything? Is that an option?"

I chuckled. "It can be."

"Good. Can it start with getting naked? Or at least, like, a few layers less?"

"Yeah, we can start with that." I took a deep breath and reached for the hem of my hoodie.

"Only if you're sure," Spencer said. "I don't want you to be uncomfortable."

"Thank you." I leant down to kiss him softly. "But I want this too."

I sat up and pulled my hoodie and t-shirt off at once, letting my eyes linger on the wall above Spencer's head for just a second longer. Then Spencer whistled, his hands coming up to touch my body and sending shivers across my skin.

"Fuck me, you're sexy," he said in a low, awed voice. "Can we have sex?"

CHAPTER NINETEEN

Spencer

NOAH STARED at me like he couldn't believe the words that had just come out of my mouth. But I wasn't joking. I wanted to have sex with him.

"We don't have to," I said. "Not if you don't want to. I just really want that… with you. If you do too."

I wasn't sure I was making much sense, but words were hard right then. Just looking at Noah was enough to leave me tongue-tied. It probably meant that whatever we did, it wouldn't be my best performance. I'd be lucky not to come the moment he touched me. But I could make up for it later.

Right now, I just wanted to be inside him.

"I do," Noah said. "As long as you're sure. I don't want to rush you."

"Dude, you're killing me here." I grinned. "It's not like I've never had sex before."

Noah chuckled. "I know, but this is different."

"Not really," I said. "Sex is sex. Butt stuff is butt stuff. Oral is oral. Doesn't really matter to me what parts are involved. Besides, it's not like I've never seen a penis before. Do you know how many guys like to walk around naked in dressing rooms? And I've watched enough porn."

"You still need to tell me about this rabbit hole you fell into," he said, shaking his head as he dropped his hoodie and t-shirt onto the floor before kissing me.

"Later. First, I want to fuck you."

Noah groaned, his eyes fluttering shut. "Okay. Yeah."

"Only okay?" I asked with a grin.

"Shut up," he said, looking at me with a wry smile and desire burning in his eyes. "It's more than okay. It's something I've wanted for a long time."

"Good, because I want to watch you ride me." I slid my hand down his stomach to the bulge in his jeans, loving the way Noah gasped as I rubbed his hard cock through the material. I'd thought it might be strange to feel another man's erection under my hand, but it wasn't. It was just different. I couldn't really compare it to my own or to anything I'd experienced with other partners.

I liked it, though. I liked it a lot.

But the jeans were an annoyance because they were in my way.

I reached for the button, popping it open before unzipping his fly and working the jeans open as far as I could. It was a little limited considering the way Noah was positioned between my legs, and it was starting to frustrate me. I just wanted to get my hand on his dick.

My mouth too.

I'd always loved getting head and giving oral, so I figured I'd probably like blowing Noah. I just had to try and remember all the things I'd enjoyed women doing to me over the years and replicate them. I didn't think it would be as easy as some of them had made it feel, but I hoped Noah wouldn't mind if I was a bit sloppy and uncoordinated.

And if I was, that was what practice was for. I'd always been dedicated, and if I wasn't good at something, I practised until I was. Hopefully, Noah wouldn't mind me practising on him.

"Can you lift up?" I asked, trying to tug his jeans a little farther down. "I wanna get these off you."

"Do you want to go upstairs first?"

"Nope. First, I want to try sucking your dick. And I'm too horny to move."

Noah laughed but carefully climbed off me and shrugged his jeans off, toeing his socks off at the same time, until he stood in front of me in just a pair of loose, black boxers. They had an obvious bulge in the front where his dick was straining against the dark material, and I grinned.

"Seriously, you're so fucking sexy. Come here." I beckoned him towards me and patted my thighs as I slid my legs closed. My own dick protested because it was struggling in the confines of my jeans, but I'd get to it later. Noah looked a little hesitant as he climbed onto my lap and even more so when I hooked my hands around his thighs to pull him up my chest.

"Don't worry," I said. "You're not going to, like, crush

me or anything. If you're struggling for balance, you can put a foot on the floor."

"Are you sure?" Noah asked as I ran my hands up his gorgeous thighs. Fuck, they were so thick and perfect.

"Yeah, I am." A small voice in the back of my head wondered whether Noah wasn't used to his partners wanting him like this. But I was desperate to have him on top of me so I could see as much of him as possible. His crotch was now the perfect height for my mouth, and with some minor adjustments so I didn't crick my neck, I was able to comfortably lean forward and trail my lips across the skin of his thigh.

It was covered in soft, dark hair, and I liked the way it felt under my lips. I gripped his thigh with one hand while I ran the other thumb across his cock, watching it jump under the material. I grinned as I gently reached through the slit in his boxers to grasp his cock and pull it out. Noah gasped as soon as I touched him, and I smirked, loving how sensitive he was.

His cock was shorter than mine but slightly thicker with a soft reddish-purple head that had precum beading on the silky skin. I pumped it slowly, getting used to the weight and feeling in my hand. My eyes kept flicking between staring at his cock and watching Noah's expression. His mouth was slightly open, and he kept pulling at his lip as he tried to keep his eyes on me, but every so often his eyes would flutter closed as he focused on the sensation.

"You'll have to tell me what you like," I said. "Don't be afraid to correct me. I… I work better with directions."

Noah groaned. "Okay, fuck, I can do that."

I swiped a bead of precum up on my thumb and lifted it to my mouth. It tasted slightly different than mine. Noah's was a little sweeter. It made me want to taste more.

Leaning forward, I guided his cock towards my lips, slowly running my tongue across the head. It was soft but still firm—again, it wasn't really comparable to anything I'd experienced before. Noah moaned softly, cursing under his breath as I licked him. His voice had a shuddering edge to it like he was dangerously close to losing control.

I looked up into his eyes as I carefully wrapped my mouth around the head of his cock, letting the weight of it rest on my lips. Noah groaned, and I smirked. I was definitely going to enjoy this.

I pumped his shaft with my hand as I took a little more of his cock into my mouth. My tongue slid around the edge of it, and I realised this was going to take more coordination than I'd thought. I wanted to tip my metaphorical hat to all my previous girlfriends, especially Millie, who'd been able to do this thing with her tongue I was now convinced wasn't even physically possible.

"Shit, yes… just like that," Noah said. "Do you like it?"

I hummed around his cock before giving it a tentative suck. Noah groaned again, and I sucked a little more into my mouth.

"Fuck, that's it. Go slowly. You don't have to take it all."

That sounded like a challenge, but even I wasn't foolish enough to try swallowing his cock straight away. I had no idea how sensitive my gag reflex was, and I definitely didn't want to chuck up all over him. That would be the least sexy thing *ever* and something I'd never recover from.

"Fuck, Spencer, you look so good like this," Noah said, reaching his hand out to caress the top of my head, carding his fingers through my hair. "You look so fucking good with my cock in your mouth."

I hummed around him again and slowly started to move my mouth and my hand together, attempting to get some sort of sucking rhythm going. But even with my adjusted position, it was awkward. I didn't want to stop, though.

I knew I'd told Noah that I wanted to fuck him, but the idea of stopping to go upstairs and find lube and condoms and everything was distressing as fuck. Maybe we could come back to that later. It wasn't like this was going to be a quick one-time thing.

Noah groaned again. "Mmm, yes. Can you take a little more? Fuck! Yes, that's it. Focus on the rhythm and use your hand too. Mmm, fuck, Spencer, you're doing so good."

A burst of pride exploded in my chest like someone was setting off fireworks. I loved hearing Noah praise me like that. I loved knowing I was doing a good job for my first time.

My whole focus narrowed to sucking him, working his cock with my hand and mouth, determined to make him feel good. I didn't know if I'd be able to make him come, but I wanted to try. I'd never tasted cum before, and even if I didn't like it, at least I could say I'd tried it.

"Shit, mmm, yes… just… mmm, like that," Noah's voice was soft and rough, his thighs trembling under my touch like he was trying not to fuck into my mouth.

Fuck, that idea was sexy.

I pulled back slightly, letting his cock slip from my mouth with a slick pop, strings of saliva still connecting me to him. "You can fuck my face," I said, taking a second to process just how wrecked my voice sounded.

"No, I… You're doing great."

"I know," I said, giving Noah a wink. "Not bad for my first time. But I want you to come, and if I can't do that by myself, then I want you to help. I want you to use me to get yourself off."

"But… I… Didn't you want to fuck me?" Noah asked.

I gave him the best approximation of a shrug I could. "We can do that later. I don't want to move until you've come in my mouth. I want to taste you, Noah."

He groaned again. "Fuck, you have an amazing mouth."

"I know," I said again. "And now I want you to use it."

"Okay, but you can stop me any time you want. Just tap my thigh. And you can control it with your hand."

"Relax, babe. I've got you." I winked at him and sucked his dick back into my mouth, using my other hand to gently encourage him to move his thighs. Noah groaned and thrust gently into my mouth as I squeezed his shaft with my hand, creating a hot, slick tunnel for him to fuck into as I took as much of his dick as I could.

Which wasn't as much as I wanted. Again, I was going to have to practice.

I focused all my energy on making Noah feel good, squeezing and working his cock as he fucked into my mouth. Groans, gasps, and muttered words filled my ears along with the slick, wet sounds of me sucking his dick. It was sexy and fun and everything I'd been missing in my last few hook-ups, not to mention my life in general. My own cock strained painfully inside the confines of my clothes, and I wished I had another hand so I could jack myself off at the same time.

But then I'd probably lose my rhythm, and that wasn't fair to Noah. He was my focus right now. I could have my turn later.

"S-Spencer," Noah gasped, his hips giving a stuttering thrust as his cock stiffened. "I'm... fuck, I'm going to come."

I hummed and kept going, not wanting to be the reason he suddenly lost his orgasm. I wasn't there to edge him like that. That would just be mean.

Noah's body tensed before he cried out, his cock pulsing on my tongue as he filled my mouth with cum. I struggled to swallow it, the hot, salty liquid spilling out between my lips and running down my fist. I let Noah's dick roll out of my mouth, his cum dribbling out as I looked up at him. Noah's face was flushed, his lips slick and open, his eyes gazing down at me with an expression of awe and adoration like he'd never seen anything like me before.

His chest was heaving as he leant down to kiss me, his tongue sliding across my bottom lip as he licked some of his cum out of my mouth.

"Fucking hell," I murmured. "That was hot."

"Yeah? You liked it?"

"Yeah. I really did." I licked my lips and frowned. "Not sure about the taste, but I guess I'll get used to it."

"You don't have to," Noah said.

"I know, but I want to. I know that probably wasn't,

like, the best BJ you've ever had, but luckily for you, I like practising. I'm dedicated like that."

Noah chuckled darkly. "I can't wait." He kissed me again, deep and slow, spreading his body out on top of mine. "But first, I'm going to repay the favour." He kissed down my jaw and my neck, drawing happy little noises from me as I relaxed into his touch.

He quickly disposed of my t-shirt, dropping it onto the floor with his clothes before slowly working down my chest and stomach, exploring the ridges of my muscles as he went and trailing his tongue down the dips in my hips as he reached my jeans. My dick was screaming for relief, desperate for even the barest hint of touch, and I was afraid I'd jizz in my boxers if I wasn't careful.

That totally wasn't what I wanted from this moment.

I sighed in delight as Noah popped open my jeans, lifting my hips so he could tug them down my thighs. Pulling my jeans off like this wasn't the sexiest thing ever, but who gave a fuck about that. I watched as Noah tilted his head down and pressed his lips lightly to my straining cock. My underwear felt like a vise, and I was two seconds away from just ripping them off with my bare hands.

Noah must have realised how desperate I was because he didn't torture me any further. He just grasped the waistband of my boxers and gently pulled them down, releasing my cock from the confines of its fabric prison.

I groaned as Noah ran his thumb up my shaft before wrapping his fingers around me. There was a devious smile playing across his face. "You have such a nice dick,

Spencer," he said. His voice was quiet, but every word sank into my soul. "I can't wait to have it in my ass one day."

"Yeah... Fuck, that would be so hot," I said, losing the ability to form words as he began to jerk me slowly. "Fuck, please, Noah. Will you... Fuck, I'm not going to last long..."

"Are you asking me to suck you?" he asked coyly. "Do you want to know what it feels like to have my mouth around your cock?"

"Mmmhmm." I nodded so hard it made my head hurt. "Please."

I watched as Noah shuffled down the sofa, then lowered his head, wrapping his perfect, plush lips around the head of my cock. His tongue flicked out to collect the beads of precum that had gathered on the swollen head before he sucked me down, slowly taking me deep into his mouth.

"Fuuuck!" I cried out at the intense rush of pleasure, my hand shooting out to grip one of the back cushions on the sofa so tightly my knuckles were almost white. Noah's mouth was perfection, and everything became a haze. It felt like the world had slowed and dialled every sensation up to a hundred. I couldn't focus on anything except the overwhelming feelings flooding my body.

I knew I hadn't gotten laid in a while but still. Nothing had prepared me for how amazing this would feel.

"Noah... I'm... Fuck, I'm close," I said as heat coiled in my muscles like a prepared spring. Noah hummed around me, his fingers caressing my balls as he sucked me deeper, pushing all my buttons as if he already knew exactly what I wanted.

My orgasm hit me like a ton of bricks, and I came with a

shout, my hips jerking off the sofa as I pumped my release into Noah's mouth. A feeling of utter bliss washed over me, wringing me out until there was nothing left in my muscles but jelly. I glanced down my body, trying to focus on Noah. I realised he'd swallowed my cum, which was ridiculously fucking hot, and he was smiling at me as he released my spent cock from his mouth.

"Good?" he asked, and I snorted.

"Don't… don't ask stupid questions," I said, and Noah laughed. He crawled up my body and into my arms, the two of us lying naked and content on the sofa as I tried to come back to myself.

"I'm glad. And you're not freaking out, so that's a bonus."

"Why would I freak out? I told you, I want this with you." I tilted his head up to look at me. "I'm not going to suddenly freak out and run away just because you're a man. This isn't some experiment for me. I like you, Noah, like a lot, and that was fucking amazing." I kissed him softly, then grinned. "I can't wait to do it again."

"Me too. Just give me some time to catch my breath."

"Same," I said and pulled him closer to me. I loved how warm and soft his body felt against mine. Noah was so perfect for cuddling that I just wanted to hold him forever. My mind began to drift as we lay there, and suddenly, I remembered what I'd told myself I'd do when I saw Noah again. I didn't know if this was the best time, but if I didn't do it now, I'd either forget or chicken out. "Hey, can I ask you something random?"

"Sure."

"A couple of guys at the gym are putting a five-a-side football team together for the league they run down at the leisure centre, and they asked me if I wanted to join them."

"That sounds fun," Noah said, twisting slightly in my arms so he could look at my face. "Are you going to do it?"

"I don't know. That's the problem." I sighed. "When I retired, I was told not to play again because it could really do me damage, but that was, like, nearly eleven years ago. And they were talking about professional-level stuff, not just a kick-about league. So, I mean, I have a legit reason to say no, but…"

"But you don't want to."

"Yeah, I really want to play again. But I left that behind me," I said, feeling a swell of unexpected emotion rise in my chest. "I had to. Because giving it up was the hardest fucking thing I've ever done, and the idea of playing again, even casually, is making me feel all…" I waved vaguely with my hands.

"Discombobulated?"

"Yeah, that. Just all confused and stuff. Because it could be awesome and give me a chance to do something I thought I'd never get to do again, but also, like, what if I get injured again and make everything worse? What if all I can focus on is how shit it is that football isn't my life anymore? That everything should have been so different, and it's not, and…" I cut myself off before I could ramble any further. "Sorry, it sounds so stupid to get so worked up over this. It's not like it's a big thing."

"It is, though," Noah said gently. "At least it is for you. Football was your whole life, and a professional career was something you'd worked so hard for, but the decision to stop wasn't one you actively wanted or chose. It was forced upon you, so of course that's going to have ramifications for how you feel. And you've spent the last ten plus years not playing at all, and now this offers you the chance to play again, but it's also opening up all your old emotional wounds."

"That's what it feels like. I tried to forget about it all, but now it's just all come rushing back. And I just feel so weird. Like I want to play, but also, I never want to look at a football again. Ugh, I wish I could just make a decision."

"Did you ever talk to anyone when you left?"

"Like a therapist?" I shook my head. "Not really. I mean I had a few transition things through the club, but that was about it. I didn't really think I needed it. Maybe I should have talked to someone, though."

"You still can if you want," Noah said. "There's no time limit on this."

"Maybe." I wasn't convinced, mostly because I thought it might make me feel worse. "But I do need to decide about the league soon. I promised Chris I'd let him know by next Friday."

Noah thought for a second. "Why don't you give him a tentative yes and say you need to get your ankle checked by a doctor—because that's probably something you ought to do anyway—and then that'll give you a bit more time? You can warn him you might have to drop out or only be able to play a little."

I nodded. "Yeah, that would work. I'll ring the doctor in the morning too and see if they can squeeze me in at some point to get it checked." I looked down at him and smiled. My heart kind of felt like it was purring, which was nice but weird. I'd never felt this way about anyone before, but there was something about Noah that just felt right.

"Thanks," I said, "for letting me vent to you."

"That's what I'm here for," he said, kissing me softly. "I'll always be here to listen to you and help however I can. You'd do the same for me. Besides, you saved me from utter baking embarrassment, and I owe you a lot for that."

"I don't wanna keep score," I said, returning his kiss. "No points, only… kisses."

He chuckled and brushed his lips against mine. "I'm on board with that."

CHAPTER TWENTY

Spencer

My post-blow-job talk with Noah had started to unknot a few more of the worries in my chest I'd felt about football. I'd told Chris about it being a tentative yes and that I had some stuff to sort first, and his enthusiastic response had had me grinning for hours. Apparently, they were all just excited to potentially have me on board, even if I just played for five minutes, because they wanted it to be something we all did together.

The whole idea of it being just a fun thing we did as friends was something I hadn't even considered, and I started to wonder if I'd been looking at it all wrong.

I'd been thinking of it as something serious, even if it was just a rec league, but Chris, Sean, and Andrew had just been thinking of it as another fun, sporty thing we could do. Andrew had even said in the group chat that he didn't care if we were shit as long as we enjoyed it.

Which Sean and Chris had booed him for in GIF form, and I'd just laughed.

They were still looking for another couple of people, though, which was why I was heading up to Will's farm to try and sweet talk him into joining us.

Cliff Top Farm sat nestled around the edge of the Castle grounds and rolled into the land beyond it. It was mostly a sheep farm, but I knew Will had diversified the farm's income over the past ten years with some unique holiday cottages—made from old shepherd's huts and repurposed horseboxes—and a livery yard complete with both indoor and outdoor arenas and some enormous stables Will and his dad had constructed themselves in two of the old barns.

His parents still lived at the farm in an old cottage near the gate, but they'd stepped back from the bulk of the farm management several years ago. Will's mum, Sandra, now managed more of the cottages while his dad, Mark, helped Will out where he could and spent the rest of his time looking after his beloved trio of highland cows.

Since I knew Will was always busy, I'd sent him a text on Wednesday morning to ask if I could drop in. I could've just asked him over text, but Will was more likely to say no if I didn't corner him. The man lived and breathed his work, and while I knew farming wasn't something he could easily take a holiday from, he could at least take a couple of hours off a week to play football. The world wasn't going to end if he did, even if he didn't believe it.

I pulled my car into the yard and parked next to Will's mud-splattered Land Rover. It was a very grey and drizzly autumn day, and even here, set back from the sea, I still felt the chill of the coastal breeze trying to get through my hoodie. Will's two working dogs, Nellie and Moss, pottered out of the nearby old stable Will had converted into their pen to see who it was, and Nellie wagged her tail when she realised it was me.

Being working collies, they weren't particularly cuddly, even if they were both gorgeous. I'd always loved dogs but had never really considered getting one because I was so busy with the coffee shop. But maybe that would change in the future. If not, I'd have to be happy stealing snuggles from Lane's old collie, Sparrow, whenever I could.

Will must have heard my car because he appeared from one of the nearby buildings, wiping something off his hands with an old rag. He was wearing the same navy overalls he always did and a solid-looking pair of boots that had straw clinging to the bottom of them.

"Hey, Spencer, you all right?" he called as the dogs bounced up to him, clearly thinking it was time to get back to work.

"Yeah," I said. "You?"

"Not bad, not bad. Just changing the oil and filters on the bike. You want a cuppa?"

"Go on then," I said with a grin and followed Will to the back door of the stone farmhouse, toeing off my trainers and lining them up next to his boots. Will stripped his overalls open and tied the arms around his waist before he wandered through to the kitchen, grabbing the kettle to fill it up.

"Grab a seat," he said, gesturing at the large, slightly battered wooden kitchen table in the middle of the room.

One end of it held a couple stacks of paperwork next to several old issues of *Farmers Weekly*. I pulled out a chair and sat while Will dug in the cupboard for some mugs. "There's buns in the tin if you want one," Will added. "Mum was baking for the cottages again, and we had some left over. Should still be all right."

I reached for the large tin patterned with brightly coloured chickens that was lined up beside Will's laptop and popped it open. Inside were a couple of sticky-looking fruit buns with large sugar crystals studded across the glazed surface. They looked delicious, and even though I'd spent the morning baking for work, I was never going to say no to more cake.

"How's things?" I asked, not wanting to dive straight into my question. I didn't want Will to feel like I was only there to nag him.

"Busy, but not too bad. Cottages are fully booked for half-term. Luckily, Mum's been taking care of that because I've had the sheep to sort, but yeah, it's not too bad." Will nodded, and as I studied his face, I realised he looked tired. I knew his parents helped out as best they could and he had a couple of farm hands too as well as someone to manage the livery yard, but still, Will looked like he needed a break or at least someone to help share the mental load. But I couldn't remember the last time Will had dated anyone. "How's things with you?"

"Pretty good actually," I said, smiling as I pulled the bun apart and tried to catch any sugar falling onto the table.

"Yeah? You and Noah get things figured out, then?" Will asked. I stared at him, eyes wide, and he chuckled and shook his head. "Was it supposed to be a secret or something?"

"I... er... I mean... I've not long figured out I was bi," I said. "And the whole thing with Noah is pretty new. So it wasn't like a deliberate secret, more that we just weren't really telling people yet because you lot are so nosy."

Will nodded. "I figured."

"How did you know anyway?" I asked, still baffled by Will's question. Did the man know everything? Could he read minds or something?

Will shrugged. "Just by watching you two. There was the going to the Castle together, the looking like I'd just kicked a puppy when I suggested you go with Oliver, the sneaking off together, the way Laurie swooped in to take Alex away..." He grinned fondly at me. "I didn't know you were trying to be subtle about it."

"And did you... did you know I was bi?" I asked. "Because if you did, you could've told me ages ago!"

"I had a hunch," Will said. "But it wasn't really any of my business. I figured you either hadn't worked it out or you had and didn't want to tell people, so it wasn't up to me to say anything. I figured you'd get to it in your own time if you wanted people to know."

"Okay... but how? Because it's only become obvious to me recently. Am I really that dense? Or are you just psychic?"

"Not psychic just observant." Will chuckled and started to pour hot water into the two mugs on the counter. "Remember when we were sixteen and Georgie Wood joined the football team?"

"Yes…" I dug through my memory to find what Will was talking about, the image of Georgie resurfacing in my mind. He'd been a year older than us and had just moved to Heather Bay. He'd been fit as fuck with the most amazingly defined thighs that had been highlighted by his shorts, and this soft, dark hair that swept across his face, and…

Ah, fuck.

"Yeah, I see it now," I said, shaking my head. How had I ever thought that my feelings for other men were just platonic, just guys being guys?

"You literally couldn't stop staring at him," Will said. "You nearly walked into the fucking goalposts once trying to talk to him."

"He was so cool! And he was proper fit too." I sighed. "I always thought I liked looking at other guys because they were, like, physically fit, y'know? Or I like their legs or their shoulders or something. I just thought it was like a regular thing."

"Mate, I love you, but you are properly unobservant sometimes."

"Yeah, I know," I said. "At least I figured it out now. And Noah's been amazing about it."

"I'm glad," Will said. "You two are good together."

"You think so?"

"Yeah, I do."

I grinned as I took the mug of tea from Will. I was glad nobody had made a big deal about me and Noah being a thing, at least not so far anyway. Maybe it was time to tell the others, although they might have already figured it out if we hadn't been very subtle about everything.

Then again, nobody was as observant as Will, so we might've gotten lucky.

Will walked over to the table and pulled another chair out, putting his mug on the table as he reached for the tin of buns. "Was that all you wanted to talk to me about?"

"No, there was actually something else." I tore my last piece of bun in half, resisting the temptation to squish it into a ball just to give my hands something to do. "Couple of friends of mine from the gym are looking to put together a five-a-side team for the league the leisure centre is running. I think I'm going to give it a try and wondered if you'd want to come with me?"

Will took a sip of his tea, and I saw him thinking. "You think you'll be okay playing?"

I smiled. It was so typical of Will that his first thought was concern for me. "Yeah, I think so. It's rolling subs, and I can play carefully. I'm going to get myself checked by the doctor next week too. And I... I think it'll be good for me. Noah and I had this long chat last night about it. For ages I've just locked football away and tried to forget about it, even though that's impossible. My feelings are still mixed because I'm not sure I'll ever really get over what happened, but I can't just keep pretending it didn't. I might not always like that it did or that it totally changed my life, but I can't change the past. And if this gives me a chance to do something I've always loved, then maybe it'd be good for me to try again. Does that make sense?"

"Yeah, it does," Will said. "I'm glad you're talking about it with him."

"Me too." I took a long sip of my tea, letting it warm me from the inside out. There was something cosy about sitting there with Will. It made me realise I didn't see enough of him. "You avoided my question, though. Are you going to come too? We need at least one or two more people, and you were always really good. And it'd be good for you to take a break once in a while."

"You sound like my mum," Will said. "And I come to the pub every week."

"I know, but that's one night. Come on, the farm's not going to burn down if you leave it for a couple of hours to play football. You can't be a hermit out here forever."

Will chuckled. "I wouldn't exactly say I'm a hermit. Just busy."

"Even busy people can take a night off to do something fun," I said, giving him my best pleading look. "Come on, Will. Please. For me. And the other guys are really nice too. Plus, I can promise no toxic, homophobic sports bullshit from them since they're all queer too. It'll be fun!"

"If I say no, are you just going to keep nagging me until I say yes?"

"Probably," I said. "I'm annoying like that."

"Fine," Will said in an amused but resigned tone. "I'll play."

"Yes!" I did a little happy dance in my seat, and Will laughed. "It'll be awesome, I promise."

"I can't guarantee I'll be any good, though."

"That's okay, neither can I. We can all be shit together."

A new sense of excitement began to bubble away in my chest, and I knew I'd made the right choice. Despite my swirling emotions, I knew I couldn't wait to get out there again with a ball at my feet, even if I didn't do anything more than casually defend.

Now I just had to hope I could remember how to play.

CHAPTER TWENTY-ONE

Noah

I WAS LYING on the sofa reading when the flat's buzzer sounded. I lowered my book and frowned, wondering who it could be. Alex was still at work, and as far as I knew neither of us had ordered anything.

And if it was Alex, and he'd done something like forgetting his keys again, he'd have messaged me instead.

With a soft groan, because I'd been lying down for too long in one position and everything had gone to sleep, I heaved myself off the sofa and headed over to the intercom. "Hello?"

"Hey, it's me!" Spencer's voice was instantly recognisable, and the bounding, happy note in his voice made me grin from ear to ear. "Can I come in?"

"Sure," I said, pressing the button to open the downstairs door. "It's open."

"Awesome! Thank you!"

I reckoned I had about thirty seconds before Spencer came careening through the front door, which wasn't enough time to do more than run my fingers through my hair and tug the ratty, old t-shirt I was wearing back into place. I wasn't exactly the epitome of style and glamour at the moment, more exhausted teacher halfway through half-term, realising they had to go back to school on Monday.

I'd been aiming to get more of my work done than I had, and I really needed to spend the end of the week putting some conscious effort into it. Otherwise the start of next term was going to smack me in the face and send me staggering.

There was the briefest of knocks on the front door of the flat before it opened, and Spencer's face appeared. He was beaming, his grey eyes practically dancing, and he looked about two seconds away from exploding. I wondered what had made him so happy.

He bounced across the room and swept me up in his arms, kissing me deeply before I'd even had a chance to say hello.

"Hey," he said softly. "I missed you."

"I only saw you yesterday."

"I know, but I still missed you. Didn't you miss me?"

"I did," I said, almost embarrassed to admit it, but I didn't know why. Maybe it was because I didn't want Spencer to think I was clingy. But he'd already said he missed me, so that should have nullified any of my worries. I decided to just keep talking and hope my brain decided to shake off whatever early relationship worries it was dreaming up. "You seem happy?"

"I am!" He kissed me again, and I could have sworn he was vibrating. "I went to see Will and asked him if he'd come play football with us. And he said yes! It's going to be so awesome." He stroked my cheek softly, gazing down at me with such a fierce intensity I thought I might melt. "Thank you for talking about it with me yesterday. Even just acknowledging everything helped, especially because you don't think I was being weird or silly about it."

"You're welcome," I said. "You definitely weren't being silly. And I'm glad Will's joining you. He needs to get out more."

"Right? That's what I said! He seems to think that if he leaves for, like, five minutes something's going to explode. He needs to chill out a little. Maybe get laid."

I chuckled. "You're not going to go on some outlandish quest to find Will a boyfriend, are you?"

"Nah," Spencer said. "Although… my mate Andrew is single… You never know, they might hit it off."

"Didn't you say he's always really busy, though?" I thought back to last night when Spencer and I had lain on the sofa together, and he'd told me all about his friends from the gym. He already wanted me to meet them all and had insisted we'd all have to get together for pizza or something.

"Yeah, that's true. I'm not even sure how he's fitting football in to all the other stuff he does."

"I think Will needs someone to be there for him, not

someone who he's going to feel like he lets down or hardly sees." I shook my head. "I don't know. It sounds weird saying it, but Will basically needs someone who's going to slot into his life and help him pick up the slack. Farming is more a lifestyle than a job, and he needs someone who'll understand that."

"Yeah, I know what you mean," Spencer said with a nod. "By the way, Will knows about us."

"Oh? Did you tell him?" We hadn't really talked about telling people, only that we wanted to keep it on the down low until we'd figured things out. I knew Alex had sort of guessed, and Theo and Laurie knew because Spencer had confessed to telling them, but I hadn't realised he wanted to tell everyone else.

"No. He guessed."

"Really?"

"Yeah, apparently he thought it was bleedin' obvious." Spencer laughed. "He asked me if it was supposed to be a secret, then laughed at me. I don't think anyone else knows, though. Will's the only really observant one."

"That's true," I said. "Lane told me Will said it was obvious how hung up on Oliver he still was before he'd figured it out for himself. Apparently, Will told him he was in denial."

Spencer nodded seriously. "Will's clearly psychic or something. He's definitely got superpowers."

I chuckled softly. We still stood nose to nose, and every so often Spencer would punctuate his sentences with quick, soft kisses like if he didn't kiss me he'd somehow suffer for it.

"God, you're so amazing," Spencer said. "I have the most amazing boyfriend in the world."

"B-boyfriend?" I felt my skin heating. One single word seemed to have reduced me to nothing more than a puddle on the floor. It was like all my wishes had suddenly come true—all the things I'd dreamt about finally manifesting themselves in reality. Which was either sweet or disturbing depending on your point of view.

"Yeah, is that okay? Don't you want to be my boyfriend?"

"I do," I said. "More than anything."

"Good, then be my boyfriend," Spencer said, pulling me even closer to him as he claimed my mouth in a passionate kiss that made my head spin and my heart race. My arms wrapped around him, holding him against me as one kiss melted into another. We'd barely been apart for a day, but the heat in his touch made it feel like it had been months.

I took a step back, then another, walking Spencer towards the sofa. It was harder than I'd expected, but neither of us wanted to let go and actually focus on moving, so we hit a few things along the way.

I was pretty sure I'd have a lovely bruise on my thigh tomorrow morning from where I'd hit the edge of the table.

Eventually, we made it to the sofa and collapsed onto it, half-laughing to ourselves but still kissing as if the world might end if we didn't. Our hands slid under clothes, reaching for every available bit of skin we could find. Spencer's lips trailed across my jaw and nipped at my earlobe before moving down my neck. I tilted my head back and groaned.

His cock was hard against my hip, and I ground up against him, teasingly offering him the chance at more. Spencer growled and sucked a mark onto the base of my neck, leaving me gasping and laughing and desperately hoping the collar of my shirt would cover it up if it was still there on Monday. My students would never let me forget it if they saw me with a hickey, especially after I'd told them to cover them up before.

"Spencer," I groaned as my nails skimmed over his back.

"Yeah? What do you want?" His voice was soft with a delicious underlying note of eagerness like he needed to know what I wanted so he could please me.

"You. I want you."

"Mmm, you want me to fuck you?" he asked. "Want me to make you come on my cock?"

"Fuck, yes!" I gasped as Spencer ground down against me, his hand sliding underneath me to squeeze my ass.

"I've been dreaming about it. Can't stop thinking about how perfect it's going to feel around my dick." He nipped my neck and pressed another sucking kiss to the skin. "You're going to look so fucking amazing riding me, Noah. You're so fucking sexy. I can't wait to watch you come all over me."

I moaned because I wanted that more than anything.

Spencer lifted his head and grinned at me. It was clear he knew how much he was riling me up and that he was loving every second.

"Kiss me," I said, and Spencer obeyed.

If I could, I would have lived on his kisses.

We were utterly lost in each other with no thought of anything else. Which was why the front door opening and Alex's disgruntled "For fuck's sake!" was the equivalent of being shoved headfirst into an icy pool.

Spencer and I leapt apart like startled cats, our heads clattering together as we tried to sit up. Pain ricocheted through me, and I yelped.

"Shit, are you okay?" Spencer asked.

"Yeah," I said, closing my eyes in the hope it would dull the pain as I tentatively touched the spot on my temple. "Are you?"

"Yeah, I think so."

I glanced over Spencer's shoulder to see Alex looking at us with folded arms and pursed lips. He didn't look upset, just more annoyed. Or like he was vaguely contemplating disowning both of us.

"Hey," I said with a forced casual air, like he hadn't just caught me getting hot and heavy with his older brother on our sofa. "Good day?"

Alex raised an eyebrow, but his lip twitched, and I knew he was trying not to laugh. "Seriously? That's what you're going with. 'Good day?'"

"Well, y'know, just being friendly."

I knew then that he wasn't mad at me because he laughed. "Yeah, okay, let's go with that." He looked between Spencer and me and sighed. "God, this is weirder than I thought it would be."

"Sorry," Spencer said sheepishly. "Are we making you uncomfortable?"

Alex pinched the bridge of his nose. "Yes but also no.

Like I'm happy you've sorted your shit out and I don't have to put up with either of you moping around, but that"—he waved a hand in our general direction—"*that* I'm not so comfortable with. I don't think *anyone* wants to see their best friend and their brother dry humping on their sofa."

"Sorry," I said. "I lost track of time."

"It's fine," Alex said. "Maybe next time you could just, I don't know, find a bedroom or something? I'd rather not stumble into a live action porno starring you two in my living room. That would just be next-level fucked up." He turned and headed for the stairs. "I'm going to go and get changed."

"Sorry," Spencer called after him. "It won't happen again."

"It better not," Alex said.

As soon as he'd gone, Spencer and I looked at each other, unable to stop ourselves from grinning like naughty kids. "Fuck," I said with a laugh. "At least we know he's okay with us."

"Yeah, it could've been worse," Spencer said. "He didn't start yelling or anything."

"Nah, if he was proper mad, he'd have been silent," I said. "We would've just gotten glared at."

Spencer nodded. We both sat properly on the sofa now with several inches between us. Neither of us seemed to want to risk shuffling any closer just in case Alex suddenly popped up behind us.

"So," Spencer said, "what do you want to do now?"

I pretended to think for a minute. "Do you want to go and find a bedroom? Pick up where we left off?"

"That sounds like an awesome plan. Do you wanna come back to mine? I think it'd be a bit awkward trying to have sex with my brother downstairs. Like, we can try to be quiet, but he's gonna know."

"Perfect," I said. "Although, I do have to come back here later. I promised Alex we could start watching the *Underworld* series tonight, and I don't want him to feel like I'm abandoning him for you."

Spencer nodded. "I don't want him to feel like that either. I don't want this"—he waved his hand in between us—"to get in the way of your friendship."

"You're so sweet, you know that?" I leant over and kissed him. "I'm just going to tell Alex I'll be back later, then we can go."

"Don't be too long," Spencer said. "Or I might get lonely."

I laughed. "Really?"

Spencer grinned. "I don't know. I might. I do get lonely sometimes."

His words were meant as a joke, but I felt the real pain behind them. "Don't worry. You'll never be lonely as long as I'm around. I promise."

I kissed him again, trying to pour as much affection into the gesture as possible. Because I never wanted Spencer to feel like he was alone. This relationship might have been new, but it was already clear to me that I was developing deep feelings for him. My childish wish had been for us to be together, whether we were compatible or not, but now it was becoming increasingly obvious just how well we fit together.

I knew we were still in the honeymoon phase where everything was rose-tinted, and I knew I shouldn't rush. But deep down, I got the feeling Spencer really was the only one for me, and that I'd never find another man as perfect, even if I searched for a thousand lifetimes.

CHAPTER TWENTY-TWO

Spencer

I was so excited to finally get to fuck Noah, but I was a little nervous too. I hadn't done anal in a while, and I didn't want to hurt him. I didn't want to get inside him and come straight away either. I wanted the sex to actually be good.

But Noah seemed to love telling me what he wanted, and I really got off on that. All I needed was for him to keep doing it and for my dick to show a little restraint.

I felt the heat simmering between us—like there was something bubbling under the surface just waiting to be unleashed—as we headed back to mine. It was like our desire was two seconds away from boiling over and making a mess everywhere.

We just needed to make sure it happened in private.

As soon as my front door closed, Noah was in my arms, his fingers tangling in my hair as he dragged me in for a desperate kiss. "Upstairs," he growled, his mouth barely breaking away from mine. "I need you inside me."

I groaned and grabbed his hand, dragging him towards the stairs. I was half tempted to pick him up and carry him to my room, but there wasn't a lot of head room, and giving Noah a concussion wasn't on my bucket list.

Two flights of stairs had never felt so far in my life; it felt more like climbing Everest.

I barely managed to turn on the light and glance around my room before Noah was kissing me again, pressing his tongue into my mouth and utterly claiming me with his kisses. I melted against him, wanting nothing more than to give myself to him. My cock throbbed, and I groaned as it brushed against Noah's own growing bulge.

"I need you," he murmured. "Please, Spencer, I can't wait. I fucking need you inside me."

"Whatever you need," I said as I stepped back to start shrugging off my clothes, not caring if I looked elegant and sexy. This wasn't the time for some super sexy burlesque-style striptease. This was just about getting naked as fast as possible. In front of me, Noah was doing the same, and as he dropped the last of his clothes to the floor, I stopped moving and stared. "Wow."

I'd seen him naked before, but every time it continued to blow my mind just how sexy he was.

He was soft and strong and round and just… I didn't have the words. The only way I could describe him was with some indeterminate growl.

I reached out and ran my fingers down his chest. His chest hair was darker and slightly curled, but it was still soft, and there was something about it that ratcheted the heat up inside me. My own chest was smoother, and the only hair was so white blond it was almost unnoticeable at first. I'd waxed it a lot when I was younger and had only started growing it out when I'd retired, and by that point it had virtually given up.

"I'm not—" Noah started to say, but I silenced him with a kiss.

"Yes, you are. Don't you dare say you're not sexy because to me you're the sexiest person I've ever seen." I kissed him again, wrapping one hand around him and trailing it down his spine until I reached his ass. "You're like god-tier sexy." I pulled back and looked down at him with a smile. "And you're not allowed to be mean to my boyfriend. He's fucking awesome, and I won't stand for it."

"You won't?" he asked with a teasing smirk.

"Nope. And if you are mean to him, I won't make you cupcakes ever again."

Noah whistled. "That's a pretty evil threat."

"I know, it's more of a deterrent than anything, though," I said, my lips practically pressed against his.

"Guess I'll have to be nice, then."

"Guess you will." I grinned and kissed him sweetly, letting my tongue caress his bottom lip. Noah groaned into my mouth as I squeezed his ass cheek, then slid my fingers across the furred muscle, dipping them into his crack. Noah pushed back into my hand as my fingers caressed the furled, fuzzy skin of his hole.

"Fuck," he murmured. "Give them to me."

"Can I…" I thought back to some of the porn I'd seen on

my trip down the gay-sex rabbit hole. "Can I try eating you first? I want to know what you taste like."

"Are you sure?"

"Yeah, I wouldn't have asked otherwise," I said. "Please, Noah, let me taste you."

His answering kiss was full of heat. "Yes. I want to feel you eat my ass." He stepped away from me and strolled over to the bed, climbing onto it and settling onto all fours, then looking over his shoulder at me with the most gorgeous pair of fuck-me eyes. "You can jerk yourself off while you do it if you want," he added. "But don't come. I want you to do that inside me."

"Okay." I nodded. "I can do that."

Since my bed was so big, it wasn't too hard to arrange both of us on it, so I didn't feel like I was about to fall off. I pressed a series of lazy kisses down Noah's spine before I reached his ass. His cheeks were thick and round, and I knew they were going to look so good sliding up and down my cock. I squeezed one cheek with my hand and kissed the top of his crack before gently pulling his cheeks apart.

I'd always been an ass man. There was just something about a thick, juicy butt that did it for me. And I knew I'd be happy to worship Noah's as often as he'd let me.

I lowered my mouth and gently ran my tongue across his hole. This wasn't the first time I'd eaten ass, but it was the first time I'd gotten a deep, needy moan in response. A smile played across my lips as I flicked my tongue again, eliciting another moan from Noah.

I would *definitely* be doing this again.

My tongue caressed the sensitive skin as I kissed and

licked and sucked his hole, drawing more delicious sounds from his lips. There were a few broken words too, but it was hard to make out more than "More" and "Fuck" and "Oh fuck, Spencer." The last one especially made my self-satisfied smile widen.

I reached between Noah's legs and gently wrapped my hand around his shaft. He must have been aching and desperate for my touch, considering the way he thrust into my hand. My own cock was just as hard, and I was so fucking desperate to give myself some relief, but I resisted the urge because I knew that once I started, I wasn't going to want to stop until I'd come.

And that kind of defeated the purpose.

Noah's hole was beautifully slick now, and while I knew it wasn't going to be a good substitute for lube, I didn't quite want to stop just yet. Slowly, I slid the tip of my finger into his hole alongside my tongue. Noah gasped and pushed his ass back onto my face. I grinned because I must have done something right.

It didn't take long to work a finger into him, still using my tongue to tease the sensitive skin while my other hand slowly worked his shaft.

"You look so amazing like this," I said, breaking away to press a kiss to his ass cheek.

Noah glanced over his shoulder, his face flushed. "Yeah?"

"Yeah." Slowly, I slid my finger out of him and released his cock, moving up alongside him on the bed so I could kiss his perfect mouth again. "I just want to spend all day playing with your ass, making you moan on my tongue and my fingers, and seeing how many times I can make you come. I want to fuck you over and over again until we're too exhausted to move. I want to feel you come on my cock and watch you cover me in your load. Fuck, I can't wait to feel that."

Noah moaned again. "You're going to ruin me."

"Good." I grinned at him and winked. Noah muttered something under his breath that sounded like "Fuck me."

"I'm going to get lube and stuff," I added. "Then I'll fuck you."

"You know," Noah said, giving me a soft kiss and sitting up on his knees. "I had all these ideas about telling you what to do, but now…"

"I still want you to do that. I love it when you tell me what you want," I said. "Then I know I'm getting it right."

"You're going to be the death of me."

"The sexy death of you." I winked at him again and rolled off the bed to rummage in my bedside cabinet for the fancy new lube and the box of condoms I'd bought. I'd already remembered to unwrap the bottle so I didn't have to spend ten minutes trying to peel the plastic off, and I climbed back onto the bed and clicked the lid open.

"Lie on your back," I said. "I want to see your face while I get you ready for my cock."

Noah nodded and shuffled up the bed, lying down and spreading his legs for me. He hooked his forearms under his thighs, and I let out a little happy sigh at seeing him all spread out in front of me. It was a mental image I'd be jerking off to for weeks.

"Tell me if you want more or less or something different," I said, moving myself between his legs. "I want you to tell me what you want."

"I will," Noah said. "Start with one, but you can go up to two pretty quickly. I'm usually fine with just that, but if you want, you can use three. Do you know how to find my prostate?"

"I think so." I grinned. "I did a bit of reading and watched a few videos. Mostly because I was curious."

"Has anyone ever found yours?"

"Yeah, I think one of my exes did. She was really good with her fingers, and she'd just get the angle right, and it would be like… like holy fucking shit good."

"That sounds about right," Noah said. "Just take it steady, and don't yank them out."

"Dude, this isn't my first time using my fingers," I said with a wry smile. "Well, it is on a dude, but I mean, like—"

"I know what you mean. Now get them inside me because I'm getting desperate over here."

I was tempted to tease him for being bossy, but I was at my limit too. I needed to be inside him more than ever.

The lube was cool on my fingers as I drizzled it across my digits, but I hoped it would warm up quickly. Kneeling between Noah's thighs, I slowly pressed my finger back into him, loving the way he groaned as his body pulled me inside.

It didn't take long to work up to two fingers, scissoring him open and using my other hand to tease his cock, occasionally lowering my mouth to press teasing kisses to the hard, silky shaft.

"More," Noah said. "Please, Spencer. Give me more."

"Are you sure? I don't want to hurt you."

"You won't. Don't make me beg."

I groaned. "I'd love to hear that."

Noah smirked. "Maybe one day. If you're good and give me what I want. Which right now is your fucking fingers quickly followed by your cock."

A deep moan rumbled in my throat as I leant over him to kiss him fiercely, trying to show him everything he did to me as I slowly pushed another finger inside him. The sounds Noah made were sweet and delicious, the kind I wanted to drink down over and over because hearing them once was never going to be enough.

"Lie down," Noah said. "I want to ride you."

"Fuck yes, please do that."

I rolled onto the bed beside him, quickly grabbing the box of condoms and pulling one out. It was easy enough to rip the foil open and roll one onto my cock, using the left-over lube on my fingers to slick it up. Noah watched me with hungry eyes before swinging his leg over to straddle my hips.

He looked so fucking perfect on top of me, and I knew this image would also be going in my spank bank, especially the expression on his face as he started to slide down onto my cock.

"Fuck," I groaned, my hands going to his thighs and clinging on for dear life at the sheer intensity of the pleasure pulsing through me. Noah's ass was hot and tight, squeezing my cock as he took all of me, resting his hands on my chest as I bottomed out. I let out a deep, shuddering breath as I tried to control the urge to thrust up deep inside him until I filled him. "Shit, you're so tight. It feels... Fuck, this is incredible. You feel so good."

"So do you," Noah said, sounding a lot more controlled than I did. He leant down and brushed his lips against mine. "I'm going to ride you now, but I don't want you to move. I don't want you to fuck me, not yet. I just want to use your perfect cock to fuck myself. Does that sound good?"

"Mmm, yeah... that sounds, fuck that sounds so good. Use me, Noah. Please. Use me however you want. I want you to come."

"You're so sweet, did you know that?" His voice was a low murmur, and every word sent shivers racing across my skin. "And don't worry, I'm planning on riding you until your perfect skin is covered in my load. Then you can fuck me. I want to know what it feels like when you come inside me."

Any further words I'd been planning to say died on my lips as Noah began to roll his hips. All I could do was hang on and stare in awe at the gorgeous man in my lap who was riding my cock like it was the best fucking dildo in the world.

Maybe to him it actually was. That was a pretty awesome thought.

My hands moved up to grip his hips as Noah began to bounce up and down, my eyes mesmerised by the way his thighs moved and the sight of his hard cock bobbing in front of me. My senses were being bombarded with sensation, and it was threatening to overload my system in the most spectacular way.

Noah cried out as he shifted his hips and began to ride me faster. I guessed he'd found the perfect angle to hit his sweet spot, and I knew from past experiences that moving now could ruin everything. I was not about to fuck this up by adjusting my position even an inch. Instead, I watched, trying to memorise every detail so I could revisit it later when I was alone at night and desperate for Noah's touch.

"S-Spencer," Noah cried, his eyes locked on mine and shining with desperation. He reached for his cock and began to jerk himself off. "I… I'm… Fuck, I'm so close."

"Yeah, that's it," I said. "Come for me, baby. I want to feel it."

Noah rose up and slammed down on my cock, riding me harder and harder until he cried out, his whole body stiffening as his ass tightened around me, pulling me deeper inside his channel as he painted my skin with hot, sticky cum.

"Fuck, baby, that's it… Shit, you look so fucking amazing Noah."

Noah tilted forward, a sated smile on his face as he kissed me. "God, your cock is just… Mmm, it's perfect." He ran his tongue along my lip, his breaths still coming in pants. "Fuck me, Spencer."

"You know… you know I'm probably not going to last," I said with a weak chuckle as I slowly began to rock up into him. The way he'd squeezed my shaft when he'd come had nearly sent me over the edge, and it had only been through sheer force of will that I hadn't burst.

"I don't care," he said. "Besides, I don't really want to be here all night."

I snorted, then groaned. "Good, because we're not going to be."

Noah sighed happily. "Fuck, that feels good. Now give it to me hard."

I growled and gripped his hips harder, giving him everything I had. Pleasure burned through me, white hot and all-consuming. I felt the edge approaching at full speed, and it was all I could do to push out broken words to tell Noah that he was about to get his wish.

Noah kissed me deeply, and that was it. With a deep groan, I pulled him down onto my cock, thrusting deep inside him and filling the condom as my orgasm flooded me, hurling me over the edge into a void of endless bliss.

I didn't quite know when or how I came down. I just remembered Noah snuggled up in my arms. He was smiling up at me, and we were both still naked and covered in half-dried cum.

"Well," he said, "that was fun."

"Yeah… just a bit." I laughed breathlessly and leant over to kiss him. "We should probably do that again some time."

"Oh, we're definitely doing that again," Noah said, and I felt his smile against my lips.

I grinned, my mind still spinning. If that was what sex with Noah was going to be like, then I didn't think I'd ever be able to get enough.

CHAPTER TWENTY-THREE

Noah

"I can't believe I have to go back to school on Monday," I said, looking out over the beach where the Saturday afternoon sun was already starting to turn the water gold. I'd met Spencer at Novel Tea when he'd finished his shift, and now we were walking hand in hand along the front with no real destination in mind.

"You sound like me," Spencer said. "Except that was, like, twenty years ago? Wow, I'm getting old."

I chuckled. "You're not old."

"I'm thirty-two," he said. "That's kinda old."

"Only if you were going to die at forty."

"I guess." We'd stopped walking and were leaning against the beach wall. "Anyway, I thought you liked school?"

"I do. Most of the time anyway," I said. "Teaching is hard. It's not just the kids; it's the paperwork, the planning, the meetings, the marking. There's not nearly enough time to do everything at school, so I always end up working evenings and weekends and holidays. Teaching doesn't ever really stop. It really is one of those jobs you do because you love it." I chuckled softly and looked out over the beach. "It's definitely not one you do for the money or because you want an easy life. I don't even think half my PGCE cohort are teaching anymore."

"Why do you do it, then?" Spencer asked. His body was pressed against mine, offering me something warm and comforting to lean against. "If you don't mind me asking? Alex always said you were the smartest guy he knew. You could've done anything, so why come back here to teach?"

I looked over at him and smiled. "Would it be cheesy of me to say because I wanted to make a difference?"

"No. Why would it?"

"I don't know." I'd never really talked about my job in detail with anyone other than Alex before, and we certainly hadn't discussed my reasons for taking it. I'd had a couple of professors at uni tell me they thought I'd be a good researcher or academic, but both of those careers seemed so strange and distant to me—like things I just couldn't picture myself doing. "Everyone always told me I could do these great things for science, but they never felt like my dreams. I'm just one man from a small town in Yorkshire, and I've always felt like I belonged here. I know Oliver always had these big plans of leaving, and everyone said I needed to go out and live my life, but when I was a student, I missed being here so much. I think it would have been different if we'd all gone our separate ways, but Alex and

Lane were still here, and I missed them more than anything."

I paused for a second, trying to put the big, complex feelings I'd always had into words. "When we were at school, there was this sort of… expectation, I guess, that the smartest people would leave, and that would be it. But I love Heather Bay, and coastal towns are often the ones that struggle most educationally because of lack of funding or students or good teachers. And I guess… I saw how many teachers wrote off kids in my class because they didn't think they'd amount to anything more than just staying here, like that was an awful fate. But also, I wanted all my students to know they can do whatever they want, no matter who they are. So if they want to go to Cambridge, or be the first in their family to get a degree, then I will cheer and fight for them every step of the way, and if they choose to stay here, then I will cheer for them too. I know I'm just a science teacher, but I want every one of my kids to feel supported, and I think that because I grew up here, I understand more than most what it's like. The world is big and scary, especially if you've never really been outside the Yorkshire moors, which is at least half my students, and I want to make the world a little less intimidating." I chuckled and shook my head, suddenly embarrassed. "Sorry, that was quite a ramble."

"No," Spencer said. "It wasn't." He leant over and reached for my chin, turning my face to his before kissing me gently. "You're amazing, Noah. Like, I already knew that, but now I just think you're even more amazing. You do this job, which sounds like the most stressful thing in the world, and you love it. I genuinely don't know how you do it. I mean, I just remember what I was like at school."

"I'm sure you weren't that bad," I said. "Besides, I went to school with Lane and Alex—it was like the ultimate rocker-class clown combo."

Spencer snorted. "Yeah, I can see that. I remember Mum's endless levels of exasperation with Alex. Neither of us were really academically minded."

"Not everyone is," I said. "And I wish more teachers would remember that. You just have to find something each person is good at. Look at you and Alex now. You own and run the most popular coffee shop in Heather Bay. That's amazing."

"Thanks," Spencer said with an embarrassed smile. "Someone asked us today if we'd ever consider opening another location."

"Seriously?"

"Yeah. I don't think Alex and I have ever thought about it before. I don't even know how we'd go about it."

"Do you think you'd consider it, though?" I asked.

"I don't know? Maybe?" Spencer shrugged, then grinned. "I'll do whatever Alex tells me. He's the boss. I'm just one of the bakers."

"I think you're a bit more than that," I said, nudging him gently. "But that's awesome. Whatever you do or don't decide to do, I'm proud of you. Both of you. You've built something incredible that people love."

"Thanks." He looked out at the beach for a second, where a terrier was enthusiastically chasing a ball across the sand. "It's funny. This might not have been the life I'd planned, but it's still a good one." He turned his head and smiled at me, pure warmth radiating out of his expression. "Especially now that I have you!"

"Me?"

"Yeah!" He reached for my hand and squeezed it tightly. "I know this is really new between us, like *really* new, but I've got a good feeling about it."

"Me too," I said. I could hardly believe this was real, and yet it was, and everything Spencer had said felt true. We'd been together for less than a week, but it felt like so much longer. "Maybe it's because we've known each other for so long."

"I think so," Spencer said. "I just wish I'd realised sooner how fucking gorgeous you are. Well, realised that me thinking you were cute wasn't a straight feeling."

"Everything in its own time. That's what my grandpa used to say."

"I wish that my own time had been sooner, though. Then we could've had even longer together than the time we're going to get."

"Oh? And how long's that?" I asked, wondering if it was too soon to be dealing in such absolutes. I'd never had this sort of conversation with anyone before, not even in the two-year relationship I'd had when I'd moved back here to start teaching. But this was Spencer, and everything was different with him.

He shrugged, still grinning. "I don't know, probably forever if I get my way. Is that weird?"

"No, it's not. I'd be happy with probably forever too."

"Good, I was worried I sounded really creepy like I was going to kidnap you or something."

"Wait," I said, grinning as I remembered a conversation from one night during the summer. The first night Lane had brought Oliver to the Sleeping Goose and Spencer had attempted to make him feel at ease in the strangest way possible by talking about which one of us was the most likely to have a secret murder dungeon and be a serial killer in their spare time. "Does this mean *you* have a creepy murder basement you haven't shown me yet?"

"I mean, I wouldn't say it's creepy," Spencer said. "But I do have a cellar. I was thinking about painting it green, but I don't think that'll work."

"Hang on, all along you had a cellar of your own, and you never mentioned it?" I asked, almost unable to hold back my laughter. "Even when you said out of everyone I was the most likely to have a murder dungeon and get away with it? And you've pretty much had one all along."

"I know. Pretty sneaky, right?" He winked at me. "I was thinking of turning it into a home gym. Right now, it's just full of boxes."

"I like that idea," I said. "But definitely not green." I leant against his arm and watched the terrier chase its tennis ball into the waves. At the other end of the beach, I saw a couple of kids kicking a football around as the sun started to sink lower.

"Hey," I added, "you're going to the doctor on Tuesday, right? About your ankle."

"Yeah," Spencer said. "I'm a bit nervous. At first, I was

hoping they'd say I couldn't play, but now I want them to say yes."

"I'm sure they will. It's not like you're asking them to play in the Premier League again."

"I don't know," Spencer said with a chuckle. "Some of these rec leagues can be vicious. I really hope I can remember how to play. I haven't even touched a football since I retired."

I watched the kids again, an idea forming in my mind. Turning my head, I glanced along the row of colourful shops that made up the front. A lot of them were seasonal and only open for a few hours in the off-season if at all. There was one open now, though, and I could see just what I wanted hanging by the door.

"Wait here," I said, letting go of Spencer's hand. "I'll be back in a minute."

He raised an eyebrow. "Where are you going?"

"I just need to grab something. Don't go anywhere."

"Okay," he said, sounding amused and slightly confused. "I'll wait."

"Great." I kissed his cheek, then hurried off towards the shop, grabbing my phone out of my pocket as I did and tapping out a message to Alex that I then copied and pasted and sent to Lane, Laurie, Bastian, and Will.

The shop owner was just starting to take everything down and pack it away when I reached the door, but he was happy enough to grab me what I wanted: a large, yellow football.

I didn't think it was regulation, but that didn't matter. It was just to give Spencer something to kick about to see how he felt. I didn't think his skills were the sort he'd completely forget, and while he might be a bit rusty, I was betting he was still better than anyone else I knew.

Declining a bag and thanking the shop owner, I hurried back towards Spencer, clutching my prize in one arm. He'd gone back to watching the beach, but as soon as he heard me, his head turned, and his eyes lit up in shock.

"A football? Why have you got a football?" he asked, his frown deepening, and it was adorable that he hadn't quite twigged what my plan was.

"Come on," I said, reaching for his hand with my empty one. "You said you don't know if you can still remember anything, so let's see what you've got. And this way, you'll be able to see how you feel moving your ankle around before you go to the doctor."

Spencer slipped his hand into mine, but he still didn't look convinced. "What if... what if I suck, though?"

"Does it matter?"

"Er... I... I guess not?" He didn't sound convinced, and I grinned.

"Exactly, it doesn't. You can practice, and you can get better again," I said. "Besides, we're literally just going to have a kick about on the beach, and you're playing against me. If I can even hit the ball, I'll consider that a win. Athleticism and I aren't exactly best friends, unless we're in a pool, then maybe I'd stand a better chance."

Spencer chuckled. "Okay, let's do it."

We walked over to a little set of concrete steps that led down to the sand. The tide looked like it was going out, the few boats in the bay bobbing low in the water. The sun was still sinking, and I reckoned we still had about half an hour of light before it would be too dangerous to continue. The tide might have been going out, but everyone who'd grown up here knew never to mess with the sea, especially when it was dark or stormy.

I put the ball on the sand and gently tapped it with my foot, pushing it over to Spencer and giving him my most encouraging smile. "Go on then, show me what you can do."

CHAPTER TWENTY-FOUR

Spencer

As soon as my foot made contact with the side of the ball, it felt like all my worries melted away.

I gave the ball a gentle tap, nudging it from one foot to the other, trying to get a feel for the movement again. I knew I was going to be rusty, but as Noah had reminded me, if I sucked, then I could just practice.

But just feeling the ball there, against the edge of my trainer, brought everything flooding back. There were no nerves, though; it just felt like my brain was dusting off some very old files and trying to reboot that part of my memory—like football ran on Windows XP, and I was now trying to run it on updated everything.

I tapped the ball again, harder this time, and sent it spinning across the sand. I grinned. It wasn't quite what I'd intended, but that didn't matter. I jogged after it and carefully manoeuvred it with my left foot, seeing how my ankle felt.

It helped that I'd always been right-footed, preferring to do everything with that foot rather than my left, which was the one that had been damaged. It meant I wouldn't need to use my left foot for more than dribbling and the occasional pass if it came in at the wrong angle.

I moved the ball around, turning it in a small, controlled circle before looking up and around for Noah. He stood watching me near the steps, hands in his hoodie pocket, with a beaming smile on his face.

"To you," I called, giving the ball a firm kick towards him with my right foot. It skittered across the beach but didn't end up too far from where I'd intended. Noah walked over and nudged it with his foot like he was getting a feel for it. It made my chest swell with emotion because this wasn't Noah's thing at all, but he wanted to do it for me.

I'd never felt this way about anyone before.

And I'd meant what I'd said to him, even if I'd tried to make it seem like I was joking. Although this relationship was still brand new, I'd never met anyone that things felt so right with. There was just something about Noah that made everything feel easy and like I could be myself around him, and he'd never want me to be anyone else. In the past, I'd always thought I had to be a certain way in relationships like I had this image, this façade, I couldn't let down because I'd never been convinced the person I was with would like what they saw.

But maybe because I'd known Noah for so long and I'd

never been anything but myself with him, I didn't feel like I had to be any different when it was just us. I could just be the same Spencer I'd always been.

I just got to show him new parts of me as well, and he seemed to really like those things too.

I grinned to myself, wondering if Noah would be up for coming back to mine afterwards for a quickie before he went home to watch another movie with Alex. I didn't begrudge my brother anything, and I didn't want him to feel like I was stealing his best mate, but at the same time, I was almost annoyed I had to give up an evening of fun with Noah.

Mostly because I hadn't had nearly enough time to explore his body, and I knew our time would be more limited once term started again.

"Okay, this is probably not going to come anywhere near you," Noah said before kicking the ball towards me. It rolled my way with more speed than I'd anticipated, curling off to one side, and I had to jog over to retrieve it. "Sorry!"

"You're fine," I called, collecting the ball with my foot and slowly dribbling it back and forth, using some random shells as little markers.

I was so wrapped up in myself I didn't hear anyone else approaching until Alex's voice cut through my thoughts. "I heard you were looking for victims."

"He means volunteers," Lane's voice added. "Come on, grumble bum. This'll be fun."

I glanced up, my mouth falling open to see all our

friends walking down to the beach, all grinning and wearing trainers and hoodies. Even Will was there.

"What?" I asked, scooping up the ball and walking over to them. "What's all this?"

"We heard you were practising," Will said casually. "Thought you might like some people to practice with."

"We can't promise to be any good," Laurie said, popping out from behind him.

"But we can try," added Theo, who was bundled up in an enormous pink hoodie. "Wait, do we need to know the rules?"

"No biting of ankles," Lane said. "And no throwing people in the sea."

"No contact at all," Oliver said. "This isn't supposed to be violent."

"Wait, we can't even pull on people's hoodies? Not even a little bit?" Lane asked. "How am I supposed to stop Alex from cheating?"

"What the fuck? Why would I cheat? How the fuck would I cheat?" Alex exclaimed, shoving Lane playfully. Lane shoved him back, and I laughed. I couldn't believe they were all here. I wondered how they'd even known. It had been such a spur of the moment thing from Noah…

I glanced at my boyfriend, who was smiling quietly from one side of the group. He noticed me watching and shrugged. I assumed he'd put the call out when he'd gone to the shop. I just couldn't believe they'd all just dropped everything to turn up and play with us.

"You always cheated when we were at school," Lane

said with a grin. "You used to move the jumpers and make the goal smaller."

"No, I fucking didn't," Alex said. "That was you."

"Wait, do we need teams?" Bastian said. He and Anders had just arrived.

"In which case, I'm going in goal," Anders said. "Then I don't have to run."

"Oooh, there's ten of us, that's a perfect split," Theo said. "I call dibs on being on a team with Spencer. He can be the captain of Team One, a.k.a. the best team."

"Don't I get a say in this?" I asked although I didn't mind. I just loved how into it they were all suddenly getting, even though only a few of them had ever even vaguely expressed interest in sport before.

But this was what my friends did—they showed up for each other, no questions asked, because that was what you did when you loved people. And I knew some guys hated using that term about any form of friendship, but it was the truth. I loved these men with everything I had because I knew they'd always be there for me whether I'd known them all my life or just a couple of months.

I really was one of the luckiest men in the world.

"No," Theo said. "You're on Team One with me. You can pick everyone else, though."

"We're not picking teams like we're in school," I said quickly, not wanting anyone to feel left out. I'd never been picked last, but I'd always imagined it was a horrible experience. "Everyone can just choose where they go."

"Wait," Alex said with a wry grin. "Do we need a rule about couples? I don't want to be on a team with Lane and

Oliver if they keep stopping to make out every two minutes."

"We're not thirteen," Lane said. "We can make it through one game of beach five-a-side."

"Can you?"

"Don't be a dick," Lane said and nudged him again. "Fine, no couples on one team. Oliver, you go with Spencer. I'll start making up Team Two. Alex, you come with me before you shove your brother in the sea. Noah, do you want to go with Spencer?"

"I, er, I can't," Noah said, speaking up for the first time since they'd all arrived. In the light of the setting sun, I saw colour tinting his cheeks as he smiled sheepishly at everyone. "Not with the no couples rule."

I grinned at Noah and shrugged. We'd talked about telling more people, but we'd not figured out a when or where. But this seemed as good a time as any. I walked up to him and cupped his jaw in my hand, the football still tucked under my other arm as I drew him into a dramatic kiss. I turned to the group. There was a moment of silence, and everyone looked between us.

Then the whole group exploded in chatter.

"Ahh, I'm so glad you figured it out," Theo said giddily, practically throwing himself into my arms for a hug. "I knew you would."

"Wait. Did you already know?" Lane asked. "Who else knew?"

"I didn't *know* know," Theo said. "I didn't know it was official or anything."

"I knew," Alex said grumpily. "Mostly because they

won't stop making out on my fucking sofa."

"That was one time," Noah said. "And you didn't see anything."

"I saw more than I needed to," Alex said, but he was smiling. "You're like my second brother. Imagine how weird that was for me!"

"Don't make it awkward," Lane said. "Okay, who else knew?"

"Will did," I said, giving the farmer a teasing smile. "Because he's psychic."

"I'm not psychic," Will said with a shake of his head. "You're just really fucking obvious. I just can't believe none of the rest of you noticed."

"I had an inkling, but I wasn't sure," Oliver said. He was leaning against Lane's shoulder, and the builder had his arm around Oliver's waist.

"Why didn't you tell me?" Lane asked, kissing Oliver's temple. Oliver shrugged.

"I didn't want to make things strange if I was wrong. And I figured if I was right, we'd all find out eventually when they were ready to tell us."

"We weren't going to keep it a secret forever," Noah said, slipping his hand into mine and squeezing. "We just wanted some time to figure it out for ourselves before you lot got involved."

"'Got involved'? What do you mean 'got involved'?" Lane teased.

"Come on. I know you," Noah said with a soft roll of his eyes. "If you'd known, you'd have been constantly asking questions and offering advice and trying to crash our dates."

"To be fair, they did that anyway," I said, chuckling softly.

"Only because we didn't know it was a date," Will said. "You should've just said."

"Wait, when was that?" Theo asked.

"Fright Night."

"Ohhhh, I thought so! That's why we kept trying to steal Alex so he wouldn't interfere."

"Oh my God," Oliver said. "I'm so sorry. Why didn't you say anything when I insisted we all go together?"

"We were only just figuring it out," I said. "And you'd still have come anyway."

"No, we wouldn't have," Lane said.

"Eh." Alex waved his hand, grinning. "We probably would."

The sun was starting to set faster, and I knew we were going to be out of light soon. Noah must have realised it too because he clapped his hands, interrupting the discussion between Lane, Oliver, Theo, and Alex.

"Okay," Noah said using his best teacher voice, which I had to admit was kind of hot. "We can finish this later. Right now, we need to decide on teams if we want to do anything before the light goes. So me, Lane, Alex are part of one team, with Oliver, Spencer, and Theo starting the other. Where's everyone else going?"

"I'll go with Lane," Laurie said, sliding away from Theo towards where Lane and Alex had moved to. "I'm guessing that makes him the captain, then?"

"If you like," Lane said. "But I'm not sure we need captains."

"Yes, we do," Theo said. "And this isn't a competition, but the losing team are definitely buying the winners hot chocolate."

"I'll go with Oliver and company," Bastian said. "Then Anders can go with Lane."

"Only if I get to be in goal," Anders added. "I'm too old to run."

"You're not old."

"I never said that. I said I'm too old to run. There's a difference."

"Guess I'm with you, then," Will said to me, giving me a nod and a smile. "Just like old times."

"Just like old times." I grinned, then looked around the group. "Let's do it."

We made a couple of quick goal markers out of sand and driftwood, and since I already had the ball, it was easiest for me to kick off. Soon the beach was filled with the sounds of raucous laughter and swearing as we attempted to play some version of football. None of us were very good, but that didn't matter. Just moving around with the ball at my feet was enough to start sloughing the rust off my system.

My body felt good, and the underlying worry that I'd touch the ball and somehow break in half hadn't materialised. Instead, all I felt was the sheer joy of playing again, and when I neatly slid the ball between the makeshift goal posts and past Anders, everyone cheered, and passers-by would have thought I'd scored the World Cup winner for England.

And while that might have been my dream once, I was starting to realise that this would be enough in its place.

Because I didn't need a fancy footballing career with England caps to make me happy. I just needed my home and my friends and the man who was changing everything.

It was probably too early to say that I loved Noah, but I was going to think it anyway. Because nothing had ever been truer.

CHAPTER TWENTY-FIVE

Noah

The piercing shriek of the first bell echoed in my ears as I pottered into my lab with an enormous mug of tea in hand, ready to register my form for the first time this term.

Because it was Halloween, I had dutifully dug out the old lab coat I'd smeared with fake blood several years ago as a fun but gentle way to scare my students. I'd also come in early to place a few decorations that wouldn't get in the way or be a hazard around the lab classroom, which meant there was a very large, purple, glittery spider sitting on my front bench with a top hat on and several fake pumpkins on the sides since none of my classes had practicals today. I'd also taped some Halloween bunting to the front.

It was a cursory effort, but it would do.

"Morning, all," I said as I looked around the motley collection of teenagers sitting in front of me. They were in year ten, which meant they were a raging mix of stubborn, hormonal fourteen-and-fifteen-year-olds, who largely didn't think I knew very much and thought they knew everything. But when they weren't being argumentative, they were a genuinely interesting and funny group, who'd been astounded I actually knew most of their pop culture references.

Apparently, at least half of them hadn't expected me to know what a meme was, despite the fact I was barely twelve years older than most of them.

"Morning, sir," came the semi-enthusiastic response. Probably because I was also holding a large tub of Cadbury Heroes in the other hand, which they'd already twigged was for them. Which it was because it was both Halloween and their first day back, and all of us were going to need chocolate to survive.

"Nice coat, sir," said Jack Harris, who had a reputation for being a bit of a troublemaker but mostly just reminded me of Lane. He sat on one of the desks at the back, surrounded by his friends.

"Thanks."

"What did you cover it in?"

"The blood of year tens who put their feet on my desks," I said deadpan as I put my tea down and gave him a pointed look. A couple of people laughed, and Jack hopped down. "Right, let's make this as painless as possible, then you can all have some chocolate and go to wherever you're going next."

"English," added another voice. "We've got more Shakespeare." There was a collective groan.

"How fun," I said with a wry smile. "Don't worry, if you come back here at lunchtime, I'll let you watch *Frankenstein* or something."

"Seriously?"

"Yeah, it's raining, so you can hang out here," I said. Mostly they were supposed to be outside at lunchtime, but most of the teachers kept the classrooms open for our forms to come and hang out since they weren't allowed to leave the school premises, and there wasn't much outdoor shelter.

The school only had about nine hundred students aged eleven to eighteen, so it wasn't like we had to do split lunch shifts or didn't have room for them to be indoors. Besides, I'd rather they hung out here than annoy the elderly librarian, Mr. Finch, or get caught making out in the music rooms again. "I'll find a classic monster movie for you. It won't be gory or anything, but it'll be fun."

"Cheers, sir," Jack said with a grin. "Can we have some chocolate now?"

"Two minutes," I said. "Let me do the register first, or Mrs. Healey will be down here to lecture me." Mrs. Healey was the head administrator, and both teachers and students lived in fear of her grumbling and her endless talks about punctuality and efficiency.

Jack winced, then threw me a mock salute. "All right, sir, carry on."

I chuckled and shook my head, opening the school tablet and pulling up the registration list.

Despite my initial grumbling, the day turned out better than I'd expected, especially when virtually all my form had turned up at lunch, armed with some Halloween cookies from the canteen, to watch as much of a film as we could squeeze in.

They'd had a choice between the Hammer Horror versions of *Frankenstein* or *Dracula*, and while *Dracula* had won, it had been very close, and there had been a lot of vehement disapproval, so I'd promised them that if they behaved and I didn't hear any complaints about their behaviour, I'd make it a regular thing.

There was already a heated discussion going on about what they wanted to watch after that and whether it was too early to start Christmas movies.

I'd just chuckled to myself and made a mental note to dig out more classics for them.

My last class of the day were my year elevens, who were already wading towards their GCSE exams with grim resignation, but I'd tried to make their lesson fun by spending the last twenty minutes talking about whether Frankenstein would ever work in real life.

Afterwards, I spent a few minutes packing up the stuff I needed to take home for marking before leaving for the day. Hareford Grammar wasn't too far from the centre of town, and it was only a twenty-minute walk back to my flat. It was one I made most days, unless I had a ton of books to bring home, but I still wasn't used to the hills.

But as I'd had a lot of work to bring from home that morning, I'd driven to work in the old car I'd bought right after university. I only needed it occasionally, and it did make things so much easier, even if trying to find a parking spot on our street could be a nightmare.

The earlier drizzle had let up by the time I left, although it was virtually dark by the time I made it home.

Which was probably why I didn't notice Spencer standing outside, wrapped in a coat and holding a white cake box, until I almost walked into him.

"Hey," I said. "I didn't know you were waiting."

"You're fine," he said, leaning over to kiss me. "I just wanted to bring you something for your film night." He lifted up the box and grinned. "And would it be weird to say that I wanted to see you again? Even though I literally just saw you yesterday."

"It's not weird. I missed you today. Being back at school was strange." I pulled my keys out of my pocket and unlocked the building's front door. "I think it's because we've just existed in this bubble for a week, and now I have to go back to work."

"How was it?" Spencer asked as he followed me up the stairs to the flat. "Did you set anything on fire?"

I chuckled. "Sadly not. But I did get to make a pig's foot wave at my year sevens, and I got a Halloween cookie from the canteen at lunchtime. They weren't as good as yours, though. How was your day?"

"It was fine. Just did some baking for the next few days, went to the gym… nothing special."

We'd reached the flat, and as I let us in, I was filled with this strange feeling of future familiarity. Like I could see us doing this on a regular basis—meeting outside, walking in together, and talking about our days or making plans for the evening or the weekend. Doing normal, everyday things together and building a life with each other.

Both Spencer and I had admitted we were experiencing a rapid onset of feelings for each other, but neither of us seemed to view this as just some brief infatuation that would burn itself out in a few weeks. There was a weight of certainty to my emotions I'd never experienced before, a feeling of *rightness* like something had clicked inside me.

I'd met people who'd said they'd known, right from the first moment they met their partner, that they were the one. Someone I knew had said she'd known the first moment she saw her husband, before he'd even said anything, that he was the one she was going to marry, and they were still together nearly twenty years later.

And now I was starting to understand what those people had meant when they said they just knew.

I didn't know how to explain it, but all I could think of was that as sure as I knew lightning strikes produced ozone or copper flames were blueish-green, I was sure Spencer and I had a future together.

"How's your ankle today?" I asked, trying not to give away the fact that I'd just casually realised how much all this meant to me. "Is it sore from yesterday?"

"No, not really." Spencer sounded surprised as if he hadn't expected his body to react as well as it sounded like it had. "I'm a little sore all over, but it's probably just from running across the sand."

"That and picking me up to stop me scoring."

"I just wanted a kiss," Spencer said innocently.

"Yeah, right," I said, putting my stuff down, then walking over to take the box out of his hands, giving him a kiss over the top. "Can I open this?"

"Of course. You're not just supposed to look at it."

I shook my head and grinned before carefully teasing the edge of the box up with one hand. Inside were six perfect ghost cupcakes, each with different expressions piped in chocolate across the fluffy marshmallow icing. "Oh, Spencer, they're amazing. Thank you."

"You're welcome," he said. "I thought you and Alex might like them."

"You really are the sweetest," I said, sliding the box onto the edge of the table before drawing him into a hug and kissing him softly. "I don't deserve you."

"It's just cupcakes."

"It's the thought, though," I said. "I really appreciate it."

A pink tint flared across Spencer's nose, and he shrugged. "I just thought you might like them," he said again like he really didn't have any idea why I appreciated this as much as I did. "Since you had a busy day and everything."

Maybe my bar for relationships was really that low, but showing up with a box of homemade cupcakes just because he thought I'd like them really wasn't something most men would do. But Spencer seemed to think it was normal. How on earth had he still been single?

"Do you want to stay for a bit?" I asked. "Maybe have some dinner?"

Spencer glanced back at the door. "I don't want to intrude. This is your thing with Alex."

"You can at least stay for a drink," I said. "Even if it's just a cup of tea."

"Tea sounds great actually."

"Okay, then tea it is."

I made us some tea, and by the time Alex came back, the pair of us were sitting on the sofa with two empty mugs and two cupcake wrappers after I'd persuaded Spencer he could have one of mine.

"Hey," Alex said, looking at the pair of us as he kicked off his shoes and stretched. "How was school?"

"Not as bad as it could have been. Got to freak out some year sevens."

"Cool." He glanced at Spencer. "You staying for the film?"

"Nah, it's fine. I don't want to intrude," Spencer said, standing up, but Alex just waved a hand at him.

"It's fine. Sit down. I'm going to get changed and order pizza. You okay with spicy pepperoni and barbecue chicken? I'll get some garlic bread too."

"Er, yeah," Spencer said, looking at me to see if he was really allowed to stay. "That sounds great."

"Cool," Alex said and headed for the door. "Noah, do you want to find the film and get it set up? I'll be back in a minute."

I watched him go, a smile playing about my lips. Spencer was looking back and forth between me and the door his brother had disappeared through.

"I don't get it," Spencer said quietly. "I don't want to intrude, and he said he didn't want us to be gross in front of him. But then he does that."

"That's Alex for you. It means he wants you to stay. That's the most open invitation you'll ever get." I grinned and handed him the Blu-ray I'd grabbed off the shelf earlier. "You stick this in. I'm going to throw some joggers on."

"Okay," Spencer said, still not sounding convinced as I kissed him and followed Alex.

Alex's bedroom door was ajar, but I still knocked and waited before sticking my head around it. Alex was sitting on the edge of the bed in his boxers, scrolling through his phone. His room, as per usual, was a mess, but Alex said he always knew where everything was, so I didn't question it. He was fastidious about the rest of the flat, especially the kitchen, but his room was the one place you could trust to look like it had been hit by a hurricane.

"Hey," I said, "are you sure about Spencer staying? He doesn't want to butt into our evening together."

"Why would I mind? He's my brother and your boyfriend."

"I know, but…" I walked over and sat on the bed next to him. "You're still my best friend, and I don't want us to lose what we have because I'm dating Spencer."

"That's sweet," Alex said. "But it's also complete bollocks. I mean, I know I'll still be your best mate, but things are going to change between us. They were always going to when one of us got a serious boyfriend."

"I… I mean, it's only been a couple of weeks…"

Alex chuckled and looked at me, his grey eyes soft for once. Alex might come off as a bastard sometimes, but he was a squishy, soft one at heart. One day, I hoped he'd find someone who could worm their way inside the walls he'd built over the years and flatten them because if there was anyone who deserved to be loved, it was Alex.

People had asked us a lot over the years if we'd end up together, but the truth was neither of us could be the person the other needed. We were more like brothers than anything else, and while I loved Alex with all my heart, I'd never be *in love* with him. And I knew he'd say the same about me.

"Come on," Alex said. "It's obvious when I look at either of you. This might be new, but it's not some fast and dirty hook-up. It's something. I mean, you finally got my brother to admit he likes men, which I never thought would happen."

"You knew?"

Alex shrugged. "I had a hunch. He spent *so* much time watching fan vids of footballers as a teenager—the sort of ones where they're all like shirtless and everything. I was just waiting for him to figure it out. Didn't think it would take this fucking long to be honest. That's Spencer, though." He shook his head fondly. For all their bickering, I knew Alex loved his brother. He wouldn't have worked with him for so long otherwise.

"Anyway, that's not my point. I don't think Spencer would've done that for just anyone, and you… you've always had a crush on him, but I've seen you two together when you think nobody is looking. There's just something there. Call it another hunch. If you're not still together in like two years, I'll… I don't know, get a tattoo or something."

"Seriously? A tattoo?"

"Yeah." He grinned. "Tell you what, if you two don't get married or end up in an equally serious relationship, I'll get a tattoo, and you can choose the design. And if you do, then you have to get one. Chosen by me."

I snorted. "Wait, are we betting on my potential heartbreak?"

"If you want to look at it like that," Alex said. "But I think we're betting on you being happy for once."

"Fine," I said, holding out my hand so we could swear on it. "But I hope you're right."

Alex gripped my hand and grinned slyly. "Come on, when have I ever been wrong?"

CHAPTER TWENTY-SIX

Spencer

My foot tapped rapidly on the floor of the doctor's waiting room as I glanced around the various notice boards and read all the posters for the hundredth time in ten minutes. One of the women opposite me had a baby in her lap that kept staring at me. I pulled a couple of silly faces, watching them break into a wide-eyed smile of delight.

I'd never really thought much about babies until we'd started running Novel Tea and I'd been exposed to them a bit more. Now I thought they were funny, cute, and complete menaces to my clean floor. Nothing was as painful as scraping up bits of mushed-up cake and biscuit, but luckily, I forgave the culprit every time because they were too freaking adorable to be mad at.

I wondered if Noah liked babies. How did gay couples even have children? Did they adopt? Was surrogacy a thing? I knew it was on TV, but it might be different outside of America. Was it weird that I was thinking about having a baby with Noah? Maybe. But if I didn't tell him, then I could at least pretend I wasn't already planning a future for us.

If we ever did want kids, though, I'd totally be down for it. They could even come to work with me sometimes, and I could teach them how to bake. I was sure I'd seen tiny chef hats for kids. That would be so freaking adorable. They could play football too—kids football was always adorable because it was like watching a group of enthusiastic puppies chase a ball up and down the pitch.

"Spencer Matthews?" said a warm voice, and I looked up to see the doctor standing by the double doors of the waiting room. She was a petite woman with an orange cardigan and bright yellow shoes. I decided I liked her already. I hopped out of my seat and made my way over to her. She smiled at me. "Hi, I'm Doctor Varley. Follow me. We'll be in room three today."

The surgery was pretty small, and I followed Doctor Varley down a short corridor towards her room, ducking inside and taking a seat on the padded chair. She sat down opposite me and gave me another cheery smile. "What can I do for you today, Spencer?"

"So, er, I need some advice and maybe your approval." I took a deep breath, wondering why I was so nervous. "Basically, I used to play professional football when I was like, in my early twenties, and then I was tackled really badly, and it broke my ankle." I wiggled my left foot slightly. "I had, like, two surgeries on it, and it's sort of fine now, but I was always told I shouldn't play again because it might damage it more, so I retired. But I was wondering if I'd be able to join this five-a-side league with my mates because it's not like it's professional level, and it's rotating subs, so I can easily come off. And, yeah… I was just hoping that would be possible."

"Okay," she said. "Let me have a quick look at your file, then we'll have a feel of your ankle. Do you want to pop your shoes and socks off for me?"

She turned to her computer and started flicking through various tabs on my medical record while I reached down and unlaced my trainers. It hadn't been an immediate no, so that was a good start. Doctor Varley hummed and muttered something under her breath.

"Right, let's have a look at you," she said, rotating back to face me before standing up and walking over to the padded bench, pulling some tissue across it. "If you can hop up here, I can have a look at both of your ankles. Your left was the one that was injured, right?"

"Yeah," I said as I walked over and climbed up, stretching my legs out in front of me and rolling up my joggers to give her better access to my ankles.

"Perfect. Hopefully my hands aren't too cold, but I apologise if they are."

Doctor Varley started with my right ankle, giving it a feel and flexing it in various directions while asking about my levels of activity, my initial recovery, the physiotherapy I'd had, and whether I ever had any pain. She was really easy to talk to, and by the time she moved onto my left leg, I felt like I'd practically told her my life story.

I tried to relax as she repeated her tests on my left ankle, hoping it wasn't suddenly going to give out. I felt that it wasn't quite as flexible as my right, but I hoped that wouldn't be a mark against me. There was a calm but serious expression on her face, and I wondered if that meant she was gearing up to give me bad news.

"Okay, you can pop your shoes and socks back on now," she said, giving me a smile as she released my ankle.

"How does it feel?" I couldn't wait a minute longer for an answer. It felt like my heart was in my throat.

"Good. You still have a good range of motion, there doesn't seem to be any pain when I flex it, and I think the muscles you've built up are nicely supporting your joints. It's hard to tell what it's actually like inside without X-rays, so I would like you to get some done. I'll get you a referral letter, then you can ring up the community hospital and get an appointment, and we can go from there."

I let out a long breath as the crushing weight on my chest began to lift. "Do you think I'll be able to play?"

"I don't want to say an absolute yes until I've seen your X-rays, but considering you've never had any issues since the surgery and the level of movement and fitness you have, I think you'll be fine. But it would be a good idea to get some ankle supports and make sure your boots or trainers are also providing plenty of support. I'd also avoid tackling or being tackled where possible, although I know that's hard, and it might be worth looking into sports massage therapy, just to make sure you're supporting and strengthening it as much as possible. They might be able to give you some additional stretches or exercises to do." Doctor Varley smiled at me. "How does that sound?"

"Good," I said. "Really good. Thanks."

"Good, I'm glad. You seemed very nervous."

"Yeah, I was." I slid off the bench and onto the cool floor, walking over to retrieve my trainers and socks. "When my friend first asked me, I was going to say no mostly because I wasn't sure if I could play again and also because of a bunch of other reasons. But my boyfriend suggested I at least come and get checked out. He knows how much this means to me, and I'm glad I listened to him instead of just pretending it wasn't a big deal."

Doctor Varley nodded. "He sounds like a smart man. And I'm glad you came too. Some people would just go off and play. But I think as long as you don't try to be Jordan Green, then you'll probably be fine."

I grinned. "Greenwich fan?"

"My wife is from London," she said. "I've become a fan by association over the years. It's hard not to be."

"He's nice," I said. "I met him a couple of times when I was with them. I went on loan to Norwich, though, and that was me."

"He seems like a nice guy. And his relationship announcement was certainly something."

"Yeah, it was." I still remembered watching the clips of that on Twitter, staring at my screen.

It had been after the World Cup two years ago, and both Christian King and Hugo Serin had given a press conference where they'd both come out and announced they were both in serious relationships, although not with each other. Someone in the media had tried to start some shit, asking about whether their teammates would be comfortable with that, and Jordan Green, who'd always had a reputation as someone with zero tolerance for shit, had called them out.

He'd then proceeded to announce his own bisexuality and declare his love for his boyfriend, who also happened to be his manager's brother.

But two years later, they were still going strong, and I knew he, Christian, and Hugo had done a ton of advocacy work around LGBTQ+ inclusion in football.

At the time, I'd just thought it was a really admirable and brave thing to do, never considering that one day I might be in that position myself.

I guessed I was lucky in a way. I didn't have to plan some big coming out or try to keep my relationship a secret because it might destroy my career. I'd just told people Noah and I were dating and that was it. None of our friends had really cared. They'd been more preoccupied with the fact that none of them had noticed.

I still hadn't told my parents, but they were a much lower priority on my list. I'd get to them eventually, but it wasn't like I saw much of them anyway despite the fact they still lived locally. Alex and I hadn't exactly lived up to their expectations, and while both of us had shrugged it off over the years, it was easier to just stick to ourselves than to open up that can of worms.

Doctor Varley and I chatted for a few more minutes before she let me go, promising I'd get my referral for X-rays in the post in the next few days and giving me a polite but firm warning that just because it felt okay to her, didn't mean I could suddenly go gallivanting off and pretending to win the World Cup.

Slow and steady only.

I promised to be good, and I meant it. I wasn't going to put myself at risk like that. Maybe I would have done once upon a time when I was young and reckless, but now I didn't want to deal with that level of stress.

Besides, if I totally fucked up my ankle, it would mean more surgery, and that was something I wanted to avoid at all costs. Plus, Alex would never let me hear the end of it if I abandoned him to run Novel Tea while I was stuck at home with my foot in plaster. He'd make me come in and sit at a table and ice biscuits or something.

Or even worse, do all the ordering and accounting.

I strolled out of the doctor's with a smile on my face, pulling out my phone to tell Noah everything. I knew he was busy teaching since it was only just past eleven, but I wanted him to know anyway.

Then I pulled up my thread with the rest of the team and typed out a message for them. They all knew I was coming to get my ankle checked, and I'd promised Sean I'd let them know as soon as possible. He'd already messaged me three times this morning, so I figured it was time to put them out of their misery.

Spencer *Anyone know where I can get some good ankle supports and AstroTurf boots? =D*

CHAPTER TWENTY-SEVEN

Noah

THERE WAS ALWAYS something calming about slipping into a swimming pool. The water seemed to wash away my stress and revitalize my aching muscles, my ears full of nothing but the sound of my own breathing and the slap of the water as my mind slipped into the calm focus of swimming up and down the lanes.

During term time, I didn't get to come as often as I wanted as I was always so busy, but I still tried to come two or three times a week to help myself relax.

The pool wasn't too busy for a Saturday morning, mostly because it was still early, and there was only one other person in my lane.

It gave me time to let the reality of everything that had happened over the past few weeks sink into my bones. I still wanted to pinch myself some days because I couldn't believe Spencer and I had gone from friends, who saw each other in the pub and in passing, to so entangled in each other's lives that going two days without seeing him felt like the end of the world.

I knew we were still in that early relationship flush and that things would inevitably change, but I hoped I never got over the wonder of having Spencer in my life.

It had been strange, but in the best way, sitting next to each other in the pub last night and holding hands under the table, trying to steal kisses here and there when we thought the others were busy and only stopping when Alex coughed pointedly. Apparently, we hadn't been as subtle or tasteful as we'd hoped.

It had been even stranger leaving with Spencer and heading back to his house, falling into bed in that beautiful, warm, yellow room together and losing ourselves in each other until we were too tired to keep our eyes open. Spencer had told me he had to get up for work early, but that hadn't mattered. I'd just gotten up with him, and we'd exchanged soft kisses over toast and coffee before he'd gone to work, then I'd gone home to get another hour of sleep.

Or at least attempted to. I'd been too awake by that point, so after an hour of trying, I'd given up and come swimming instead.

As I reached the deep end and treaded water for a second, catching my breath, I tried to push away the nagging feeling that this had all been too easy. That there had to be *something* challenging waiting for us that wasn't just small bumps in the road. Surely it wasn't going to be as simple as just falling for my best friend's brother and skipping merrily into happily ever after.

I kicked off from the wall and swam another few lengths, trying to tell myself that if I went looking for the negatives, I was just going to get entangled in my own worries. I'd be so busy looking for problems, I'd create them by default.

All I could do was keep showing up, be open and honest with Spencer, and try not to let my doubts get in the way.

Because maybe our relationship wouldn't be the hard thing, maybe it would just be all the ups and downs life threw at us, and whether we made it through those would be the real issue we had to deal with. The world was hard and messy, and it had a tendency to drop shit on you whenever you least expected, and sometimes, even the best couples got caught in the crossfire.

Spencer and I would just have to hold tight to each other and hope the other didn't want to let go.

After swimming, I went home to shower and pass the rest of the morning doing various boring but necessary jobs like the washing and food shopping and my share of the housework. The only thing that kept me going through the packed supermarket and trying to work out why the hoover was clogged was the fact that Spencer and I had another date night planned.

We'd made vague noises about going out for dinner or maybe getting a takeaway, but I didn't really care what we did as long as I got to spend time with him.

I *really* hoped he'd be up for fucking again too because I was so fucking horny it was almost unbearable. I'd spent the whole week feeling like someone had turned my libido up to eleven like I was a teenage boy all over again, only this time I had a very willing partner who I was frustratingly separated from most nights due the ridiculous necessities of adult life.

I was almost counting down to the Christmas holidays so I could spend several days of uninterrupted bliss in bed with Spencer.

"Hey," I called as I pushed open Spencer's front door using the spare key he'd given me that morning. "It's just me."

"Hey, I'm up here." Spencer's voice came from the top of the stairs, sounding distant and slightly echoing. Spencer's room was on the top floor in what I assumed was a loft conversion, which was what gave it the gorgeous sloping ceilings and views over the bay. I shut the door behind me and started to climb, my overnight bag in one hand.

As I reached the middle floor, I looked up and saw Spencer's head and shoulders appear at the top of the next set of stairs. His hair was wet, and there were still droplets of water beading on his skin, running down his perfectly firm pecs. "Sorry, I just got out of the shower."

"No need to apologise," I said, giving him a sly smile. "Can I come up, or are you indecent?"

"Do you mean am I naked?"

"Yes."

"Then, yeah, I am, but I don't think it really matters. It'll save us time."

I chuckled as I climbed the stairs. "I thought you wanted to go out for dinner?"

"I mean, we can fuck, then go out," Spencer said. He'd come out of the bedroom now and was leaning against the wall, his entire body on display. I stopped halfway up to admire him, my eyes roaming over every beautiful inch.

"Do you think we'll want to go out?" I asked, raising an eyebrow teasingly.

"Probably not, but we can pretend we might." He grinned at me. "Are you going to come and kiss me now?"

I didn't bother to answer. I just climbed the last few stairs and closed the gap between us, backing him into the wall and pressing my body against his. Spencer's arms wrapped around me, pulling me into a deep, hungry kiss as one hand fisted in the back of my hair. He groaned as my tongue pushed into his mouth, caressing his and demanding more. I slid my hands across his body, squeezing his muscles and teasing all the sensitive spots I'd started to discover. Spencer whimpered and pushed his already hard cock against me.

"You're so hot when you're desperate for me," I said, breaking our kiss to lean my head back and look at him. His face was flushed, his eyes wide with need. "And I love how eager you get for me."

"I just... I need..."

"What do you need Spencer?" I tilted my head forward and brushed my lips against his ear, my breath ghosting across his skin and making him shiver. "Tell me what you want."

"Will you fuck me?" he asked quietly. "I want to know what it's like to have you inside me."

"Are you sure?"

He nodded. "Please, Noah. I need to feel you… need your cock filling me up."

"Of course." I moved my lips back to his, kissing him softly. "Whatever you want." My gaze met his, and I smiled. "Have you ever done anything like this before?"

"Like anal?"

"Yes."

"I've had girlfriends who've fingered me in the past," he said. "I always liked it. But I've never taken anything bigger than two or three fingers."

"Okay. We can go slowly."

"What if I don't want to go slowly?" he asked, his expression gorgeously cheeky and demanding. He kissed me and pulled my lip between his teeth, drawing a moan from my lips before he murmured, "What if I want it hard? What if I want you to fuck me so deep and rough I forget my own name?"

I chuckled because, fuck, Spencer was so cute when he was like this—desperate and almost pouting. There was something about seeing a man like Spencer, so muscular and strong, reduced to putty in my hands. I knew it would be even sweeter when he begged for my cock later. The temptation to give in and give him everything he wanted was a strong one, but I still remembered my first time bottoming and how shit it had been because we'd rushed.

Spencer might have taken fingers, but taking cock was different, and I wanted him to enjoy it.

"Maybe if you're good," I said. "But we're starting slowly because it's your first time, and I don't want it to hurt or for you to hate every second."

"I don't think I will. And it's not really, like, my first time."

"Don't argue with me," I teased. "Or I won't fuck you."

"You will," Spencer said, with a sweetly smug air because he knew he was right. "You know you want this ass."

I snorted, and Spencer grinned wickedly. "You're not wrong."

"I know." He kissed me again before gently pushing me away and taking my hand. "Come on, I need some dick."

I shook my head, still smiling as I followed him into his room. The curtains were drawn, and the two lamps were on, casting a warm glow around the space. The bed was made, but I saw the normal decorative cushions had already been moved, and there was a bottle of lube and a box of condoms already on the bedside table. "You planned this, didn't you?"

"Yeah. But I've been dreaming about it all day," Spencer said, drawing me towards the bed and reaching for my clothes. "Kept getting distracted at work thinking about what it would be like to feel you inside me. Nearly burned a whole pan of caramel 'cos I was too busy thinking about your cock."

"As long as you didn't hurt yourself. Or give Alex a reason to be pissed at me."

"I'm fine. I just chucked some cream in it and made a caramel sauce. I'll use it for something." He pulled my t-shirt and jumper off then reached for the waistband of my jeans. "I don't want to talk about work, though."

"Tell me what you were thinking about," I said as he

dropped to his knees in front of me, tugging down my jeans and boxers. I stepped out of them, and Spencer threw them out of the way. He was still kneeling.

"What it's going to feel like when you're inside me. How I can't stop thinking about you." He ran his hands up my thighs and leant forward, pressing a kiss to the soft head of my cock. "I want you all the time. I'm so fucking horny, Noah. Fucking you is just… It's fucking incredible. But I want you inside me so fucking much. I need to know what it feels like to have you stretching me, filling me with your cock until I can't think about anything else." He grinned up at me. "Maybe then I'll stop being so distracted."

I caressed his face with my hand. "Or maybe you'll just want more. Maybe you'll never be able to focus again."

"I'll take that risk. I fucking need you, Noah." He slid one hand across my thigh and grasped my cock. I moaned as he slowly pumped me to full hardness before he wrapped his lips around the head and began to suck me.

I let out a shuddering breath and growled as familiar heat and pleasure rushed through me. Ever since Spencer had discovered sucking my cock, it had become his favourite pastime. But I wasn't going to complain because he was a quick fucking study and had already worked out how to push my buttons. It was like he delighted in getting me off.

My hand gripped his hair, and I thrust into his mouth, feeling his throat tighten around me. Spencer groaned, redoubling his pace and using his hand to add another delicious dimension to his efforts.

"If you want me to fuck you," I said, "then you need to stop and get on the fucking bed."

Spencer pulled off with a wet pop and smirked at me, strings of saliva dripping from his lips. He looked so debauched already with slick lips and mussed hair. I wanted to take a picture just to show him how sexy he looked.

"I'd say you ruined my fun, but I need you to fuck me." He stood up and kissed me. "But I'm going to suck you again later. It's so fucking hot when you come in my mouth."

I wasn't going to say no to that. All I could do was kiss him like it was my last day on earth.

CHAPTER TWENTY-EIGHT

Spencer

My heart raced as I grabbed the lube and a condom and climbed onto my bed, spreading my legs wide for my beloved. The knowledge that Noah was finally going to be inside me was a deep, desperate thrill, and I could barely lie still.

"Is this okay?" I asked. "Or do you want me on all fours?"

"All fours might be better for me to prep you," Noah said. "But I'm going to fuck you on your back so I can see your face. I want to see all the beautiful expressions you wear as I make you come."

I groaned and rolled onto my knees, pushing my ass into the air. "Fuck! How quickly can you prep me? I needed your dick, like, an hour ago."

Noah chuckled, and the sound made me shiver. "I'm not going to rush you. I already said that."

"Spoilsport," I grumbled, but I found myself pushing into his hand as he gently caressed my ass cheek.

"Just relax," Noah said as he clicked the bottle of lube open. "And try to bear down. It sounds weird, but it'll help. Jerking yourself slowly might help too. It's a good distraction. And if you want to stop at any time, we can. No judgement and no questions."

"Okay." It was awesome how sweet he was being about checking up on me, but fuck did I just want to grab the lube and do it myself if it would get his cock inside me faster. I knew Noah was right, though. This wasn't something I should rush—not the first time at least.

It burned more than I'd expected when Noah slowly pressed his finger into me. I let out a slow breath and reached for my dick, stroking the softened shaft and letting the little burst of pleasure take my mind off the strange burn.

"Are you okay?" Noah asked, stroking my ass and pressing a kiss to the skin above my crack. His finger was seated inside me, but he wasn't moving it.

"Yeah." I nodded. "I'd forgotten how weird the first one is, and I haven't done this in a while. It, er, wasn't the sort of thing I did with most of the women I hooked up with." It had tended to be a trust thing, and I'd only brought it up with two of my girlfriends while another had actually asked me herself. But I'd never mentioned it to my flings or one-night stands because there just wasn't that connection.

I trusted Noah, though. More than I'd ever trusted anyone.

The burning began to ease.

"Okay, you can move it now. Or add more. Whatever you want to do."

Noah kissed my butt cheeks, then slowly started to pump his finger in and out. It felt strange at first but not for long.

By the time he added a second finger, I was desperate for it.

It burned again, but I kept stroking my cock. Then Noah curled his fingers and pressed against my prostate, and I nearly yelped at the burst of sensation that raced through me. "Holy fuck," I said with a shaking laugh of disbelief. "Please do that again."

I heard the smile in Noah's voice as he answered me. "Of course."

Noah worked me open with soft, calculated precision, making me moan and gasp as he stretched me. His fingers teased my prostate and made me beg for more, but we both knew he was going to make me wait for it. By the time he had three fingers pumping in and out of my hole, my cock was hard as a rock, and I was sweating.

I was *this* close to grabbing him, pinning him to the bed, and straddling his hips.

But I craved his gentle control. I needed him to fuck me the way he wanted, telling me exactly what to do because I knew he'd make me come harder than I'd ever imagined. I'd told Noah I wanted him to fuck me so hard I'd forget my own name, and while I knew the pace was up to him, potential brain fog was definitely on the table.

I'd only ever had sex that came close to what I shared

with Noah with one of my exes in London who'd opened my eyes to all the ways sex could be good.

But intimacy with Noah had already surpassed that, not only in the physical sense but in the emotional sense too, and I knew this would be the final nail in the coffin. After tonight, I'd never want to have sex with anyone else because I already knew they'd never be better than Noah.

There was just something about being with him that was incomparable.

"How're you doing?" Noah asked.

"I'm so fucking ready," I said. "Please, Noah. I need more… I need your cock inside me."

"Are you sure?"

"Yeah, I'm fucking sure. I couldn't be any more sure."

"Good." He slid his fingers out slowly and kissed the base of my spine. "I just wanted to check."

"I appreciate it," I said, lowering myself onto the mattress with as much grace as I could muster—so it was more of a walrus-style belly flop than anything else. I rolled onto my back and wiggled up the bed, piling the pillows under my head as I watched him roll on the condom. "You're so sweet. I don't think I've been with anyone who cares as much as you."

"Is that a bad thing?" Noah asked. He crawled up the bed towards me, slotting between my thighs and lowering his mouth to mine.

"No," I whispered. "It's an awesome thing."

Our kiss was one of those ones that alters the universe a little bit. The sort where you broke apart afterwards knowing that something had changed, and neither of you would ever be the same person again.

I wrapped my hands around Noah's neck and pulled him closer, spreading my thighs around him as Noah's hand reached between us to guide his cock into my waiting hole.

"Breathe for me," he said. "Bear down and tell me if you need me to stop."

"Okay." I nodded, kissing him again. I groaned as he breached me, trying to force myself to relax. Even having taken three of Noah's fingers, I wasn't prepared for the stretch and burn that his dick would bring.

"Fuck," I groaned, and Noah hesitated. I shook my head. "Don't stop, please. I want it all. I just… Fuck, it's so intense. Is it always this intense?"

"Sort of. It gets easier the more you do it."

"Makes sense." I tipped my head back onto the pillows, breathing deeply and keeping my eyes locked on his as he pushed inside me.

Noah stilled as he bottomed out, giving me another kiss. This one was softer, though, and kind of sweet. Then he kissed my nose, and I grinned. "You're so gorgeous," he said. "I don't think I'll ever get over how gorgeous you are."

"I feel the same about you."

"Yeah but… why me?"

I snorted. "Bit of a weird time to ask, isn't it?"

Noah chuckled. "I guess, but now you can't avoid me."

"I wouldn't want to." I gave him a kiss in return. "And the reason it's you is because you're literally the most gorgeous and amazing person I've ever met, Noah. And I need you to believe me, but if you don't, I'm going to keep telling you until it gets annoying."

"I could just distract you," he said, raising an eyebrow and smirking.

I was going to ask how he planned to do that, but then Noah slowly started to rock his hips, and it became really fucking clear how easy it would be for him to accomplish that.

It was a little strange at first, but then the pleasure started to build, washing over me like waves on the sand. His thrusts were deep and slow, melting me from the inside out.

"Do you like that?" he whispered.

"Uh-huh." I nodded, barely able to vocalise what I was feeling. "It… fuck… it feels…"

"Good?"

"Yeah." If good meant so freaking amazing that I wondered why I hadn't done this sooner.

Noah kissed me as he drew his hips back, thrusting in harder and starting to add a little more pace to his rhythm. I groaned and gasped as his cock rubbed over my prostate, adding a new dimension to the pleasure pulsing through me.

I grasped onto Noah, clinging to him like he was the only thing that was going to stop me from getting washed away. His body brushed over my cock with every thrust, and the friction was driving me wild, but it wasn't enough to send me over the edge. It was just holding me there and torturing me.

"Touch yourself," Noah said. "I want you to come for me."

Nodding, I slipped one hand between us, moaning loudly as I gripped my cock. I started to jerk myself hard and fast, gasping as Noah began to speed up, fucking me harder and faster and making it difficult for me to remember what I was even supposed to be doing. It felt like the intensity had been turned up to a million, and all I could do was let my body take over as my mind melted into a haze of pleasure.

I cried out Noah's name as my muscles began to burn, my balls pulling tight before I shot my load between us, my cum coating our skin. Noah groaned, and I felt my body pulling him deeper. His mouth met mine as his thrusts became more erratic, and I knew he was close.

Noah came with a grunt and the broken utterance of my name, his lips on mine. We were both panting and sweaty, but we couldn't stop kissing like we didn't want the connection between us to end.

Later in the week, when I was sweating my butt off on the treadmill and thinking about all the things I wanted to try with Noah, my phone rang.

The sharp sound in my earbuds caught me off guard and nearly sent me flying across the gym. I had to hit the emergency stop button to regain my balance while I tried to answer my phone.

"Hello?" I said, my voice rough and my breaths coming in pants.

"Hi, is this Spencer Matthews? It's Doctor Varley, from the surgery. Is now a bad time?"

"No." I shook my head, even though I knew she couldn't see me. Beside me, I saw Sean slow to a walk, trying to pretend he wasn't listening in. "Sorry, I'm just at the gym."

I hopped off the treadmill and started walking away from the line of machines so I could hear her better.

"Ah, that makes sense," she said. "I just wanted to give you a call because I've got your X-rays here."

"Already?" I'd only had them done on Tuesday, and I hadn't been expecting any kind of fast turnaround.

"Already. We got them through this morning, and I was able to have a quick look at them."

"And?" I barely felt my heart beating, even though I knew it was. It was like I'd forgotten how to even breathe as I waited for her next words.

"It's a lot better than I think anyone could have predicted. I can see where it's been pinned, but it looks very healthy, and considering the extent of the injury you suffered, it looks great. I've seen worse healing on much more minor fractures."

"What does that mean?" I asked. I needed to hear her say it out loud before I started celebrating.

"It means that I'm happy to say you can play five-a-side," Doctor Varley said. "Just remember to wear ankle supports and get supportive shoes. Also, don't push too hard and try and avoid being tackled where possible, but I know that's easier said than done."

"Seriously? Thank you so much. That's freaking amazing!"

"You're very welcome. I hope it all goes well. Any problems, then obviously let us know, and we can take it from there."

We finished off the call, and I hung up, unable to stop a broad grin from breaking onto my lips. I knew I wasn't going to be able to keep this news from my friends.

I practically bounced across to where Sean, Andrew, and Chris had gathered. They were looking at me with pensive expressions, and I was pretty sure Sean had heard I was on the phone with the doctor.

"Everything okay?" Chris asked, doing his worst to try to appear casual.

"Yeah," I said. "That was just the doctor letting me know about my X-rays."

"And?" asked Sean.

"Do you really think I'd be smiling if it was a no?"

"Fuck yes!" Sean cried, doing a fist pump, then pulling me into a hug. "You're okay, then?"

"Yeah, just gotta make sure I don't get tackled too hard and wear good shoes."

"We can deal with that," Chris said, giving me another hug as soon as Sean let go. "We better get practising."

"Good thing I booked a pitch for tomorrow then, isn't it?" Andrew said with a grin.

I laughed. "Good thing I already bought some boots too."

"Think we can play now?" Sean asked, glancing out the

window and down at the artificial pitches that were overlooked by the gym. They were all currently empty. "I bet we can squeeze on for half an hour, even if it's just the four of us."

"Wouldn't hurt to ask," Chris said. "I'll go find someone."

I hadn't been holding my breath that we'd get permission, but it turned out they'd had a cancellation. Which was how the four of us found ourselves having a kick about on the AstroTurf in the afternoon sunlight.

Andrew passed the ball across to me, and I jogged down the pitch with it before passing it to Sean. I was still grinning, and I didn't think I'd ever be able to stop.

Six months ago, I'd never dreamed I'd get to do this or have someone amazing like Noah in my life. It didn't seem possible, and I half wondered what I'd done to deserve it.

But I wasn't going to question it. I was just going to bask in the happy glow that surrounded me and make the most of every moment.

CHAPTER TWENTY-NINE

Noah

"They're fucking kidding us, right? Like, come on, this is ridiculous," Katie said, grabbing another chocolate biscuit out of the packet while angrily stacking student books into a box.

"It's Ofsted, Kat. They're not exactly known for their long lead times. At least they didn't just turn up unannounced," I said, taking my own biscuit and looking at the various lesson plans laid out in front of me.

This week had been chugging along quite nice and normally until lunchtime, when an emergency meeting had been called to announce that Ofsted, the government office responsible for inspecting a range of England's educational institutions, would be here first thing tomorrow morning to start their inspection. This had sent everyone into what Katie had described as "battle-mode" and we'd all been told, in no uncertain terms, to make sure all our books were marked, all our lesson plans were up to date, and that everything was ready in case our lessons were observed.

We'd sort of known it was coming since it had been four years since the last inspection, but we hadn't known when since they never gave more than half a day's notice.

I'd actually been through the process twice before since I'd not long joined the school when they'd last been inspected, and it had also happened while I was on one of my placements during my teacher training year.

They were always the most ridiculously intense few days, followed by a nervous wait to find out how we'd done. Even though Hareford Grammar was a very good school, there was still a lot of expectation placed on us to keep up that reputation.

Which was why Katie and I, along with all the other science staff, were still in the building two hours after school had ended, making sure everything was ready.

"I really hope they don't decide to come and sit in with me tomorrow," Katie said. "I've got to teach human reproduction to my year sevens, and I'm not sure how impressed the inspectors will be at me making the kids stand up and shout *penis* and *vagina* very loudly until they've stopped giggling."

"It works, though," I said with a grin.

"It does. Which is why I do it." Katie reached for another biscuit. "What have you got tomorrow?"

"Mixed bag. Got two of my year elevens for chemistry, then some year tens—they're a pretty good bunch, so that should be fine. I've got 8L after lunch, though, and they've just hit that teenage *shan't* phase. They're being right pains at the moment."

"Maybe an inspector being there would scare them into behaving," Katie said.

"Fingers crossed." I took another biscuit and sighed. "Be even better if I didn't see them at all."

"We can only pray." Katie tapped the spines of the exercise books, counting them under her breath. "I hope you didn't have any plans for the next two days by the way."

I chuckled under my breath. "I was supposed to be having dinner with my boyfriend this evening. Guess that's totally out the window now."

I'd already messaged Spencer to let him know I'd have to put our plans on hold until Ofsted was over. It sucked because we'd actually been planning to go out for dinner for the first time, something we still hadn't actually achieved without getting distracted. And now it wasn't even being cancelled for a fun reason, just a hideously stressful one. Part of me had been worried Spencer would be upset that I was cancelling at such short notice.

Instead of any kind of annoyance, I'd just gotten a long message asking me if I was okay, if I needed anything, and telling me that everything was going to be great because I was "a freakin' awesome teacher with a hot body and a cute ass". It had made my day, and I'd taken a screenshot of the message to save for tomorrow when I was sure I'd feel crap.

"Pretty much," Katie said. "Also, excuse me, but when did you get a boyfriend? Why is this the first time I'm hearing about this? I thought we were friends."

"We are. I've just been keeping it quiet. But his name's Spencer. He's actually a friend of mine."

"Oh, how did you meet?"

"He's, er, he's my best mate's older brother."

Katie stared at me with a delightfully outraged smile that I knew meant I'd be telling her the whole story. "Mr. Hawthorn, how could you keep this from me? Your best friend."

"Are you my best friend?"

"I'm at least your work bestie," she said. "You have to tell me everything. It'll make this whole, horrible day better. Please?"

"Fine," I said, rolling my eyes fondly. "What do you want to know?"

When I finally extracted myself from Katie's interrogation an hour later, it was nearly seven, and I was exhausted. I was glad I'd brought my car because I had one more round of books to take home and mark because although we only checked and marked each class every two weeks, the school wanted them all up to date just in case. My breath fogged in the air, and the November chill nipped at my cheeks as I climbed into the car and shot off a quick message to Alex to let him know I was on my way home.

The roads were pretty quiet, and as I drove, I realised they'd started putting up the Christmas lights. It would probably only be another few weeks before the whole town was ablaze with twinkling lights, looking like something out of a postcard, especially if it snowed.

It didn't take me long to get back and heave everything out of the car. I was determined not to have to make two trips because I was too exhausted to climb up the stairs more than once.

"Hey," I called as I stumbled in.

"Hey." The response was the one I'd expected, but not from the person I'd expected. Spencer was sitting on the sofa next to Alex, a warm smile on his face as he hopped up and strode over to me, taking the large box of books out of my hand.

"Hey," I said again. "I didn't know you were going to be here."

"He wouldn't stop nagging me about when you'd be back," Alex called. "He's been nothing but a nuisance all evening."

"I've not been *that* bad," Spencer said. "I just wanted to know so I could help."

"Help?" I knew I sounded totally bewildered, but I was still processing the fact that Spencer was there.

"Yeah. I know this is probably going to be super stressful for you, and I just wanted to know if there was anything I could do to help. I mean, I can't like mark books for you or teach lessons or anything like that. But I thought I could bring you some dinner so you don't have to order anything or deal with Alex's cooking—"

"Hey!"

"And I brought you some lunch for tomorrow too," Spencer continued, his smile never wavering. He stepped closer and wrapped me up in his arms, his embrace leeching all the stress from my muscles. "I don't want to get in your way, though, so if you need me to bugger off and come back at the weekend, then I can do that too."

"Stay, please," I said. "I'll work better if you're here."

"What am I?" Alex grumbled. "Fucking chopped liver?"

"If both of you are here. You know I can't concentrate if it's too quiet." I'd always found silence off-putting for work. It just made the room feel too oppressive like there was this strange weight pressing down on me from all sides. But quiet music or films or TV shows I'd seen a hundred times were the perfect accompaniment. It was why I tended to mark in the evenings while Alex and I watched TV. It also meant I could quote at least ten different shows word for word, which had been helpful for the odd pub quiz or two over the years.

"If you're sure," Spencer said.

"I am." I kissed him softly, then sighed. "I don't suppose you've got that dinner? I've been surviving on chocolate biscuits since lunchtime, and most of them were already gone by the time Katie and I got to them."

Spencer kissed my forehead softly. "Of course. You go sit down. I'll sort it." He looked over my shoulder at his brother. "Alex, how does your oven work?"

Alex huffed but pulled himself off the sofa, grumbling as he headed for the kitchen. "First, I'm a fucking calendar, then fucking chopped liver, now I'm the fucking butler."

"I think it's more like fucking sous chef?" Spencer teased as he released me with a wink and gently pushed me towards the sofa while he followed his brother into the open kitchen.

"Don't fucking argue with me," Alex said. He was a

head shorter than his older brother, and he had no problem prodding Spencer in the chest with a wooden spoon. "And please tell me you actually brought enough for me too, or am I going to starve?"

"You're not going to starve. I brought some for you too." Spencer batted the spoon out of the way and patted his brother on the head. "I figured I'd have to pay tribute to the sofa gremlin before I was allowed in."

"You're such a twat, you know that?"

"Yeah, but I'm your brother, so what can you do?"

"Don't fucking push your luck," Alex said, but he was grinning.

I chuckled from my seat at the end of the sofa as I watched the pair of them bicker, feeling an overwhelming sense of joy at the whole situation. This whole day had been an emotional rollercoaster of stress, anxiety, and exhaustion that had turned me upside down and spun me round so fast it felt like I'd never be able to find my feet again. I'd been expecting to ride this hell ride for the next few days with relief only coming from small snippets of Alex's banter and any snatched hours of sleep I could manage.

But instead, it felt like I was being offered the opportunity to get off for the evening—to sit down on solid ground and watch my worries go on without me. It didn't mean I still didn't have work to do or that Ofsted still wouldn't be there in the morning, but for now, I could breathe.

And it was all because of Spencer.

He really was everything to me.

He was still bickering with Alex about whatever was in the oven, but when he glanced across at me, he gave me another of those smiles that made it feel like I was sitting in the summer sun and a little wave. "Do you want a drink?" he asked. "Wait, you probably do, that was a silly question. Alex, where are your glasses again?"

"I can get one myself," I called, but Spencer just batted my words away.

"Nope, you're going to sit there and relax until dinner. I can get you a drink."

I did as I was told, gratefully accepting the glass of Coke Spencer brought me and inhaling the delicious scents wafting out of the oven. I occasionally joined in with the conversation Alex and Spencer were having, but mostly, I was just enjoying their company and the chance to lose myself in something other than work.

Dinner turned out to be this incredible chicken, leek, and mushroom pie with a rich, creamy white sauce and topped with thick, buttery pastry that melted in my mouth. Spencer had even brought the ingredients to make mashed potatoes with butter and cream and added some tender-stem broccoli on the side so we could at least pretend it was vaguely healthy. It was the sort of food that could only be described as Comfort with a capital C. Like I'd been wrapped in a warm, cosy hug that promised everything would be okay.

And because it was Spencer, he'd even made ramekins full of apple crumble, producing a tub of vanilla ice cream out of our freezer to go alongside it.

Afterwards, I felt so full and sleepy I wasn't convinced I'd be able to get any work done, but then he'd kissed my forehead gently and told me how proud of me he was. It had been like a little injection of energy into my veins, and I'd sat and marked books while he and Alex played *Mario Kart* on the Switch.

"You should stay," I said to Spencer later when I was preparing to go to bed.

He chuckled softly, pulling me into another hug. "Is that a suggestion or a demand?"

"I mean, it's not a demand, but I really want you to stay. Please."

"Sure," he said. "I didn't want to leave anyway."

We climbed the stairs and went through our nighttime routines, circling around each other like we'd been doing it for years instead of weeks, before climbing into bed. Spencer wrapped me up in his arms, the same way he always did when we shared, and I put my head on his chest.

"Thank you," I said quietly. "For tonight. I really appreciate it."

"No worries," he said. "I… I didn't want you to be stressed. This whole thing sounds like a freaking nightmare to be honest. I'm glad it's only two days."

"Me too." I yawned. "Then I can try to forget about it until we get the report."

"You're going to do awesome. I promise."

"Because I have a cute ass?"

"Yeah, and just because you're awesome." He tilted his head down and kissed me gently. "I love you, Noah."

"I love you too," I said, happiness suffusing through me. I rolled over in his arms and gazed down into his eyes, seeing nothing but love radiating back at me.

"I know it's probably too soon," Spencer said. "It's only been like a month, but the way I feel is like nothing I've ever felt before."

"Who cares about time? There's no set scale we have to adhere to. The universe doesn't make laws about love."

He grinned. "Good, because I was worried you'd be scared off."

"Never," I said. "I think I've loved you since that first day you taught me how to bake."

"Really?"

"Yeah."

"Wow," Spencer said. "That's pretty cool. I think for me it was when Alex tried to do us a first date… I didn't know it was love, but when I look back, I think it was, even then." He nodded like he was confirming it to himself. "I'm in love with you," he said softly. "That's pretty fucking awesome."

"Pretty fucking awesome indeed."

CHAPTER THIRTY

Spencer

"Are you ready?" Sean asked as I pulled on my new football shirt in the leisure centre's changing room. The shirt was bright blue with my name and number across the back in white and a little rainbow flag printed on the chest. Andrew had organised them since we all had to match, and he'd gone the whole hog and gotten us personalised shirts.

"I think so," I said. "Feels weird to be playing some sort of match again."

"You'll be great," Sean said. "Just take it steady and don't try any theatrics. They're not exactly PSG or Real Madrid."

"We're fucked if they are." I chuckled. I still couldn't believe how quickly our first game had come around. It seemed like only yesterday Chris had first asked me about it, and now we were about to play our first matches. The past six weeks had flown by.

It had taken me a couple of practices to get my act together and start remembering how to play, but that was mostly because my body was more akin to a nineties computer than the latest iPhone. But once I'd remembered, I'd started being able to pass and defend with ease. I still avoided tackling people where possible and found it easier to steal the ball mid-pass than attempt anything that could end in clattering contact, but on the whole, my anxieties about being rubbish had largely faded.

But playing a game was different.

Sure, we weren't exactly putting pressure on ourselves to win, but that didn't stop my brain from attempting to add mental pressure to the whole scenario. Part of me seemed to think I was about to go up against Chelsea instead of some other local lads, and another part kept reminding me I didn't know the other guys, and they could easily do me an injury if they weren't careful.

I'd talked to Noah about it last night just before we drifted off to sleep, and he'd listened to my rambling thoughts as if it wasn't the umpteenth time I'd gone through them. He'd just nodded quietly and made me do some breathing exercises that had put me to sleep faster than I'd imagined they would. He'd also mentioned I should probably bring up my worries with my new therapist, Dean, after I'd finally conceded that it might be helpful to talk about everything that had happened, even if it was in the past.

I hadn't been sure at first, then Dean and I had spent my first session talking about sport and comparing old injuries, and I'd realised he was more of a kindred soul than I'd anticipated.

"Looking sharp," Andrew said, dropping his bag down next to me and pulling on his own shirt. "Good thing we're playing on AstroTurf, though, because otherwise we'd probably end up covered in mud."

I chuckled. "That just reminds me of playing as a kid and getting grass stains all over my shorts."

"Man, your mum was so pissed," Will said, and I turned to grin at him, not realising he'd come in.

"I don't know how she expected me to stay clean," I said.

"Probably not by celebrating on your knees."

Everyone around me let out an undignified snort, and I laughed. "Guess I'll have to find something different this time around."

"Yeah, AstroTurf shreds your skin," Sean said. "And if you're planning on celebrating later, you probably don't want bloody knees. Trust me."

"Do I want to know?" I asked with a grin.

"He tried to do some sliding celebration when we were playing at uni," Chris said, giving his husband a wry look. "Then tried to blow me later. Whimpering in pain wasn't quite the vibe I was going for."

"Especially when you're not the one responsible," Sean said with a wink.

"And that's all we need to know about your sex life," Andrew said, throwing a pair of socks at Sean's head.

"What? I've heard much worse from you."

"When?"

"Like that time you told us you hooked up with that guy at your zombie LARP and got fake blood all over your ass. I'm still not even sure how the fuck that happened? Did he literally dip his dick in the stuff?"

"Fun as this conversation is," Chris said. "We've gotta go. Zach and Mason are downstairs waiting for us."

There was a flurry of activity as we finished getting changed and stuffed everything into the lockers before making our way down to the leisure centre's AstroTurf pitches. Zach and Mason, two friends of Andrew's from his regular LARP group who he'd roped in to fill the rest of the spots, were waiting for us.

But they weren't the only ones.

Wrapped up against the chill of the late-November afternoon and sat in the tiny, covered stand on the other side of the fence surrounding the pitch, were all my friends. They were sipping hot drinks in takeaway cups and talking among themselves, but when one of them, Lane from the looks of it, noticed us, they all cheered.

"Jeez," I said, trying to pretend I wasn't both touched and a little embarrassed by the fanfare. "You'd think we really were playing Chelsea."

I saw Noah sitting sandwiched between Alex and Lane, wearing a thick coat and a knitted hat with a fluffy pom-pom on the top. It looked freaking adorable on him, and when he noticed me looking, he gave me a little wave. I waved back, my initial embarrassment receding as I realised just how much this meant to me.

They'd all given up their Saturday afternoons to come

and watch me play in some local five-a-side league like it actually meant something.

And maybe it did. This might not have been the Champion's League final or the World Cup, but they all knew, to some degree at least, what I'd been through and what this moment signified.

The weight of the gesture settled on my chest like a warm, fluffy cat—cosy and comforting.

"I didn't realise we were going to have an audience," Sean said.

"Me either," I said.

"Guess we really better not fuck this up, then," Will said. He patted my shoulder. "Come on. Let's go and get started."

There were a couple of matches being played today, and I soon realised our friends weren't the only spectators, although they did turn out to be the loudest. We played two matches with a break in between, which gave us enough time to catch our breaths. The halves weren't long, but it was still more intense than I was used to.

We'd all decided I'd start and see how I got on because rolling substitutions meant I could tap out at any time. It was strange lining up for kick-off on the small pitch, and it reminded me of being back at school, especially when I looked over and saw Will's determined grimace, the same expression he'd worn at the start of each game for as long as I could remember.

Nervous excitement bubbled in my stomach, and I suddenly wondered whether I should have eaten more than some leftover bits of cinnamon bun for lunch. Then the referee had blown the whistle, and all my thoughts were whisked away on the wind.

Despite our jokes during practice that we'd probably suck at first, we'd played better together than any of us had anticipated.

Our first opponents were a group of older guys who Chris knew from the gym and were regulars in the league. They were fit and agile, but I was still faster, and despite their best attempts at defending, I still managed to slide a goal past them.

The sound of the ball hitting the back of the net was one I'd never forget as long as I lived. It echoed sweetly in my ears, and from the way everyone was cheering, you'd think this was more than just a Saturday league.

I couldn't stop grinning as we went back to our starting positions to kick off, and a few minutes later, I decided to swap out with Mason to stop myself from pushing my body too hard. I felt myself getting fired up, and I knew that if I wasn't careful, I was bound to do something rash in my pursuit of glory. And this was rec football, not the Premier League.

Winning did not mean I had to flog myself to death or sacrifice everything. In fact, I thought Noah would be pretty pissed if I hurt myself trying to win a Saturday league match. And then I'd just get a hard stare instead of a fun celebration this evening.

As I'd looked over at him while I was catching my breath, it was easy to see the pride radiating out of him. Not just because I'd scored but because I'd stopped too. I was putting myself first. Heck, I was even proud of myself.

We ended up winning our first match two to one with Chris scoring the winner not long before the final whistle. We'd celebrated the win with both hugs and long drinks of water, all of us complaining about how spending hours doing cardio in the gym seemed to mean nothing on the pitch.

At the break, I'd wandered over to talk to Noah. He hopped down out of the stands, and when he reached me, he slid me a Snickers through a gap in the fence.

"For your blood sugar," he said. "You're doing awesome. Are you having fun?"

"Yeah. I almost wish we'd done it sooner. I know they've been running the league here for a couple of years now." I shook my head. Wishful thinking wasn't going to get me anywhere, especially because of how reluctant I'd been to join in the first place. Without Noah pushing and supporting me, I might not even have taken the leap.

"You're here now, though, and I'm proud of you."

"Cheers." I reached out and interlinked my fingers with his through the fence quickly. "Are you still coming back to mine later?"

"Of course," he said. "And this time, I'm actually going to cook for you. I still need to make up for the pie you brought me."

"You don't owe me. You're my boyfriend. It's what we do for each other." I grinned, and from behind me, I heard someone calling my name.

"You better go," Noah said. "I'll meet you afterwards. Good luck!"

"Thanks. I love you."

"I love you too."

I squeezed his hand before I released him, then jogged back across to my team, Snickers in hand. We still had a few minutes, so I ate it quickly and watched another match wrap up.

"Can we go two for two do you think?" Sean asked.

"We can try," I said. "It's not like they're PSG."

Chris chuckled. "I'm glad you decided to join us."

"Me too. Thanks for nagging me about it."

He shrugged. "I was pretty sure you'd say yes. I just had to wait for you to figure out you still wanted to play."

"Do you and Will share superpowers or something?" I grumbled, flexing my feet and stretching out my muscles.

"Yeah, it was buy one, get one free," Will said with a grin.

"Got Clubcard points and everything," Chris added.

"Next time you see them on offer, let me know," I said. "They might come in useful."

Five minutes later we all trooped onto the pitch for our second game against a team of guys I sort of recognised from around town. I didn't know any of them by name but having watched them play earlier I'd thought they'd be a bit of a challenge, especially because I'd seen at least one of them try to make a heavy tackle.

I started again, and it only took a few minutes for one of them to come charging at me, but it was easy enough to sidestep him and pass the ball across to Will, who set off at speed and easily slotted it into the goal. I'd forgotten how fast Will could be when he wanted. It was probably from chasing after errant sheep or something.

I rotated off not long after, but following the brief half-time, I came back on because Zach's ankle was hurting. We were already up three to one at that point, but I secretly thought four would sound much nicer.

The other team were defending fiercely, though, and I didn't think it was going to happen until I found myself on the edge of the pitch and totally unmarked. Andrew flicked the ball across to me, and by the time the other players had realised, it was too late. I sprinted down the short pitch and shot the ball into the bottom corner of the goal.

"Not bad," Will said, jogging up to me and giving me a hug. "You might be good at this football lark."

I grinned. "I don't know. Think it might just be luck."

"It's definitely talent. You're just modest as fuck." He nudged me gently.

"I could say the same about you. Glad you decided to leave your lonely mountain for once?"

"Eh, I suppose." He grinned and handed me the ball. "Think we can make it five?"

"Guess we'll have to find out," I said, taking the ball from him and walking back to the centre of the pitch. I glanced across at Noah, and his beaming smile was brighter than the sun glinting off the sea in the middle of summer.

This might not have been Wembley, but I didn't care. Because I had everything I wanted right where I was.

CHAPTER THIRTY-ONE

Noah

WATCHING Spencer play and seeing the sheer, unabashed joy on his face made me smile so brightly it actually made my face hurt. There was something about seeing him utterly in his element and having the time of his life that made my heart melt.

Spencer had always seemed like a pretty happy guy, but there was so much difference between the relaxed, smiling man I'd hung out with in the pub every week and this bouncing, beaming man who radiated pure delight. I was so glad he'd decided to take Chris up on his offer, and I knew he'd have regretted it if he hadn't.

"It's like watching one of the dogs on TikTok," Alex said. "You know, the ones who look like they're sugar-high toddlers."

"He's having fun, though," Lane said. "And Spencer's

always been like the human equivalent of a golden retriever."

"That's true." Alex nodded sagely. The referee blew his whistle, ending the match, and the whole team jumped on each other, whooping and cheering and spinning each other around. Alex stood up and gave me a wry smile. "I'm guessing you're going back to Spencer's?"

"Yeah. But I'll be back tomorrow afternoon. Maybe we can watch a movie or something."

"All right." He patted me on the shoulder. "Be good."

"Am I ever not?" I asked.

"Do I need to remind you about their bloody house-warming?" Alex gestured at Lane and Oliver with one hand, and Lane laughed.

"Hey, that was nothing to do with me. That was all Laurie."

"What was all me?" asked Laurie from farther down the line. "What am I being accused of now?"

"Nothing new," I said.

"Good, because I haven't done anything."

Spencer waved at me as they all started heading off the pitch and back to the changing rooms. I stood up alongside Alex, and we climbed out of the stands, closely followed by everyone else. They all pottered off in their own directions while I headed into the leisure centre's reception area to wait, watching several parents attempt to corral a bunch of rowdy children who all seemed to be there for someone's birthday party.

I smiled to myself and remembered my own eighth birthday when I'd persuaded my mum to bring me, Alex,

Lane, and Oliver down for the inflatables session, and we'd spent two glorious hours playing on the giant, blow-up obstacle course and going down the slide as many times as possible before my mum took us home for pizza and ice cream and an enormous chocolate-fudge cake.

Luckily, there had only been four of us, which had probably been enough. I couldn't imagine wrangling a bunch of excitable kids, even though I regularly dealt with large groups of teenagers.

I got the feeling Spencer would be good with kids, though, because he'd be able to mirror their excitement but also be able to convince them to calm down. He'd probably make a really good dad one day.

That was a conversation for the future—one that I could definitely see us having.

Everything with Spencer felt so certain, and while the road ahead might still be unclear, I could already see the stops along the way. It probably should have scared me, but all I felt was excitement at the prospect of sharing my life with him. I'd had a crush on Spencer for so long that this had always felt like an unrealistic dream, a silly fantasy that I was willing to waste my time on, but now that it was real, it was more than I'd ever imagined. More than I'd ever wished.

I supposed all those fairy stories really did come true sometimes.

Or maybe it was all the birthday wishes I'd used up over the years, when I'd wished over and over for Spencer to notice me. I'd never asked for him to fall in love with me, though. That had always felt like a step too far.

"Penny for your thoughts?" Spencer asked, suddenly appearing behind me and making me jump. "Oh, sorry. I didn't mean to startle you. Are you okay?"

"I'm fine," I said with a semi-relieved chuckle. "I was just lost in thought." I nodded my head at the group of kids. "Just thinking about my eighth birthday when I convinced my mum to bring me here with Alex and co."

"Was it for the inflatables? Man, they were so awesome! I used to love coming here for that. One girl in my class at primary school had her party here, and we got the whole thing to ourselves. It was so cool."

"Seriously? How many of you were there?"

"I don't know, like, thirty? Her mum invited the whole class."

"Wow," I said. "I don't think I'd have the energy for something like that."

"Yeah, it was pretty chaotic." Spencer grinned. "It was fun, though. I think if I ever had kids, I'd want them to have cool birthday parties like that."

"Me too," I said, reaching out and quietly slipping my hand into his. "Do you think you'd ever want kids?"

"Yeah, I think so. Kids are pretty awesome. We get some who come into Novel Tea quite regularly, and they're always fun, even the super little ones. They have such tiny fingers and toes. It's kinda weird but cool too." He looked down at me and squeezed my hand. "What about you?"

"I think so too."

"They can't be any worse than your teenagers, right? Like, if it was one baby verses all your fifteen-year-olds, you'd definitely think the teenagers were the scary ones?"

"Honestly, I'm not sure. The teenagers are scary on the outside, but at least I can talk to them. They can be vaguely reasoned with," I said with a chuckle. "Even if they do think I'm *really* old."

"You're not old."

"They asked me if I knew what a meme was."

"Shit, really? Don't they know we, like, invented memes? Where do they think that shit comes from?"

"The funniest thing is half of them are all super invested in this gaming creator who's like our age. They just think because I'm a teacher I'm somehow detached from reality or like I hatched from a cocoon or something."

"That would be really cool," Spencer said. "That would make you like Mothra."

"I'd take that. Kaiju are pretty awesome."

"They are! We should totally watch *Pacific Rim* later. That film is fucking A." Spencer paused, then hummed for a second. "Huh, I've just realised that one of the reasons I like that film is because Charlie Hunnam is like, really, really fit. I always just thought I was looking respectfully but maybe not."

I laughed and pulled his hand to start walking towards the exit, dodging around the excited kids who all looked and sounded like they were two seconds away from exploding. "It's okay. You don't have to look respectfully. He is *very* handsome."

"Yeah, I think that whole cast is like hot as balls," he said. "I think there's a couple of movies like that... like, er, *Pirates of the Caribbean* and *The Mummy*."

"I believe Twitter has dubbed those the bisexual awakening starter movies," I said. "Just because of how beautiful everyone is."

"They're right. It's probably why I love them. I'd just never realised before."

It was already dark outside, and the cold air nipped at any exposed skin. Spencer had brought his car, so we both headed for that and drove back towards his little house under the glow of the town's twinkling Christmas lights. It was only a few days until the start of December, and my form had already started asking me when we could decorate the lab for Christmas.

"By the way," I said as we wound our way through the streets. "I never said congratulations. You did amazingly today."

"Thanks. I actually had a lot more fun than I thought I would," Spencer said. "I was pretty nervous before we started, like I was worried I'd forget everything or people would play dirty, but as soon as we started, I forgot all that. Now I just want to do it all again!"

"When's your next game?"

"Next Saturday. We're going to practice twice during the week, and then we're playing once next weekend, then we've got a weekend off, then it's two games the week after that. It's kinda like a rotating schedule so everyone gets breaks and nobody has to play too many games at once. But there's ten teams in the league, and we're playing everyone twice between now and the end of February. Although, I guess if the weather gets rubbish, it might go on longer. It'll depend on whether we can use the pitches."

"Cool. I'll try to come to as many as possible. Although

if it's pouring rain and blowing a gale, I might tap out. I love you, but I don't know if I love you that much," I said with a grin.

"You don't have to come to any, you know."

"I know, but I want to," I said. "Besides, it gets me out of the house, and I get to watch you run around in tight shorts, so it's not exactly a hardship."

"You like my shorts?"

"Yes, I really do." I reached over and put my hand on his thigh. "You have the most amazing legs. And there's something about you in shorts and football socks that's just really sexy."

"Hmm good to know," Spencer said like he was storing that information away to use for deliciously nefarious purposes at a later date. "So what do you want to do this evening?"

"I don't mind. What about you?"

"I do kinda want to watch *The Mummy* now that you've mentioned it. I know I said *Pacific Rim*, but I think *The Mummy* is edging it out, especially because *The Mummy Returns* is also fucking awesome. Oh, we should do a double bill!"

"That sounds perfect," I said. "And I promised to actually make you dinner as well."

"Okay, we have dinner and movies planned. What else?"

"I don't know," I said teasingly. "Is there anything else?"

"You should totally fuck me," Spencer said, and I almost laughed at his directness. It always charmed me the way he was never afraid to ask for what he wanted. I loved that about him. "I took a shower at the leisure centre, but their showers aren't great, so maybe you could fuck me when we get home? Then I can shower, and you can make dinner, and we can just veg on the sofa. Until I get bored… I might have to give you a blow job in the middle of the movie."

That time I did laugh. "Do you really think you'll get bored?"

"Probably. The films are awesome, but I fucking love playing with you, and I don't know if I'll be able to keep my hands to myself." He looked over at me, a cheeky smile on his face and a question in his eyes. "Would that be okay? I don't wanna do anything you won't like."

"I'm definitely not going to object, but thank you for asking."

"Always." He pulled up outside his house, and as soon as his car was parked, he leant over and kissed me deeply. "I love you. You know that, right?"

"I love you too."

"Awesome." He did the cutest and most ridiculous fist pump. "Okay, let's go! I wanna get dicked."

He shooed me out of the car, and I couldn't help giggling at Spencer's adorable antics. He reached for my hand and pulled me towards the front door. "Oh," he added as he dug in his pockets for his keys. "It's December next week, right? We should totally decorate next weekend. I've got this massive tree in the basement, and we can make mince pies and these Christmas cookies I found a recipe for."

"Sex first, then Christmas," I said, pushing him inside the house. "One thing at a time."

"Probably for the best. I wanna make sure I'm giving you my full attention." He grinned and wrapped his arms around me.

Spencer's kiss was full of heat and promises, and I knew he'd fulfil every one of them.

"I love you," he said again, his voice softer this time and laced with deep sincerity. "And I won't ever stop loving you."

"I love you too, more than should be possible."

"Nah. With us, nothing's impossible. We're wishes come true, baby."

And there was nothing more I could say to that. All I could do was kiss him, knowing what we had was the stuff dreams were made of.

EPILOGUE
THREE MONTHS LATER

Noah

THE SOUND of rain hammering on the window and wind howling down the old chimney breast greeted me as I stirred from sleep, bleary-eyed and wrapped in Spencer's arms. The warmth cocooning me was enough to convince me to stay put, especially because neither of us had any plans for the day. It was February half-term, which meant I was off, and since it was a Monday, Spencer was off too.

"Stay here," Spencer murmured, his voice rough with sleep.

"Wasn't planning on moving," I said, snuggling deeper into his arms. "It's pissing it down outside, and I'm cosy."

"Good." He pressed a kiss to the back of my head and squeezed me gently. I let out a deep sigh of contentment, happy to let myself drift in and out of sleep until we were both ready to get up. Although, I wouldn't say no to soft, sleepy sex either.

It seemed like Spencer felt the same as he slipped one hand under the old t-shirt I was wearing and slowly began to caress my skin as he trailed kisses down my neck. I groaned quietly and pressed my ass back into his crotch, slowly teasing his cock to full hardness as I ground against him. Spencer's hand slid down my stomach and into my shorts, stroking my cock slowly.

"Can I fuck you?" he asked, nipping my neck and soothing it with a kiss.

"Yes," I said. "Fuck me like this."

Spencer's hand retreated as he rolled away to look for the lube, and while he did, I quickly shimmied out of my clothes, kicking them out of bed. His bedroom, which was pretty much our bedroom these days, was still dark and lit only by the muted, grey daylight pushing its way around the edges of the curtains.

I heard the click of the lube bottle, and then Spencer's arm returned to wrap around me, reaching for my cock as his fingers slowly pressed inside my waiting hole. I groaned and tipped my head to the side so I could kiss him while he opened me. Our kisses were soft and heated, stoking a deep fire within me that begged for more.

By the time Spencer pressed his cock into me, I was desperate. He rolled me onto my stomach, planking above me as he began to fuck me slowly, pressing kisses to all the skin he could reach as his thrusts expertly tagged my prostate. Spencer really was the perfect partner—he knew exactly how to push my buttons and always gave me everything I wanted. He loved both topping and bottoming, so we switched regularly, and I adored hearing him moan my name when he came.

The friction of my cock on the sheet underneath me was too perfect, especially combined with Spencer's cock on my sweet spot.

I snaked my hand underneath me and with only a couple of quick jerks, I came with a deep cry. Spencer followed me over the edge very soon after, crying out my name as he buried himself deep in my ass, filling me with his release.

I twisted my head round, and we kissed slowly until Spencer rolled off me, snaking his hand around my waist and taking me with him until we were spooning again with his softening cock still inside me.

"Good morning," he whispered. "Sleep well?"

"Mmm, yes. And the wakeup was very nice too."

"It was." He kissed my neck again. "Got any plans for today?"

"No, not really. You?"

"Not unless you count snuggling you."

I grinned. "I do."

"Good." We lay in silence for a couple of minutes, listening to the rain. "Hey, can I ask you something?" Spencer said.

"Of course." I slowly pulled away from him, letting his cock slip out of me before I rolled over in his arms so we were face-to-face. I felt his cum trickling down my leg, and knew I'd end up lying in a wet patch, but I didn't care.

"How do you feel about moving in here?" Spencer's voice was soft and casual like he was trying to pretend it wasn't a big deal. My heart swelled, and I smiled, leaning forward to kiss him.

"I'd love that," I said.

"Awesome!"

"I mean, I pretty much live here anyway," I said with a gentle chuckle. I couldn't actually remember the last time I spent more than one night at my flat. It was probably last year.

"Yeah, but we should probably make it official," Spencer said. "Then Alex'll stop grumbling to me about it. He keeps saying we should just do it already."

I nodded, then bit my lip. I felt bad about leaving Alex in the lurch, even though I'd kept paying my rent and tried to see him as much as possible. I'd told him I didn't want our relationship to change, but we'd both accepted that it would. We just had to make sure we kept carving out time for each other, and I wanted to make sure that if I moved out, I wasn't leaving him in the shit with the rent and the lease.

Part of me was worried he wouldn't be able to afford it alone, and I'd have to make sure I actually got him to be honest with me about it because Alex was definitely the sort of person who wouldn't say anything just to make my life easier.

"We should. Even if most of my stuff is already here." It had gradually migrated over the last few months, and now my clothes were in the drawers, my shoes were in the cupboard by the front door, my products were in the bathroom, and there was a stack of books to be marked on the kitchen table. Spencer and I had just folded ourselves into each other's lives so effortlessly, it almost felt strange that we needed to make things official.

We were definitely going to be that couple who got engaged or married without actually talking about it. We'd probably annoy everyone with our lackadaisical approach to everything.

"True, but I'm sure you've still got a few bits to get and then there's any paperwork you need to solve. Gotta make sure we're not leaving Alex out to dry," Spencer said, and I loved how his thoughts had mirrored mine.

"I was just thinking that," I said.

"That's because we're awesome." He grinned and kissed me. "I love you."

"I love you too."

"Maybe Alex can rent the spare room out to someone on the cast of that period drama," Spencer said. "Aren't they finally meant to start filming soon?"

"I think so. Did you get the letter about extras? I know Theo applied. I think Laurie did too." There had been rumours swirling about the production for months because we'd heard it was supposed to start filming at the start of the year, but there'd been another issue with the casting. We knew Henry Lu had been cast as one of the leads, and the former boy-bander turned solo star, Jude Kane, as another, but apparently, there had been some issues with Jude because of who his boyfriend was.

The fact that Jude was gay didn't seem to have fazed anyone, but the fact that his boyfriend had turned out to be none other than the gay porn star Austin Carter seemed to have made the execs nervous. I had no idea how it had played out, but Theo had followed a lot of it on Twitter, and after much dramatic back-and-forth, it seemed liked Jude was going to keep the role, but the whole mess had delayed production while they got it sorted.

As Theo had pointed out, at least this was going to make people want to watch the show, even if it was because of all the preproduction dramatics.

"I did, but it's not for me," Spencer said. "I think Will's a little cross about it 'cos it's lambing season, and he doesn't want the ewes being disturbed. I haven't seen much of him lately, though. He's been a bit reclusive."

"That's normal for this time of year."

"Yeah." Spencer frowned. "Seems a bit more than normal. I wonder if it's anything to do with that guy who was hanging around?"

"The posh Londoner?"

"Yeah, that one. I don't know why. He's not really Will's type, and I don't see Will being his."

"Who knows," I said. "We'll find out at some point."

"Or we could just go up there and ask." Spencer grinned.

I chuckled. "Maybe if we still haven't seen him in another week or two. We can always send Theo in. He's good at getting answers out of people."

"We can send Theo and Alex," Spencer said. "They're like the ultimate shit-busting team."

"Like the Ghostbusters or something." I started humming, and Spencer laughed.

We spent another hour lying in bed, talking about whatever came to mind, before we eventually got hungry. I dove through the shower while Spencer went down to start breakfast, making us scrambled eggs on thick slices of sourdough toast and tea, which we ate sitting at the kitchen island.

It was still raining, so we decided just to curl up in front of the TV for part of the day. We talked about going over to my flat, but the weather wasn't persuasive. I'd go tomorrow and see what needed packing and try to see Alex too.

But all that could wait; there wasn't any rush. Like we'd said, I pretty much lived at Spencer's already. It was just sorting out the official bits.

"Do you need to do any marking today?" Spencer asked as the end credits of the episode of the epic fantasy show we'd been watching rolled.

"No, it can wait until tomorrow."

"Do you want to make some cookies? I kinda fancy some cookies."

I looked over at him. "I can't believe you need to ask me that. Cookies are always good."

"Awesome. Let's make cookies, then." We climbed off the sofa, and Spencer took my hand, leading me into the kitchen and starting to dig things out of the cupboard as he asked me what I fancied putting in them.

We went back and forth but eventually settled on chocolate chip and oatmeal with a pinch of cinnamon that made you just want to eat more of them.

Once the dough was chilling in the fridge, we watched another episode before we turned the oven on and spooned the cookie dough onto a tray. The kitchen smelt absolutely heavenly, and both Spencer and I snuck hot cookies off the tray as soon as they came out of the oven and we could pick them up.

It was one of those warm, cosy days that was utterly perfect. One of those days that didn't really have a great impact on the universe, but one of those days I'd always remember as another day with the man I loved. The man I'd always longed for, and the man who'd been around for most of my life. It had just taken us until recently to realise just how perfect we were for each other.

And when we climbed back into bed later that night, exchanging kisses and whispered declarations of love, I felt nothing but happiness.

Because this life with Spencer was everything I'd wished for, and I knew I'd cherish every moment for as long as we both lived.

The End

ACKNOWLEDGMENTS

Writing a story full of autumnal vibes during the oppressive heat the UK suffered this summer certainly wasn't on my bucket list for the year, but it was certainly memorable. It certainly helped give me something to wish for while I clung to my fan and wondered if it would be physically possible to climb into my freezer!

I would be nothing without the people who continue to support me, even on the days I struggle to believe in myself.

To Charity, not only the best PA in the world, but one of my best friends, my rock, my shoulder, and the one with the sharp stick to prod me along.

To Noah, for all the vibes. One day we'll meet in person and it will be the most glorious brand of chaos the world has ever seen.

To Carly, Toby, Rosie, and Jodi for being my people. I literally couldn't do this without any of you and I owe you a lot of baked goods, chocolate, and hugs.

To Jayne, for being my sprint buddy and nudging me along even when we were melting.

To Susie, for always pushing me to do more, for finding all the plot holes I'd missed and for your continued grace at my abuse of the comma.

To Natasha for making the most stunning covers I've ever seen.

To Lori, for being the sweetest and most helpful proof-reader I've ever met.

To Dan, who is not phased by my writing in dirty noises and for doing the best Yorkshire accents.

To my husband for the hugs, the cake, the support, and the love. You fucking rock!

Also, a special thanks to Louise for all her help with the Yorkshire-ness.

And last, but never least, to you, my fabulous readers. Whether I'm new to you or you've been here since the start, I am grateful for you love and support.

If you enjoyed *Like I Wished*, please consider leaving a review. Reviews are invaluable for indie authors, and may help other readers find this book.

Until next time.

ALSO BY CHARLIE NOVAK

Heather Bay
Like I Pictured

Like I Promised

Like I Wished

Like I Needed

Roll for Love
Natural Twenty

Charisma Check

Proficiency Bonus

Forever Love
Always Eli

Finding Finn

Oh So Oscar

Kiss Me
Strawberry Kisses

Summer Kisses

Spiced Kisses

Off the Pitch

Breakaway

Extra Time

Final Score

The Off the Pitch Short Collection

Off the Pitch: The Complete Collection (Boxset)

STANDALONES

Screens Apart

Couture Crush

SHORT STORIES

One More Night

Twenty-Two Years (Newsletter Exclusive)

Snow Way In Hell

AUDIOBOOKS

Like I Promised

Natural Twenty

Charisma Check

Proficiency Bonus

Always Eli

Finding Finn

Oh So Oscar

Strawberry Kisses

Summer Kisses

Spiced Kisses

For a regularly updated list, please visit:

charlienovak.com/books

charlienovak.com/audiobooks

CHARLIE NOVAK

Charlie lives in England with her husband and two cheeky dogs. She spends most of her days wrangling other people's words in her day job and then trying to force her own onto the page in the evening.

She loves cute stories with a healthy dollop of fluff, plenty of delicious sex, and happily ever afters — because the world needs more of them.

Charlie has very little spare time, but what she does have she fills with baking, Dungeons and Dragons, reading and many other nerdy pursuits. She also thinks that everyone should have at least one favourite dinosaur…

Website charlienovak.com
Facebook Group Charlie's Angels
For day-to-day-musings, giveaways and teasers.

Plus sign up for her newsletter for bonus scenes, new releases and extras.

- facebook.com/charlienovakauthor
- twitter.com/charlienwrites
- instagram.com/charlienwrites
- bookbub.com/profile/charlie-novak
- amazon.com/author/charlienovak

Printed in Great Britain
by Amazon

45019158R00182